Books by Fran Stewart

The Biscuit McKee Mystery Series:

> *Orange as Marmalade*
> *Yellow as Legal Pads*
> *Green as a Garden Hose*
> *Blue as Blue Jeans*
> *Indigo as an Iris*
> *Violet as an Amethyst*
> *Gray as Ashes*
>
> *Red as a Rooster*
> *Black as Soot*
> *Pink as a Peony*
> *White as Ice*

A Slaying Song Tonight

The ScotShop Mysteries:

> *A Wee Murder in My Shop*
> *A Wee Dose of Death*
> *A Wee Homicide in the Hotel*

Poetry:

> *Resolution*

For Children:

> *As Orange As Marmalade/*
>   *Tan naranja como Mermelada*
>   (a bilingual book)

Non-Fiction:

> *From The Tip of My Pen: a workbook for writers*
> *BeesKnees #1: A Beekeeping Memoir (#1 of 6 volumes)*
> *BeesKnees #2: A Beekeeping Memoir (#2 of 6 volumes)*
> *BeesKnees #3: A Beekeeping Memoir (#3 of 6 volumes)*
> *BeesKnees #4: A Beekeeping Memoir (#4 of 6 volumes)*
> *BeesKnees #5: A Beekeeping Memoir (#5 of 6 volumes)*
> *BeesKnees #6: A Beekeeping Memoir (#6 of 6 volumes)*
> Coming Soon - *Clear as Mud*

GRAY
AS ASHES

Fran Stewart

My Own Ship Press

Gray as Ashes
the 7th Biscuit McKee Mystery
Fran Stewart

© 2014/ © 2020 Fran Stewart

ISBN: (Softcover) 978-1-951368-17-3
ISBN: (Hardcover) 978-1-951368-23-4

This is a work of fiction. Any resemblance to any person living or dead is purely coincidental.

Map Design: Diana Alishouse

IThis book was printed in the United States of America.

Published by
My Own Ship Press
PO Box 490153
Lawrenceville GA 30049

myownship@icloud.com
franstewart.com

Gray as Ashes is dedicated
to the firefighters of Gwinnett County GA
and with deep appreciation
for firefighters throughout this nation

The People of Martinsville, Georgia
Some of us are not people.

Biscuit McKee - librarian
    her 2nd husband - **Bob** Sheffield, the town cop
        I call him Softfoot
    her cat - **Marmalade**
        Excuse me? Widelap is my human
the **Butterfly Brigade**
    Biscuit's sister - **Glaze** McKee
        I call her Smellsweet
    Dee Sheffield - Glaze's friend
    Madeleine Ames - writer of thrillers; Glaze's roommate
        I call her CurlUp
Captain Paula Corrigan – county arson investigator
Celia - mail carrier
Connie Cartwright – glass blower & teacher
Easton Hastings - red-headed woman
Emma & **Tim** Haversham – elderly residents of Martinsville
    their grandson **Jimmy**
Henry Pursey - minister of The Old Church, and his wife, **Irene**
    Henry's daughter, **Susan**
Hoss Cartwright - firefighter
Ida & **Ralph** Peterson - grocers
Lorna Jean Hagstrom – writer and runner
Maggie & **Norm** Pontiac - owner of goats and chickens
    I call her HenLady
    their adopted son - **Willie**
    Maggie's rooster - **Doodle-Doo**
    the goat protector - **Fergus**
Margot Schuss – co-owner of the DeliSchuss
Melissa Tarkington - owner of Azalea House Bed & Breakfast
    She is GoodCook
Nathan Young - family physician
    He is GoodHands
Nicholai Rimski KorsaCat – the doctor's office cat, known as Korsi
    His real name is GrayGuy

The three **Petunias** - library volunteers
    Esther Anderson
    Sadie Russell Masters
       I call her Looselaces.
    Rebecca Jo Sheffield - Bob's mother
Reebok Garner - Bob's deputy
Ron & Mary Fleming – new residents of Martinsville
Tom Parkman - owner of CT's Restaurant &
    the Keagan County Vocational Culinary School
       He is Fishgiver

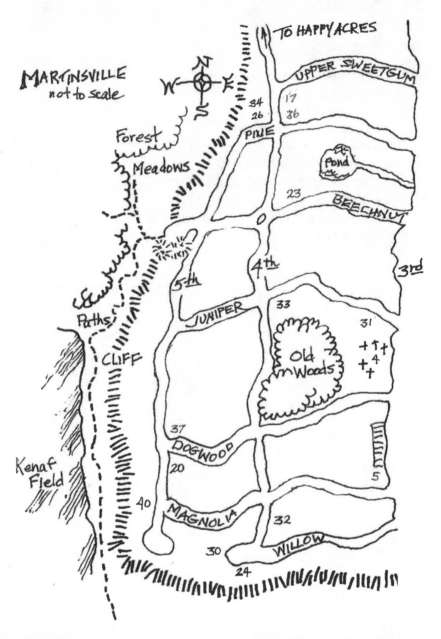

MARTINSVILLE
not to scale

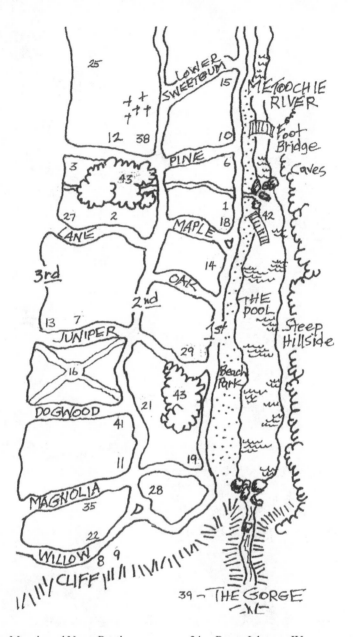

SURREYTOWN

KEAGAN COUNTY
not to scale

The Cliff

County Rd.

RUSSELL
GAP

N
W E
S

GARNERCREEK

HASTINGS

Metoochie River

BRAETONBURG

MARTINSVILLE

The Pool

The Gorge

ENDERS

The Lake

The Cliff

Chapter 1

> So, Mr. Latham, my teacher from before,
> he gave me this notebook and
> he said for me to write everything down
> about how I'm feeling
> it's not a ~~dairy~~ ~~diery~~ diary—that's for girls
> he said it's my Private ~~Gernol~~ ~~Jernal~~ ~~Juoranal~~ Notebook

~~~~~~~

THE SECOND ONE TO BURN was my garden shed, and nobody saw anything. Nobody, that is, but the creep who started the fire.

Bob and I, dressed to the nines (whatever that means—where did that saying come from, anyway?) had spent the evening at the armory up in Garner Creek, attending the Keagan County Police Association's annual ball and fundraiser. Matthew, our next-door neighbor just up the hill, had left a week ago to visit his daughter in Ohio. And Paul, right across the street, had taken Judy out to dinner. Or so he said. At any rate, wherever they were, the two of them hadn't seen anything.

If there had been a wind, the smoke might have drifted farther down Beechnut Lane. Somebody might have smelled it sooner. But there wasn't a wind and nobody smelled anything.

I smelled it.

Thank goodness Marmalade was safe inside the house. I don't know what I would have done if she'd been hurt.

I was perfectly safe.

Bob and I came home to a gosh awful mess.

Hoss Cartwright, one of the Martinsville firefighters—his name isn't really Hoss, but it was a logical nickname, given his height, his square face, and his last name—was folding the fire hose when we drove up. A group of bystanders, a few adults, but mostly gangly boys, with a few girls scattered among them, stood nearby, eyeing the fire engine and gabbling among themselves. I recognized all of them, of course. After all, this was Martinsville. Maggie and Willie were there too, waiting, watching.

"Norm and Willie and I were out for a late night stroll in the full moonlight," she told me.

Bob and I ought to do that each month, I thought. We took plenty of walks together, but there was something about a full moon. I glanced up at the bright orb.

"... course, Norm and I were doing the walking, and Willie was pretty much asleep in Norm's arms, but he's the one who saw the smoke. Norm grabbed your garden hose, but it didn't do any good. I parked Willie on your front porch with orders to stay there—he's a good boy—and I ran back up the hill to call for help, but by the time they got here," she gestured toward Hoss and the other firefighters, "the fire had pretty much taken over."

"You could have used our phone. The door wasn't locked."

Maggie looked stricken. "I didn't think of it. I just ran home as fast as I could. That's why I left Willie on your porch. His weight would have slowed me down."

WigglePants woke up and saw the smoke because I told them as loudly as I could. He was the only one who listened to me.

"Thank goodness we left our house so much later than usual," Maggie said. "Willie really should have been in bed already." She glanced up at Marmalade, who had just let out a yowl from the upstairs window. "We might not have noticed the flames if Marmalade hadn't been throwing a hissy fit in the window, just like she's doing now."

I am not nearly as loud now as I was then.

The windows were wide open, which is why we could hear Marmalade's meows so clearly. I have special sturdy pet screening so she can't accidentally fall through.

Excuse me? My balance is perfect.

Bob stepped away from Hoss and Norm and joined us. "Thanks, Maggie. Hoss told me you called in the alarm." He bent and put his hand on Willie's shoulder. "I understand you're the one who spotted the smoke, young man. Thank you." Willie squirmed with pleasure. He had a funny way of shifting from one foot to another that made him look like he was dancing. Still, he was almost asleep on his feet. They needed to take that boy home.

"I wish I'd thought to run inside and use your phone, Bob."

"You couldn't have," he said. "The door was locked."

"We never lock the door."

Bob put his hand on my shoulder. "You mean, *you* never lock the door, Woman."

"Oh."

"Well, now I don't feel so bad." Maggie peered around Norm at the moonlit darkness of our back yard. "From what I could see while the fire truck was here lighting everything up, it looked like you lost everything."

"Not everything," Bob said. "I checked the beehives. They weren't touched. The only thing damaged was just the shed."

I narrowed my eyes. That shed had all my gardening equipment in it. Bob might have sung a different tune if he'd lost his beehives or the shed up by his old house where he did his fly-tying. I was saved from making an unkind—but thoroughly justifiable—comment when Norm walked up to join us.

Maggie smiled at her husband. "We have to leave and get Willie back in bed."

I waved as Hoss pulled the engine away from the curb. Without the engine's bright lights, only the moon gave any illumination.

"Fire twuck go bye-bye."

A four-year-old ought to have better language skills than that, shouldn't he? He sounded the way my son Scott talked when he was only two.

Maggie surveyed my long dress, and her eyes wandered up to my long hair piled elegantly atop my head in an elaborate French twist, thanks to the expert ministrations of Sharon Armitage at the Beauty Shop. "You're too pretty to do anything about all that mess tonight."

"Right," Norm said. "I'll be here around six to help you two clean up. We'll get it finished before church."

"That's okay, Norm. We can handle—"

Bob squeezed my arm somewhat harder than I thought was absolutely necessary. "Thanks Norm. Appreciate it."

Norm bent and lifted Willie. The boy snuggled against his new dad as if he belonged right there. He did belong right there. His mother had died tragically in a car wreck, but Maggie and Norm loved this child to pieces. He was just what they needed.

Norm gestured, indicating the remains of my shed. "Don't try to go in there tonight. The fire's completely out, but you could break a leg if you try to climb over something and it collapses. Wait till daylight."

Maggie nodded. "He ought to know. He was a volunteer for years before we got the new fire station and professional firefighters."

She was talking to me. Bob obviously knew all this. "Norm broke his arm," she went on. "It was before you came to Martinsville, Biscuit. He walked into something that looked about like that shed of yours does now."

My former shed, I thought.

It smells very stinky.

"He twisted his ankle ..." She paused, looking up at the window where Marmy was still making noises, looking all silvery white behind the screen in the moonlight. "And he shattered his humerus."

Norm picked up on what must have been an old line between them. "Yeah. Nothing felt funny for a very long time."

I groaned. It seemed to be expected.

Are you hurting, Widelap?

Maggie tilted her head against her husband's shoulder. "Gotta take care of our men, and," she added pointedly, "keep them from doing dumb things."

"No dumber than usual," Bob said.

The three of them headed uphill and Bob and I walked inside.

The smell of smoke permeated the house. I leaned against Bob as Marmalade came pelting down the stairs toward us. "Do you think we can get this cleaned up before Peachie gets here Friday?"

"Don't worry. Norm will show up bright and early in the morning. Half the men in town will be here as well, and every one of those boys who were watching the firefighters. This is pretty exciting."

No, Softfoot. It was pretty scary.

Only men—and boys—would think my dead garden shed was exciting.

The phone rang, and Bob picked it up. "I suppose so," he said after a moment or two, "but you'll have to get here early. We're starting work on it at six ... yes, that's a.m."

"What was that about?"

"Somebody from the *Record* wants pictures. I guess our shed fire's the most excitement this valley's had all week."

The *Keagan County Record* came out every Wednesday. Martinsville's own Myrtle Hoskins had a regular column in it, and was usually the first to interview anyone with a potential story, but this sounded like somebody else. Bob would have called her by name if it had been Myrtle.

"Bob? There wasn't anything in my shed that would catch fire. Our old reel mower doesn't use gas."

"I know that, Woman."

"I know you know it. I just have to say it. I'm trying to work this through. Somebody did this to me."

"To us."

"Okay. To us."

He rubbed his fingertips back and forth across his mustache, the one I'd talked him into growing. He only did that, rubbed the mustache I mean, when he was worried. Or so it seemed to me.

"The shed door didn't have a lock," he said.

"Of course it didn't have a lock. This is Martinsville. And why didn't they just steal some trowels or something? Why burn down my beautiful shed?"

He looked at me askance and shepherded me toward the stairs. So, maybe my shed didn't look beautiful to him. And I supposed it wasn't much to look at, but it was wonderfully functional, with just the right space for everything that needed to be in there. Bob and I built it right after we were married. Well, not *right* after, but as soon as he'd recovered from our disastrous honeymoon.

I turned around on the landing and he stopped abruptly. "My compost pile!"

"What about it?"

"It's right next to the shed. Do you think it got damaged too?"

Ever the practical one, Bob said, "Let's go look. But I'd like to get out of this penguin suit first."

He was right. His white shirt blazed against the stark black fabric of his suit. I giggled, and he patted me on my behind. "Let's change, and we can start investigating."

Even though my feet hadn't been hurting—I always wore comfortable shoes—I was happy finally to slip into my old sweatpants, a paint-splattered tee shirt, and my rather grungy tennis shoes. Naturally, my fancy hairdo fell apart. Not a big loss, especially when Bob took a moment to run his hands through my hair. I sure was glad Sharon hadn't used a bunch of hairspray. A fancy do is fun for a while, but I was more comfortable on a daily basis with my hair pulled back in a ponytail. Not much call for fancy evening gowns and elaborate French twists in Martinsville.

After a suitable interlude, and armed with heavy-duty flashlights to augment the brilliant light of a full moon, we went to survey the damage.

It was extensive. The old reel mower was twisted, the garden cart was almost unrecognizable, just a frame, really. I could see the metal handle and what looked like a few wheel spokes buried under a filthy charred avalanche. The only good news was that my compost bin was untouched, except for an unavoidable dousing with water. I hoped the earthworms hadn't drowned.

The handles of all my tools were gone. Shovels, trowels, spade. I was going to have a big shopping trip ahead of me to replace them all. Maybe Peachie would go with me. We could make a jaunt up to the garden center in Garner Creek.

I hadn't seen Peachie Rose in years, ever since we met in college. We hadn't been real close friends, even though we'd shared a tiny apartment with three other girls our senior year. I'd always liked her easygoing ways and her clever quips, though. After graduation, we went our separate ways, and our friendship, if it could be called that, had been limited to birthday cards and a letter or two each year. She'd called a month ago, though, and said she was going to be in Toccoa for a week-long women's retreat and could she come for a visit, maybe three, four days. Well, of course she could. Did she think I was going to say no? Especially if she was willing to drive all the way down the length of this dead-end valley just to see me. Our old house had so many guest bedrooms, it was about time we used one of them.

~~~~~

Maggie Pontiac took Norm's left arm as they strolled up Beechnut Lane, winding her hand in against Willie's small leg. "I bet you they'll be out there looking at the mess as soon as they change their clothes."

"Won't bet against that. You'd win. But Bob helped out on enough fires with the volunteers to know what to do."

"Then why were you telling him not to go in there if he already knew the dangers?"

"Wasn't talking to him. Don't you think Biscuit's the kind of woman who'd try to plow right in there to find her favorite shovel?"

Maggie chuckled and hugged his arm tighter. She did love this man of hers.

Willie squirmed into a more comfortable position. "You did well, son," Norm said. "You showed Mama and me the fire."

"Marm-marm told me." Such a sleepy little voice.

Maggie chuckled indulgently. "That's right. Marmalade told you. She made quite a noise, didn't she?"

Willie's head bobbed. "Telled me fire." He laid his head against Norm's chest.

Almost reflexively, Maggie said, "Yes, she told you." This dear child, her son now, hers and Norm's, still suffered the aftereffects of having seen his mother die in that car accident that had left him trapped in his car seat for several days before he was found, dehydrated, starving, comatose and, when he finally awoke, absolutely terrified. No wonder he'd reverted to baby talk.

Doc had been very reassuring. "He'll grow out of it. Just shower him with love and give him your strength to lean against." Well, they'd tried. He had as much love as they could give—and that was a lot—and he had his little jobs to do, helping feed the goats, brushing Fergus (although Maggie always had to redo that job when Willie was napping—he had too much fun playing with Fergus's bushy tail). The jobs were not only to teach him gentle discipline, but also to let him know that he was a valued member of this family now.

"I'm worried, Norm. That fire was no accident."

He reached around the small bulge of Willie's back and covered her strong capable hand with his own, equally capable and moderately stronger. "No need to worry. We'll be fine."

Norm was a good man to protect their son from a conversation that might upset him. She lowered her voice a bit, even though Willie was already sleepy-limp in Norm's arms. "Why are you so sure?"

"Bob's the town cop. Somebody's out to get him. That's all it was. No doubt about it."

"But what about the fire at the IGA yesterday?"

"It was just a garbage bin. Some kid probably dared his buddy to do it. I wouldn't worry. It won't happen again."

~~~~~

My Gratitude List for Saturday
Five things for which I'm grateful:
> 1. It was the shed, not the house.
> 2. Marmalade wasn't hurt.
> 3. We have good neighbors, even though nobody saw whoever did it.
> 4. The dance—it was great fun, and I only stepped on Bob's toes three times. Well, maybe four
> 5. This comfortable bed, especially when Bob is in it

I am grateful for
        being safe
        tuna
        Widelap
        Softfoot
        this soft bed

Chapter 2

33 Years Earlier

A MISTAKE, REALLY. IT HAD just been a mistake. That was all.

She could still see it when she closed her eyes.

All she'd wanted was a hug. Nothing more. She knew the *more* would come soon, as soon as they got to the third room on the left down the hallway from the top of the stairs, but just then all she'd wanted was comfort, so she'd turned around on the top stair. That way she was practically eye-to-eye with him. She reached for him as his left foot hovered between the third step and the second. He hadn't expected her to stop. That was what really happened. He should have expected it. He should have reached out to her first. He hadn't, so when he toppled backwards, moving away from her too quickly, that wasn't her fault. It wasn't. It wasn't.

Not knowing what to do, she took a sleeping pill—from the ones she'd taken—borrowed really—from her mother. They were supposed to calm her mother's nightmares. What about the daughter's nightmares? Didn't they need calming, too? For the first time, she dreamed she was an angel. A dark angel. Carrying a sword.

They could hardly wake her when Mother came home from shopping and found him.

Poor dear, they said, the next morning. She must have slept through all the noise. Such a shame that her father wouldn't see her graduate from high school.

At the funeral, she cried. It was expected of her.

Chapter 3

So, Mr. Latham wants me to feel things
but feeling hurts
it's not much fun having no friends
I wish I hadn't moved here
I wish they hadn't made me move here
they're okay I guess, but they're old
if they were ever kids
it was so long ago they've forgotten
I keep getting tummy ~~ackhs akes~~ hurts
is this what it's like to feel?

~~~~~~

THERE WERE SO MANY PEOPLE in our yard the morning after the fire, it looked like we'd thrown a party. Doodle Doo had announced it, and everyone had accepted the invitation. The photographer from the *Record* had already come and gone. She'd asked to photograph Bob and me in front of the ruins, but Bob had declined firmly. Now, the scene was almost a repeat of that time our dogwood tree uprooted and fell over in all that rain we had a couple of years ago. Men and chain saws. Except this party was in the back yard instead of the front one, and this party was decorated not with rain and mud, but with a feathery coating of gray ashes that drifted here and there on the morning breeze every time a man put a shovel in the mess.

I would have been perfectly capable of helping Bob dig out all that wreckage. I was an independent woman in many ways, completely comfortable with tools and leather work gloves. But I looked around my warm kitchen and decided yet again that if men wanted to believe in *men's work* that was fine with me. I could pass on skinned knuckles and a sore back. If I wanted to be absolutely truthful, though, I'd have to admit how tempted I was last night to wade into that pile to see if there was anything I could salvage. Norm was probably right, though. And

Bob had gently steered me away when I tried to step into the mess.

I wiped a smudge from the bay window. Was that a paw print? *Yes.*

Of course it was. Marmy loved to watch the birds at the feeder. There weren't many birds around this morning, though. Only a few brazen chickadees braved all the hubbub generated by the men around my shed. My former shed. That bunch was going to need a lot of coffee for fuel. That was where *women's work*—I chuckled at the thought—came in.

Reebok, named for the antelope, not the running shoes, stood off to one side. I'd never seen him drinking coffee—maybe he'd like hot chocolate.

There were plenty of onlookers, and it wasn't even six o'clock yet. I could see a crowd through the window on the front side of the house—mostly women and kids. They'd like the hot chocolate too. Off to one side, a half dozen of Tom's vocational cooking school students stood talking among themselves. I toyed with the idea of asking them to whip up the hot chocolate, but wasn't sure I wanted them in my kitchen. I knew only two of them. The others were from towns farther up the Metoochie River Valley, except the short one. He was from Enders.

I pulled out the 30-cup coffee pot from the bottom shelf of the walk-in pantry and slid the big empty soup pot—now designated the hot chocolate pot—from the back of the stove to the front burner. I'd never made a place for it in the pantry. I used it so often, it seemed silly to put it away, so it lived on the stove whether it was full or empty.

The men were congregated around the remains of the shed, poking in the charred ruin of all my garden implements as if that mess held endless fascination.

Seven or eight wheelbarrows stood in a clump next to the men, having a little wheelbarrow convention of their own. One of the barrows held a selection of extra shovels; they must have been extra because all the men seemed to be holding one already. They must have each brought two just in case. Another barrow held a box of sturdy garbage bags. The men would need those if they were to haul away all the mess. I wondered where it would end up. Probably piled on the curb for Roger to take to the dump next garbage day.

I thought about asking each bystander crowded on my front walk to contribute a trowel or a rake or a shovel, but decided against it. There's something very personal about gardening tools. If I had to get another set, I wanted to pick them out myself.

Instead, I concocted the coffee and hot chocolate.

Marmy wandered in and out through her cat door, almost like a supervisor checking to be sure we were all doing our jobs.

I make sure all my people are safe.

The noise of a large vehicle drew me to the front window. Roger, bless that young man. He was ready to collect everything the men hauled to the curb. He was for sure going on my gratitude list tonight. Both for his garbage business and for how dependable he was about keeping the signboard at the Old Church up to date.

Loved that sign. This week it said something about eagles. I wished Henry would forget about the birds and preach about my garden shed. Make whoever did all this 'fess up. Sheds didn't just catch fire all by themselves.

Bob knew that. So why couldn't he catch the guy who'd done this? The fact that it had been only seven hours since we'd come home to a dead shed was totally irrelevant. I wanted that guy caught and made to pay for turning my beautiful shed into ashes.

Just in the few minutes I'd been putting together the refreshments for the men, the crowd had grown considerably. I watched the people, my neighbors, chatting and pointing, gawking and gesticulating. I knew from conversations with Bob that people who committed crimes—and it was a real crime to burn down my shed—almost always showed up to view the results. A murderer would attend the funeral of his victim. A hit and run driver would cruise past the accident scene, sometimes repeatedly.

That meant I might be looking at the person who had done this to me.

I scanned the group, searching for a strange face. Surely nobody I knew would have done this. But every face was familiar, even Tom's students whom I saw on a regular basis at Tom's restaurant where he required them to perform all the jobs, not just the cooking. They seated us, served us, bussed the tables, and cleaned up afterwards. I might not know the name, but I could identify everyone there. All of them, even the kids, except four of Tom's, were Martinsville residents. Genevieve Russell was talking to Ken I-forgot-his-last-name and a couple of his friends. They were about thirteen or fourteen years old, and good readers, both of them. I saw them in the library a lot. Although, come to think of it, Ken might have been there only because of Genevieve. He did check out a lot of books, though, and seemed to have read them when I questioned him—diplomatically, of course. The other three—I searched my memory—Dan and Jim. And Jake. Seemed like good boys, although I'd never seen Jake, the oldest one, smile. He *was* a bit surly at times.

Two of Tom's students, Austin & Bradley, the two Martinsville boys, walked toward the back yard and out of my sight. Their companions followed after a moment's hesitation. Good. They were going to help, and there were shovels aplenty.

I kept searching the crowd.

A pair of twin boys from Happy Acres, the horribly named new development north of town, stood gaping on the fringe of the crowd. Word had traveled fast. Their mother must have brought them to teach them the consequences of poor behavior, but I didn't think the lesson was being absorbed. The boys simply looked fascinated. Surely they wouldn't have done this? No, too young. Their mother would have had to transport them. I looked around for their mother, knowing I'd recognize her; she had a library card. No mother in sight, but I did spot two identical bikes dumped unceremoniously on their sides next to our mailbox. There went the boys' alibi.

Sadie's yellow Chevy pulled into the space behind Roger's dump truck and all three of my Petunias clambered out. This wasn't a party. It had turned into a circus. The three elderly women paused to let a bevy of joggers run past.

Jogging had become a rather popular sport in Martinsville. Most of those women jogged every day, some of them by themselves, some in pairs or groups. Some had graduated from jogging to flat out running. I didn't see how they managed the steep hillsides, but most of them had legs a lot younger than mine. All five of them slowed their pace, as they all turned their heads to look, but they kept jogging.

Enough of this ruminating. The Petunias would be inside in less than a minute to help. I wouldn't be surprised if Esther brought pound cake.

~~~~~~

Reebok looked up from his shovel as Miss Biscuit walked out the back door of her house. Hers and the Chief's. He tried always to remember that.

"There's coffee inside if you need it," she called out.

Reebok couldn't stand coffee.

"And hot chocolate," she said. Reebok brightened.

"Hot chocolate's for kids," muttered one of the young men who had just joined them. Reebok wilted. Maybe he could put lots of cream and sugar in his coffee. That might make it palatable.

The Chief spoke up from just behind Reebok. "If these kids want any hot chocolate, they're going to have to work for it." He lowered his voice. "Garner—round up three or four of the bigger boys. They can handle the wheelbarrows."

"Yes Sir, Chief." He almost saluted, but then he remembered that the Chief didn't like that. That was too bad. A nice salute looked spiffy. Especially if Miss Biscuit were watching.

He straightened his spine, conscious of Miss Biscuit's eyes following him. At least he hoped they were. His shovel, held ramrod straight, felt almost like an honor guard's flagpole. He didn't think it was vain to want to look your best.

He headed toward a clump of boys standing on the periphery of the crowd. "You fellas want to help?"

One of the boys nodded, but then seemed to sense the more standoffish attitude of his compatriots. Reebok liked that word. Compatriots. Sounded very organized, almost soldierly, although these four looked like they could use some good old-fashioned army discipline.

"You want our help," drawled one of the others in a tone that projected *fat chance*. Reebok thought his name was Jake; he'd have to look up his index card—he had one on everybody in town. Bright red hair. Lots of pimples. One shoulder a lot lower than the other. Probably from carrying such a heavy chip. Yes, he was right. That was Jake. Reebok never forgot an attitude. "Why should we?" Jake's words were almost a snarl.

"Hot chocolate," Reebok said, and had the satisfaction of seeing their immediate interest. He knew what made boys tick, even punks like this one.

~~~~~

Maggie set Willie down, wondering where he ever got such energy. All he did was wiggle. Or nap. That's where he got the energy. "You have to stay here with Mama," she said, careful to use that four letter word to refer to herself. *Mommy* was his dead mother, someone Willie still occasionally woke crying for at night. She waved back at

Norm and coached Willie to do the same. "When you get to be a big boy, you can help Daddy."

"Big," Willie piped up. "Like them?" Maggie looked in the direction of his outstretched arm. Reebok stood talking with four rather slouchy teens. Lordy, she hoped Willie didn't use them as role models.

"Them's big," Willie said, and Maggie saw with relief that he pointed at a pair of sturdy boys who couldn't have been more than nine or ten.

"Yes, Willie—they're big boys. And you're almost five. You're already pretty big yourself."

"Help Daddy?"

She grimaced at the hopeful note in his voice. "Not today, sweetheart, but you're such a big help with the chickens and the goats."

"Love chickens."

Maggie only wished Biscuit could hear that. People who were afraid of chickens the way Biscuit was—well, Maggie felt sorry for anyone like that.

"Big help," Willie added.

She thought he was satisfied. "Let's go home and get some breakfast in your tummy before Sunday school."

"No. Wanna shovel."

Maggie sighed.

~~~~~

The Reverend Henry Pursey stared out across the lawn of The Old Church. The signboard announcing the Sunday morning service listed his sermon topic for this morning. RISE UP ON WINGS AS EAGLES. He'd tried mightily to insist that the sign not lock him into a particular topic; he wanted inspirational sayings instead—something like YOUR WORDS MAY MAKE A DIFFERENCE. He'd even be happy with a quip of some sort. He thought a moment.

PEW WARMERS WANTED

NO EXPERIENCE NECESSARY

APPLY WITHIN

SUNDAY AT 11:00

He could almost see the sign, set up and ready. He could almost hear the chuckles. He was the minister. He ought to have some say-so about something as important as the sign. Maybe fun signs would bring more people in to the service.

Nonsense, he thought. What was going to bring a bumper crop of attendees to this Sunday's service was curiosity. They'd want to know what he had to say about these two fires. And he would talk about the fires, if he could think of what to say. He wondered idly what Father John was planning to say to his congregants. Henry sighed. He was stuck with the eagles.

Still, he was one to change his mind, and his sermon, on a whim, so maybe he wasn't stuck. Not that two fires deliberately set—he knew they'd been deliberate—constituted a whim. He'd have to address what was going on in this small community. If only he knew just what *was* going on.

This quandary of his about the signboard had been going on as long as the doggone thing had been around. Tonya Hastings, the well-meaning but alphabetically-challenged church secretary, tended to announce the sermon topic—taken from the draft on his desk—and give it to Roger to put up on the sign—before Henry was absolutely sure that was what he wanted to talk about. At least she spelled everything right on the signs, unlike her efforts with the weekly bulletin. Then again, maybe Roger caught her errors and replaced *wigs* with *wings* and *rize* with *rise*. Maybe he should start writing his sermons at home.

Irene had forgiven him, but he still felt a little awkward around her. That was another good reason to use his home office. He'd be able to stop every once in a while and give her a big hug.

No. She'd just think he was in her way. He looked hopefully at the signboard. Maybe it had spontaneously altered itself in the last minute and a half. No such luck.

He'd been all set to preach, rather poetically if he did say so himself, about that image of soaring above the pettiness of everyday life. And it was on the signboard. But then last night he'd made the mistake of looking up Isaiah 40:31 in his copy of the *Tanakh*, the Jewish Bible. It said, "renew their strength as eagles grow new feathers." Nothing about soaring. Nothing particularly uplifting. The ancient Jews believed that eagles regained their youth when they molted—that's what it said in the footnote—but that sort of renewal sounded like an everyday affair, like growing fingernails or sprouting a beard. He hated that signboard.

~~~~~

Whew! Getting such a big cleanup job out of the way was almost as good as—well, no, not quite as good as that. I glanced at Bob and lingered on the sight of his bare shoulder. Brushing teeth wasn't perhaps the sexiest thing two people standing next to each other in the bathroom could do. It was all in my mind anyway. I stepped closer to him, my own toothbrush at the ready. "Care for a duel, dear?"

"Gruddle meach?"

We'd been married long enough to have figured out each other's toothbrush talk. "I mean," I said, running my free hand down the middle of his beautifully bare back, "that we still have half an hour before we have to leave for church. I bet I can finish brushing my teeth faster than you can."

We polished off our teeth in record time. And then we lingered a bit, so we were a little late getting to the pew. The church was packed. Luckily, Glaze had saved us two places next to her and Tom.

As the wheezy organ ground into the final phrases of the prelude, I glanced through the bulletin and pulled a pen out of my purse.

"Put it back," Glaze whispered, handing me her bulletin. "I already marked all of them."

Poor Tonya, I thought. Our church secretary had no idea about the limitations of spell-check. *Rise Up As Eagles*, today's sermon topic, came out as *Rise Up Is Eagles*. How she could have missed that one was a marvel, I thought. The last time I looked, i was on the other end of the keyboard from a. Glaze had underlined *I Come to the Garden Aline* (easy to do, since i was next to o, although I doubted that young Tonya knew anything about the A-line skirts that were so popular in the 50s), *Community Averts*—she must have meant *events,* and *Please join is in prayer four our members who have suffers recent losses.*

"Three in one sentence," I muttered. "Is that the new record?"

Clara Martin, substituting for the regular organist, blared out the final chord. Clara's name was, I noticed, spelled right in the bulletin. Tonya knew better than to mess up the name of the First Lady of Martinsville. If she spelled it wrong—although I wasn't sure how even Tonya could mess up that name—Clara would probably make Hubbard, her husband and Chair of the Town Council, reprimand Tonya at a Council meeting.

I pinched my left arm—a technique I'd read about somewhere to keep me from gossipy thoughts. Each time I had an unkind thought or said an unkind word, I was supposed to pinch—hard. The idea was that eventually I'd get tired of all those black and blue spots, and I'd moderate my mind. Fat chance as long as Clara was around. Sigh. I pinched myself again.

"No," my sister whispered. "I counted four last summer." It took me a moment to remember what we'd been talking about.

Maddy turned around from her seat in front of us. "Her record was five in one sentence two years ago."

I guess Glaze and I hadn't been as quiet as we thought we were. We stood for the first hymn, which was, according to Tonya's bulletin, *A Mighty Furtress is our God*. Susan, Henry's daughter, the one nobody had known about until only recently, made her entrance a few minutes after the hymn, right in the middle of the announcements.

I could sense everybody watching her walk down the center aisle. There was something so sensuous about her knee-length hair, especially since it was a luscious shiny black, and it flowed down the middle of her back as smooth as the Metoochie River. I'd never seen it tangled. Of course, I'd never seen her at six in the morning. Maybe she looked like all the rest of us then. She turned when she reached the front pew, and I glimpsed that flawless complexion. No, she didn't look like the rest of us—never.

She sat next to Irene. I wondered if Holly, the daughter who was away at school, had patched up her quarrel with Susan.

No wonder Henry had been preaching all those sermons about forgiveness. He was asking Irene's in front of everybody. Still, she must have forgiven him, because she sat there and smiled at Susan. And then she smiled at Henry. An air current passed through the church as everyone seemed to let out their breath at the same time.

Henry lost his train of thought.

~~~~~

My gratitude list for Sunday
    1. Getting all the fire mess cleaned up so quickly
    2. Good friends – and Roger with his garbage truck
    3. Henry's sermon—about taking responsibility for one's own actions (I'm not sure what that had to do with eagle's wings, but maybe my mind drifted)
    4. Reebok – he's such a big help to Bob
    5. Bob of course—I should have put him as number one

I am grateful for
the bird feeder
leftover chicken
soft laps
my own special door
this soft bed

Chapter 4

12 Years Earlier

SHE ADJUSTED THREE SMALL VASES painted with disgustingly wide-eyed puppies. With all her artistic ability, here she was selling hand-painted knickknacks to tourists during a city sidewalk fair. Fair? It wasn't fair.

Next to her, Barb grunted. "We need to enter some competitions or something and get us some prizes. Then they'd take us seriously."

Sal passed the bottle again, below the edge of the table.

That was good, to keep it out of sight. People might not take them as serious artists if they saw what Barb and Sal were drinking. Or how much of it, although it was hardly anybody else's business. She tried not to drink too much. It put weight on.

"You have to pay to get into most competitions," Sal said. "You got any money?"

"Nope. But you can't sell paintings if you haven't won anything." Barb turned to the third of their group. "Whatcha think?"

She nodded. Barb had given her an idea, but she wasn't going to share it.

He would have wanted her to win.

Chapter 5

So, some guys at school, they said I could
hang out with them if I wanted to.
Only trouble is they're starting this club
and I'm not a member yet
they have their own table
in the lunchroom
and they won't let anybody else eat ~~their~~ there
they said they like to be ~~issolet~~ ~~isoleted~~
they like to eat by themselves

~~~~~~

TWO MORNINGS AFTER THE FIRE, the smell of charred wood still hung around my back yard, even though the men had done a great job of clearing out all the blackened detritus. Later that day, I walked down to the IGA for groceries. Ida's mouth was pinched tighter than a drawstring bag. "You know somebody set fire to one of the garbage bins behind the store Friday night?" I nodded and she wrinkled her nose. "Been trying for the last two days to get this place aired out, but nothing seems to help."

"Was anything else damaged?" I knew about the fire, but hadn't talked to her since then. And I knew there'd been no other damage. Bob had told me. Still, Ida wanted to talk about it, and what else are friends for, if not to listen?

"This infernal stink," she said. "Even the lettuce smells sooty."

"Oh, Ida. It does *not*."

She sniffed. "Maybe not, but there are blackish burn marks up the side of the building."

Ida's mild-mannered husband Ralph walked by and nodded to me. He looked fairly grim.

I reached out and touched her arm. "It could have been a lot worse, I guess."

She sniffed again. "Just let me get my hands on whoever did it."

"It was probably just a prank." Even as I said it, my gut clenched. Two fires in two days? They had to be connected.

She ran her hand through her limp brown hair. "You don't believe that any more than I do. Was it a prank to burn down your shed?"

Mind reader.

After I bought my groceries—none of which smelled like smoke—Marmalade met me on the walkway outside the IGA. I wondered idly if she might have seen who'd set the fire in my back yard.

No. I was sleeping. No one was there by the time I smelled the stink.

I hoisted the handles of my canvas bag over my left shoulder and waved to Celia, our mail carrier. She called out the window of her little white mail van, "Heard about your shed. Are you okay?"

Yes, PushOut. We are.

"We're fine." For a moment I was truly grateful it had only been the shed. What if the guy—whoever he was—had burned the house instead? What if Marmalade had been hurt?

I was safe.

"... wasn't the house."

I caught only the last few words of Celia's comment, but it was easy to follow what she'd been saying. "My thoughts exactly." I waved once more as she continued down Main Street.

I jumped in with her once, but she told me no.

Marmalade purred mightily and walked ahead of me for the two blocks until I reached home. Then she veered around the house, her tail high in the air ...

I want to look at the bird feeder.

... and I put away the groceries, wondering all the while just who could have had something against Ida and Ralph and me. Or maybe they were mad at Roger Johnson. He owned the garbage company that supplied the bins. Nonsense. Nobody could be mad at Roger.

~~~~~

Emma Haversham peered out her front window as the mail carrier slammed shut the door of her mailbox. Like many women of her generation, she enjoyed sending cards and letters—and receiving them, too, so the mail carrier's appearance was always a welcome one. Of course, frequently there were only bills and advertisements. The occasional letter made the anticipation worthwhile. She wondered if she'd hear from Eunice and George. They'd been such caring neighbors back in Atlanta. She'd invited them to come up for a few days. Maybe their answer would be waiting for her in the mailbox. It was nice to think about the possibility. And if not today, then maybe tomorrow.

She strolled down her front walkway, wondering why she'd never heard anything more from Pam, who'd lived on the other side of them from Eunice and George. They'd exchanged a few letters, but Emma had to admit that she'd been the one to institute every exchange. She always tried to ask some questions in her cards and letters, so Pam would have a good reason to write back. But Pam hadn't even bothered to respond to the last card Emma had sent—a funny birthday card with a knock-knock joke.

Sure enough, there was a letter from Eunice, saying they'd be delighted to drive up week after next. Nothing from Pam, though. That was just as well. After all this time she didn't really expect anything. And they hadn't been all that close, even before the … the … No. She didn't want to think about it.

~~~~~

Reebok gathered the small group of index cards and spread them out in a different arrangement on his desk. He looked up as the Chief entered. Leaping almost to attention, but not quite saluting, he said, "Yes Sir, Chief?"

Bob shook his head slightly and nodded toward the spread of three-by-fives. "What's all that, Garner?"

"Notes on the … the case, Sir." He really did wish his voice wouldn't break like that. He was afraid it made him sound younger than he was.

"The case?"

"Yes Sir. The arson." When the Chief didn't reply immediately Reebok hurried to explain. "I read about it in a mystery book, sir. This private eye takes notes and moves them into different positions to see if there could be connections that she hadn't seen before."

"Uh-huh. You read mysteries?"

Reebok's almost beardless cheeks flushed a bit. "I get them from the library." He didn't want to admit that he bought the ones he really enjoyed so he could read them again and again. "They're good for getting ideas, Sir." He pointed to the cards. "Like this."

Bob moved toward the desk. "Show me what you have."

Reebok stepped to one side. "Not much yet, Sir. But we'll get more information, I'm sure."

He pushed the first card toward the Chief. Reebok was proud of his careful printing. It was tidy and easy to read. This one said: GARDEN SHED BEHIND MISS BISCUIT'S HOUSE BURNED

It was followed by five others:

PONTIACS DISCOVERED FIRE

FIRE IN GARBAGE BIN BEHIND GROCERY STORE

SLIGHT DAMAGE TO WALL AT BACK OF IGA

PONTIAC SON LEFT ON FRONT PORCH OF MISS BISCUIT'S HOUSE

NO DISTINGUISHABLE EVIDENCE AT EITHER FIRE SCENE

Bob pointed to the two dates on each card. "What are these?"

"The one on the upper left is the date of the incident, Sir. The one in the upper right corner is the date I wrote the card." When the Chief frowned slightly, he added, "Just in case that information is necessary at a later date, Sir."

"Carry on, Garner. We will solve this soon."

Reebok was inordinately pleased at that *we*. He was a part of the team. With the Chief.

~~~~~

I am grateful for
> *Widelap, who forgot her list tonight*
> *walking with her when she goes places*
> *leftover turkey*
> *GrayGuy, who does not live here anymore*
> *this soft bed*

Chapter 6

12 Years Earlier

WHAT GOOD WAS schooling if you couldn't get any mileage out of it?

She fingered the latest missive from them. They asked. Was it any wonder she planned to comply?

Four issues a year. That sounded about right.

She'd need to make up some names, but that ought to be easy. Nobody paid attention to details anyway. It was the headline that counted.

He would have liked to see her name in print.

He would have been proud of her.

If he'd lived.

Chapter 7

So, the deal is
there's this ~~anishiashun annichi innishi~~ ceremony
for getting into the club.
I gotta go through that before they'll let me in
they're gonna do it too but
they said I gotta be the one to go first
since I'm the new one in town

~~~~~

THE NEXT EVENING, EMMA HAVERSHAM was almost the first person out of Axelrod's. She and Timothy barely knew the woman who had died; they'd come to the memorial service more as a matter of courtesy to the dead woman's husband, whom Timothy, a long-time proponent of helping small businesses to succeed, had mentored for the past year. The widower's Laundromat up in Garner Creek was thriving, thanks in large part to Timothy's insistence on following good standard business practices. Timothy could wax poetic about the value of a good inventory system.

Her husband followed closely behind her, but when Emma set her mind to get out of a place, she tended to leave Timothy in her wake. He must have gotten used to it by now. She couldn't help herself. She'd been like that for the six years since their house ... ever since Atlanta... and then ever since her son ... no. She didn't want to think about it. She *couldn't* think about it. She pushed the glass door open and almost ran to the middle of the drive-up area where the hearse was usually parked for funerals. No hearse tonight.

She couldn't see their car through the ranks of other vehicles. She'd insisted that Timothy park the car way back in the last row, near the woods behind the funeral home. The exercise was good for them both, but the real reason was so the car would be relatively out of sight. Ever since Atlanta...ever since what happened, she had to hide her possessions as much as possible. Now she just needed to get to the car and get home. Timothy caught up with her as she paused under the portico.

Ahead of them, a young man Emma couldn't recall having seen during the memorial service dropped a cigarette on the pavement and didn't even bother to grind it out. A thin trickle of smoke curled upward and insinuated itself under the hem of his tattered jeans. The smoke reminded Emma uncomfortably of what a body had to go through to be turned into the ashes that had been displayed in a ceramic urn at the front of the funeral home's "memory chapel."

The young fellow ignored Emma and looked out over the lines of parked cars. He yawned, not bothering to cover his mouth, and stretched his arms straight above his head. Emma thought he looked like one of those guys at the airport, signaling the airplanes at the gates. Only airport personnel didn't slouch.

Her grandson slouched like that, but Emma tried not to pester him about it. He'd been through so much in his short life. Short to her. She tried to remember what she'd been like at thirteen, but that was so long ago, and times had changed so much since then.

She took Timothy's hand. She was safe. Now. For years people had told her that she was so lucky to have married such a handsome, distinguished-looking man. But she'd never loved him for his movie star looks. She loved him because … well, just because.

Behind them, people began to emerge. Emma had just stepped out from under the portico roof when an explosion rent the air. A ball of fire, a loud whoosh, a faint sound of laughter. It all merged together into a mélange of color and noise and smell.

Their car, the solitary one parked farthest from the funeral home, was engulfed in flames. Timothy started to run.

"No, Timothy," she shouted. "Your heart!"

He slowed to a fast walk, but soon stopped. Even from where Emma stood, she could feel the heat.

When she looked around, the slouching boy had disappeared. She wished she'd looked at him more carefully. All she could remember was ill-fitting jeans and the arms stretched high. Almost like a signal.

~~~~~~

Reebok was glad both he and the chief could split the job of interviewing all the witnesses. They excused everyone who'd been inside the funeral home when the explosion occurred. That still left about fifteen people to talk with.

They'd set up a command post—Reebok liked the sound of that—in two rooms where he supposed Mr. Axelrod met with bereaved people to plan...whatever had to be planned. Reebok had never thought about the mechanics of what to do when someone died.

He placed a blank three-by-five card in the center of the desk and walked out to the large central hall of the funeral home. Only two women and one man were left. He gestured to Mrs. Hagstrom, but she shook her head discreetly and quietly pointed to Mr. Orrin. The old man did look pretty exhausted. Reebok nodded and waited while Mr. Orrin limped into the room.

It turned out Mr. Orrin hadn't known the deceased at all. He just liked to attend funerals, and no, he hadn't seen anything having to do with the fire. He'd been standing out there talking with Ralph Peterson, and their backs were toward the blaze. No, he hadn't seen anyone suspicious. And no, he didn't know the Havershams, the people whose car it was.

Reebok believed him, but he duly noted the details on a card. It paid to be thorough. He walked Mr. Orrin to the door. The Chief must have taken the other woman, the one with the dark hair, into the other interview room. Now, only Mrs. Hagstrom remained, and he beckoned her in.

He expected her not to have seen anything useful even though, unlike Mr. Orrin, she'd known the deceased woman.

"That car exploded just seconds after I walked out the door," she said.

"Did you see anyone suspicious?"

"I certainly did! A young fellow gave a signal—raised his arms up over his head as soon as we walked out."

"Did you recognize him?"

She rubbed the back of her neck. "If I'd realized what he was doing, I would have tackled him. But by the time the car exploded a few seconds later, he was gone."

Reebok stifled a grin as he thought of Mrs. Hagstrom, with her elaborate hairdo piled high on top of her head, tackling an unknown youngster. Anyway, she was about as old as his mother, and he simply couldn't see his mother doing something like that. So maybe Mrs. Hagstrom shouldn't either.

Once again he asked, "Did you recognize him?"

"I wish I could, but I don't really know any of the young people in town. I didn't pay any attention to this one, either—just noticed that he seemed to be signaling someone. And when the explosion went off, of course I looked that way, and then he was gone."

"It was a male, you're sure."

"Most girls don't slouch like that, Officer." Promising to keep an eye out for him and to report to Reebok if she saw him, she wished him "good luck with the hunt."

"If you see him," Reebok said before she left, "don't try to apprehend him yourself. Leave it to the police."

He liked the sound of that.

~~~~~

Maggie checked on Willie one last time and then snuggled in next to her husband. "You awake?"

"I am now."

"The fires, Norm. The shed wasn't the only one. You said Bob was the target, but he can't be. Not if the grocery store and that fire at the funeral home this evening are part of the same pattern."

Norm yawned. "Maybe there's no connection."

"Oh, great." She pulled back onto her side of the bed. "Now I have to worry about *three* fire starters?"

"We're safe. Don't worry."

Fine for you to say, she thought, realizing that sleep would probably be a long time coming.

~~~~~

I was at tap dance class Tuesday evening, so I didn't hear about the fire at Axelrod's until Marmalade and I got home. Bob stood and enveloped me in a warm hug.

"That was nice," I said, "but what's it for?"

"I can hug my wife if I want to, can't I?"

I pulled back and looked up at him.

"There was another fire."

I did not see that one.

Bob had gone to the scene, of course, but he said there wasn't a lot to discover except that it had been deliberately set. People described leaving the service and hearing what they described as "a great big whoosh," and a late model Subaru parked way at the back of the lot went up in flames. He and Reebok had interviewed all the witnesses, but nothing much had come of it. Still, Bob said, "It was clearly a case of arson."

Arson. A word with a nasty taste to it.

Do words taste?

Marmalade, purring away, insinuated herself between my legs. "Whose car was it, Bob? Do you know yet?"

"Yes, I do," he said. "It belonged to the Havershams. They were there at the memorial service."

"Emma Haversham?" She had a library card, so I knew her at least by sight. I hadn't talked with her very many times. She and her equally elderly husband had moved here to Martinsville from the city after she retired six or seven years ago. Maybe I should invite her to join the tap dance class.

"... only way they knew it was their car was that they'd parked out in the last row."

Whoops, I'd missed some of his words. I wondered how many. "Was the lot that full?"

"Not really." Bob looked disturbed. I wondered if there was something more to the story, something he wasn't telling me.

"She said they're trying to get a little more exercise, so they always park as far away as they can."

If they wanted exercise, I thought, they could have left their car at home and walked the five or six blocks to Axelrod's. If I remembered correctly, they lived up on 5th Street, at the head of Magnolia. Nowhere in Martinsville was too far to walk. "Do you have any idea who set it?"

He looked at me funny. "No, as I just told you."

"Sorry."

"The car was out at the back of the parking lot, so whoever set it could douse it with gasoline, pour a trail back toward those trees, wait for the crowd to walk out of Axelrod's, throw the match, and disappear into the woods, all the time blocked from everyone's view by the car itself."

He was using his patient voice, which meant I'd really better pay attention. Usually he didn't get too upset with my habit of woolgathering.

"... a single clue that I could find, other than an empty gas can, the kind anybody can buy in any hardware store. "

"Were there any fingerprints?"

"No. We asked the Captain to drive down to take a look, but

even she didn't have much to add."

If the county arson investigator was stumped, where did that leave the rest of us?

"Bob?" I hesitated to voice my concern, almost as if saying it would make it somehow more real. "Is this something we need to worry about? Ida's garbage bin, our shed, and now a car?"

Softfoot is already worried. I can tell.

He sank heavily onto the couch. "I'm already worried."

See, Widelap? I told you he was.

Marmalade normally had a loud purr. This time, though, it boomed out like a train rumbling through a station. I picked her up and sat beside Bob. She curled herself into a fluffy ball on my lap and kept on purring. Did that mean she was happy?

Yes.

~~~~~

My gratitude list for Tuesday – and Monday, too, since I forgot to write anything yesterday

    1. Bob, who is snoring softly beside me

    2. My sister

    3. Maddy and Norm

    4. Our safety

    5. Marmalade, who is snoring softly on my other side

Excuse me? I do not snore. I purr. I am grateful for

    Softfoot

    cool water

    wide windowsills

    laps

    this soft bed

Chapter 8

9 Years Earlier

THEY MAY ALL HAVE BEEN a little drunker than usual. Not her, of course. She never drank. Too many calories, and she didn't like the fuzzy feeling it left in her head. But the others were royally plastered, so nobody could remember later just whose idea it had been. She knew it hadn't been her idea, but when Ron swore up and down that it was, she didn't disagree with him. Let them think she was a genius. She'd been friends with most of them—change that to acquaintances—for more than a dozen years. They ought to know by now that she was the smartest of the lot. And certainly the best artist.

"My dad'll let us have a show." Ron hardly slurred a single word. "He's oozing with money, so why shouldn't he?"

The others all agreed, but she had reservations, considering the one work she wanted most of all to put in the show. It might be dangerous. "We could all use pseudonyms," she said. That would solve the problem.

"Pseudo, pseudo, pseudo," Ron chanted, and the others joined in with great glee.

When it came time to choose the names, though, everybody except her wanted to be Rembranch, even Celeste, whose work was about as far from Rembrandt as an octopus was from a peacock. "No, no," she told Celeste. "You need to be Matoose."

Celeste brightened. "Yeah, my work is really swirly."

Then there was Charles. "Seumouse," she said, pointing at him, "because you always paint people on picnics."

"Seurat had the right idea." Charles waved his bottle—he was far too manly to drink out of a glass. "Life is nothing but a picnic. Seurat knew it, and Seumouse does, too."

She turned away from him, from the fine line of spittle dribbling down his chin. Charles was truly disgusting. She called these people her friends? Finally, someone asked her what name she'd chosen. "La Degasa," she said. "That's what I'm going to call myself."

They bandied around the other possibilities—Monart, Mo-neigh, Breuglee, Breuglum, Caravangio, Carouselgio. Ron wanted to sign his work PISScaso, but they all knew Ron's dad would draw the line and never allow that in a gallery named for Ron's extra-rich grandmother.

Chapter 9

So, we all gotta do it alone
plan it first
do it soon
I've got an idea
but I hope
I don't get ~~cuaght~~ caught

~~~~~

ON WEDNESDAY, THE *KEAGAN COUNTY Record* sported front-page photos of all three fires. The one of my garden shed was by far the largest, probably because it was a more picturesque view than a ruined dumpster; and a car fire at night can't be easy to photograph.

Marmalade pawed at the picture. I pushed her gently away. There was a funny whitish blob on the left-hand side of the photo of my shed. Whatever it was should have been cropped. I took a closer look. Was that the end of Marmalade's tail?

Yes. I spoke to the woman with the camera, but she did not listen to me.

I folded the paper and headed for the library. Marmalade took a slight detour into the dense foliage of the daylilies around the foot of the mailbox. I wondered what she was after.

Beetle bugs. They are crunchy good.

An hour later, Esther had the preschoolers well in hand for story hour. Their laughter and delighted clapping soared over the bookshelves that separated the children's section from the large central area where we had the checkout desk. Sadie and I smiled at each other. I always enjoyed hearing the laughter of small children—but I was equally grateful for the fact that I didn't have to be the one to deal with them in large groups.

Esther was amazing that way. Good for her. She had two such groups scheduled each Wednesday. And one on Friday afternoon as well. How she stood it, I'd never know.

If they got too noisy I could hide upstairs in the cataloguing room—which also just happened to have a small kitchen and some very good loose teas I always sampled with pleasure. And on Friday, I wouldn't need to disappear, because Peachie would be here by lunchtime. That meant I'd miss all the noise of the Friday afternoon session. Marmalade appeared from behind one of the reference shelves, a long bare tail hanging from one corner of her mouth.

This one is a very small intruder.

She laid the mouse—I was glad it was dead—at my feet. "Thank you," I whispered, so I wouldn't disturb the children's story hour.

You are welcome. This is part of my job.

Lorna Jean Hagstrom shoved open the heavy oak door and breezed up to the counter. I nudged the mouse out of sight. I wished Marmalade would put the things in the trash basket.

That is not my job. That is yours.

Lorna Jean had lived in Martinsville about as long as I had. She and her husband—I think his name was Mark—had relatives in the area, a sister of hers, or was it Mark's sister? They'd been renting a house on 4th Street when I first met her—when she signed up for a library card—but they bought the old Selman house on Willow a couple of months ago after Mrs. Selman finally died. The old woman was well over a hundred years old, and the only reason she died was that a wheel on her walker gave out as she was taking her daily constitutional down to the town dock, and she pitched headlong into the Metoochie River. Drowned before anybody could reach her. The town gossip mill said that her children sold the old house for a song.

Well, I wouldn't be surprised if they did. The place was practically falling down. Old Mrs. Selman refused to have any work done on it, even though plenty of people would have been willing to help, just like they did with cleaning up the remains of my garden shed.

"Did you hear about the car fire?" Without waiting for an answer, Lorna Jean went on in a breathless voice, "I was there. It was awful. So hot I thought I'd roast, even though it was at least a hundred yards away from the front entrance."

You still feel scared.

Marmalade vaulted to the counter and meowed loudly. I picked her up and set her on the floor, but she hopped right back up again.

I want to smell her closer.

"Did anybody see what happened?" I knew the answer already,

but Lorna Jean so obviously wanted to talk about it, I let her. That seemed to be my purpose in life lately.

"No. That's the awful part of it. This was, what? The third fire in less than a week? That's terrible."

I couldn't have agreed more.

"Emma's such a nice person, too," she went on. "I met her and her husband right after Mark and I moved here. It's been six or seven years, I think. It's so sad about their son and his wife, isn't it?"

Sadie nodded, as if she knew what Lorna Jean was talking about.

"Their son?" I hadn't heard anything, which was hard to believe in a town as small as this. Usually word spread faster than chicken pox in a first grade classroom. Then again, I didn't know Emma well, so it made sense that I wasn't in the loop.

"Didn't you hear? Emma's son and his wife died in a car crash down in Atlanta a month or two ago." I was glad she sounded sad rather than excited. Funny how some people got so ghoulish when passing on bad news. "Very tragic," she went on after a suitable pause. "Emma was just devastated. She'd been taking that class from Connie, the one that meets every Monday and Thursday. She really enjoyed it, but she was so devastated by her son's death, she stopped everything. All she does, it seems, is grocery-shop on Wednesdays and go to church on Sundays."

"I don't really know her well," I said, but now that I thought about it, other than one visit here a couple of days ago, she hadn't been in the library in months. At least not that I'd seen.

"Car crashes," Lorna Jean said, "and now fires. What's the world coming to?"

Martinsville is such a small town, we weren't used to this many fires. Bob and Reebok spent hours interviewing folks, but nobody had seen anything related to any of the blazes. They asked everyone to keep an eye peeled for suspicious people. We had a firebug on our hands and no clue as to who it could be.

~~~~~~

Lorna Jean truly did wonder what the world was coming to. Somebody like Biscuit, this quiet librarian, married to that sweet police officer, didn't have to worry about anything.

Lorna Jean wished sometimes that she could be like that, but she couldn't. Not any more. It started almost a year ago, when Mark began taking lessons twice a week from Connie Cartwright. A hobby, she'd thought, but as time went on he spent more and more evening hours there. He even had a key to the studio.

"We all have them," he'd told her. "That way we can work on our own projects even if Connie's gone or is working on her own pieces."

Lorna Jean didn't like it. She'd seen other women going in there too, when she'd thought Mark would be working alone. She hadn't been able to identify the women—they were just small shadowy shapes outlined against the light from the opening door. Maybe she should have marched over and introduced herself. But she was afraid that would look like she didn't trust her husband.

Of course, she didn't.

She'd asked him about it just that morning. She'd been standing at the sink, not even looking at him.

"They're all taking the class," he'd said.

"And what about all those times Connie isn't there? I can see when her car is gone."

He had stepped forward and turned her around to face him. "We have assignments to complete, things we can do without Connie."

What assignments she wondered, but was too afraid of the answer to even ask. He was so much older than she was. Maybe he was having a mid-life crisis? A last chance fling?

He'd looked at her long and—she thought—hard. "You don't need to worry about me," he said. "I'll make sure nothing happens."

Lorna Jean shivered.

"Are you okay?" Biscuit sounded genuinely concerned.

"Just a goose walking on my grave," Lorna Jean said, and wondered why she'd pulled that ancient aphorism out of her brain. Her mother used to say that.

~~~~~~

Emma picked up one more dish, swiped at it with a blue edged dishtowel. Something had to be done, but she didn't know what. She felt so helpless—Timothy hadn't said much after the police finished questioning everybody at the funeral home, but she could tell he was upset. And that wasn't good for his heart. So many of their questions had dealt with how much insurance they had on the car. Surely nobody believed that Timothy—sweet gentle Timothy—would burn his own car,

Maybe they should have stayed in Atlanta? It had been at

Emma's insistence almost seven years ago that they'd moved to Martinsville in the first place. The vandalism in Atlanta had felt like a personal attack; she and her husband had come home to their house in an upscale neighborhood one evening and found what looked like the aftermath of a tornado in their living room and, as they discovered after they called the police, throughout the entire house. Almost all of their precious possessions destroyed. Not even stolen for somebody to sell—maybe she could have understood that—but ripped, slashed, thrown over, disemboweled, shattered. Walls with cross-shaped holes pounded into the expensive knotty pine paneling. The stove with cross-shaped dents all over it. Photo albums fed into the toilets. Chandeliers pulled out of the ceilings, as if someone had swung on them. The work of young drug-crazed gang members, or so Timothy had insisted.

The only room that wasn't touched was their bedroom, but she hadn't been able to bear the thought of staying in that house for even one more night.

The ferocity of the violence had terrified her. She'd demanded that they move, and she had to quit her job as a result. Her manager could have fired her; she couldn't—couldn't—go back to the office again. She couldn't leave Tim's side. She wouldn't let him leave hers. She couldn't make herself be alone. But her manager had understood, and Emma resigned over the phone, calling from an anonymous hotel in downtown Atlanta where they'd gone as soon as the police were through with them that night. That awful night.

Even before the break-in, though, Timothy had a good retirement income from the sale of his business. And, almost unbelievably, they'd made a bundle of money when they sold the trashed house. They'd bought it long before that particular section of Atlanta was fashionable, and then had watched the value skyrocket. Thank goodness they'd found Martinsville.

They fled here less than a week after it happened. An old school chum of Tim's was a Martinsville resident. He'd found a house for them. They had no clothes to speak of, nor any household goods. What she carried with her away from Atlanta was her fear. She brought it here, and it had taken several years to wear off. She'd finally been able to walk to the Herb Shop or the grocery store by herself, without the comforting bulk of her husband by her side. Timothy had been so supportive, so understanding. They still did the grocery shopping together, but now it was because they liked to do things with each other, not because she was desperate to have him with her.

And then, two months ago, their son and his wife died in a car crash. Some of their new friends here had supported them through that awful time. The pain had been almost more than she could bear, but she and Timothy had tried to stay strong for each other. No parent should ever have to lose a child. She was touched by how many Martinsville residents had driven all the way to Atlanta for the funeral. She hardly even knew some of them.

Up until the last few days, Martinsville had felt like home, and she loved this town, this house. But now, the violence was here, too. No connection to what happened in Atlanta, of course. She'd wasted a good deal of time crying in the hours since her car was burnt up. Torched? Wasn't that what they called it nowadays? There was no reason at all for someone to do that. No more reason than there had been for the destruction of their belongings in Atlanta. But still, this was the second time they'd been backhanded by violence.

Emma resented the heck out of the people—whoever they were—who had attacked Timothy. Twice. Timothy's house and his car. Their house. Their car. He was such a good man, such a kind man. Oh, he had his moments, the same way most men did, she supposed. But who on earth in Atlanta could have felt such anger toward him that they would destroy his house? And who here in Martinsville would even care enough to burn his car? And why, when she'd found a true home here, should this happen now?

She would not let this freeze her in her tracks. Her son's death had stopped her for a time, too, but she had to get hold of herself. Timothy was affected by her fears and anguish. She couldn't let that happen. It was just a silly car, after all. Probably a kid's prank. The boy in the jeans had looked like he was sending a signal. That's all it was. Kids … although she was vaguely disturbed that the definition of *prank* had changed so much in recent years. There was an enormous gulf between tipping over somebody's outhouse—which was about as far as pranks went when she was a youngster—and burning a car, or that shed she'd heard about, to the ground. But she was determined to learn again how to visit the library and the grocery store by herself. She would go to the IGA. She would live her life like a normal person, not like a hunted animal, like the spouse of a hunted animal. Timothy didn't deserve any of this.

She had to stop thinking about this. She'd call her sister and arrange that trip she'd been talking about. She could cook up enough meals ahead of time so Timothy and the boy wouldn't starve; then it wouldn't be such an imposition on them if she left for a few days. Timothy could take the boy fishing this weekend. She'd tell them at dinner tonight.

Timothy had gone outside about half an hour ago to wash the rental car. He'd washed their car—their former car—the afternoon before ... before it happened. Her gut clenched the way it used to do all the time right ... right after ... after Atlanta. She'd almost forgotten that feeling, the fear that everything she and Timothy owned might be taken from them again. He always told her they didn't need *things*, as long as they had each other. But somebody who had destroyed *things* could destroy *people*.

Just to be sure he was still there, still okay, she walked down the hall to the big picture window in the living room.

Timothy used a squeegee on the windshield of the rental car beside the curb. When he glanced up, she waved, and he waved back. She wanted to open one of the smaller windows that flanked the big one and call out, "I love you, I love you, I love you." But even with the sash windows open, she doubted he'd hear her. His hearing had deteriorated so much in the past few years.

Anyway, it would be silly to yell out the window. Someone was walking past, pausing to exchange a few words with Timothy. So she wouldn't shout her love. She'd just think it.

She laid an arthritic hand over her heart for a moment. It wouldn't be fair for her to go visit her sister. Not now. She'd have to stay here and deal with the aftermath of the car fire. She couldn't run away and leave Timothy handling all of this. Especially with the boy here now.

She worried about her grandson. He was a good kid. Always had been, although she hadn't seen as much of him as she would have liked to once she and Timothy moved up here to Martinsville. Well, now they'd have four or five years together until he went off to college. Maybe eventually the hurt would heal enough that he'd open up. She hoped he had a teacher at school that he could talk to.

Maybe she could take up the classes from Connie again. That would take her mind off all this. She hadn't finished the last vase Connie had assigned. Maybe she would drop over there this evening and see if she could complete it before Connie came back from…from wherever she'd gone. And Mark might be there. Such a sweet young man. Not that he was that young, but compared to Emma, everybody seemed young. He was pleasant to talk with, and he reminded her so much of her son. Mark's glasswork was considerably better than hers, but that didn't bother her. He took it seriously. For her, it was just a hobby.

She waved at Timothy one more time and walked back to the kitchen. Sliding open the top drawer beside the refrigerator, she removed the key Connie had given her. She'd go over there to the studio once she was sure Jimmy was settled in for the night—he usually did his homework in his room, and then she wouldn't see him until she tiptoed in after he was sound asleep. She could never resist tousling that thick hair of his. Often Timothy would go with her and they'd marvel at Jimmy's gangly sprawl and how much he looked like Timso at that age. Jimmy was such a dear. But far too quiet, except when he had nightmares. No wonder, after what he'd been through.

Eventually, she might be able to get her grandson interested in doing something with glass. He was good with his hands. And he seemed to be doing a lot of writing. She'd come upon him several times, but each time he'd whipped his notebook out of sight, so she hadn't said anything. That was such a hard age. He was probably writing love poems to one of the girls at school. She hoped the girl wouldn't be mean to him.

Emma jotted a few items on her grocery list. She'd just been to the IGA a few days before, but she wanted to bake cookies with Jimmy this weekend. She'd need flour. And some more sugar. And if Eunice and George were coming next week, she'd have to stock up a bit for that. And ice cream. Jimmy loved ice cream.

She studied the list. Too much for her to carry by herself, and even if Timothy came along to do the hauling, the ice cream would likely melt before they made it up the hill. She'd ask him to drive her down.

~~~~~

Paula Corrigan punched her brother's phone number and he picked up on the second ring. That was a record. He usually took five or six to answer.

"Lunch tomorrow?" She never had to identify herself. Ever since she was eight, ever since the fire, her voice had been distinctive. Something about smoke-damaged vocal cords, the doctors had said. They thought she'd grow out of it, but she never had.

"Is it that time of year again?"

"Yeah." She brushed the prematurely white lock of hair off her forehead. "And I know you didn't forget, so quit pretending."

He didn't even try to defend himself. "It'll have to be breakfast this time. I've got a lunch meeting with the Board."

"The Board." Paula infused the word with as much bewilderment at his chosen career path as her damaged vocal cords would allow.

"Yes. The Board. So where do you want to eat?"

"As if we ever eat anywhere else? I'll meet you there at 0500."

"Oh-five-hundred it is. Good thing the Delicious opens so early."

They hung up without saying goodbye.

They never said goodbye. Never. Not since that day their big sister threw them both out of a third-floor window.

~~~~~

I took a circuitous route home that afternoon. Marmalade and I ran into Tom Parkman, and as always he ducked back inside his restaurant to get a small take-home bag of salmon for the Furball, as he called her.

Thank you, Fishgiver.

Marmy wove between his legs. I'm sure she knew what was in the bag.

Excuse me? How could I mistake that smell?

Tom looked a bit frazzled.

He feels tired.

I wondered if he'd taken on more than he could chew …

I do not see him eating anything.

… what with that new school he'd started. "How's the school going, Tom? Is it as fulfilling as you'd thought it would be?"

"It's been a slow start. I'm down to only ten students. This semester, two of the six new ones dropped out."

"Couldn't take the pressure?"

He shrugged. "Not exactly. It was more that they couldn't figure out how to take responsibility for their own actions, and they didn't give me...the school...a chance to teach them how." He looked off over my shoulder, his eyes unfocused, as if he saw his dream out there somewhere.

I waited a moment. "How are the others doing—the ones who are left?"

His brown eyes glowed. "Great. Just great. The six older students—the ones I have left from last year—have progressed admirably."

"You sound like an advertising brochure."

He grinned, a bit sheepishly. "We've had a few glitches to work out, but for the most part they see this as their best chance for a good job, and I'm beginning to convince them that they can have a career as restaurateurs." He grinned again, a little sheepishly I thought. "They don't think of it in quite that light yet."

I started to reply, but my attention was drawn to shouting from the back of the restaurant. Tom looked over his shoulder. "They still have so much energy. Don't see how they do it." As we watched, a group of boys—young men, I supposed—rounded the back corner of the building and sprinted across the parking lot, then doubled back toward the lawn in back, where Tom sometimes catered wedding receptions.

They remind me of puppies.

As I watched, one of the shortest of the boys—the blond one with a snub nose—skidded to a halt and threw a basketball as hard as he could toward one of the others. It made vicious contact, and I looked at Tom to see if he'd do anything about it, but he'd already turned away from them.

"I know it doesn't look like it," he pointed his thumb back over his shoulder as the two boys grappled for a bit. The rest of the group soon disappeared around the corner. "But some of them are talking about eventually owning their own small-town diners. You can't get much better than that."

"Sure beats washing dishes for somebody else for the rest of their lives," I said.

"That's right. And that was about all any of them had to look forward to with failing school grades. Now they have a chance." He glanced at his watch. "Speaking of chances, I need to get back in there. Break time is over, and here's a chance to teach the four new ones the best way to flip a burger."

"I admire your enthusiasm," I said.

He laughed. "Yeah—who else would get ecstatic over spatula-work?"

"Better you than me." I waved, and Marmalade led me all the way home.

~~~~~

My gratitude list for Wednesday
>   1. Sandra, Sally, and Scott, my three wonderful children. I can't imagine losing a child—even though mine are grown up and on their own. Of course, Emma's son was grown, too. How did she ever cope? I wish I knew her other than just by sight— and by library card. Maybe I could have—NO. Nothing could possibly help when someone loses a son. But maybe I could have cried with her.
>
>   Get to the point, Biscuit McKee! This is supposed to be a gratitude list, not a journal.
>
>   2. Bob, who was gone so long after he found out Daniel Russell had been attacked. I'm glad he made it home finally.
>
>   3. Marmy, who's yawning. So am I.
>
>   4. The library – MY library!
>
>   5. Lorna Jean. I'd like to get to know her better. Just so she doesn't ask me to go jogging.

I am grateful for
>   *Salmon from Fishgiver*
>   *claws and teeth to catch the intruders in the book place*
>   *the bugs I catch in the funny wavy plants*
>   *stretching*
>   *this soft bed*

Chapter 10

9 Years Earlier

SHE KNEW EXACTLY WHICH PIECE she'd enter in the show. She'd never signed it—that might not be safe. Somebody might remember.

She opened her closet, pushed aside the few clothes she'd bothered to put on hangers, and pulled out the canvas. Propped on an easel beside the window, her black and white masterpiece—it *was* a masterpiece—still could bring tears to her eyes.

She'd captured the strength of his shoulders, the angle of his jawline. The streak of premature gray—silver really—at his temple was just suggested. She'd worked so hard to get exactly the right balance of fact and enigma.

Too bad the subject of her portrait had never seen it. Would never see it.

She toyed with the middle word of the title. Should it be *Hated*? Or should it be *Loved*?

Chapter 11

So, I'm not sure I want to go first
but I don't have much choice
do I?
I wish Mr. Latham was here
so I could talk to him
about all this

~~~~~

REEBOK CALLED JUST AS DOODLE-DOO crowed on Friday morning. He did that earlier each day, or so it seemed. The rooster. Not Reebok. Anyway, it was exactly 5:31. Why do I always look at those stupid red numbers when I'd rather be sleeping? Bob seldom said anything when he had to head out early like that, but this time he turned to me with a warm, quiet kiss. "Stay safe, honey," he said. "Go back to sleep."

Back to sleep? Ha! Fat chance of that, what with the phone call—and what did Bob mean about *stay safe*? Like there was something going to happen? Bye-bye sleep, especially with Marmalade prancing around on my tummy.

We need to go see something.

Oh well, I'd heard Reebok's high tenor voice on the phone—not words, so I didn't know the whole story, but the tone—I could hear the panic he couldn't control—so I was out of bed and into the bathroom before Bob was out the front door. Maybe the call had to do with Daniel Russell, the young boy, thirteen or fourteen years old, who'd been beaten so badly last night. I knew he was in the big county hospital up in Russell Gap. How ironic that he was being cared for in a town that bore his family name. There were a lot of Russell's in Keagan County. Sadie was a Russell before she married Wallace. I wondered if Daniel might be a great-grandnephew of hers. I'd have to ask.

Bob had told me the ambulance hadn't even stopped at the

Montrose Clinic, the closest hospital in this end of Keagan County. Daniel's head injury was way beyond the skills of the doctors there. The boy was unconscious, unable to identify his attacker. I hoped he hadn't died. That would have sent Reebok into a tailspin, I was sure.

Come outside. Hurry.

I dressed quickly and, shortly before dawn, with Marmalade right underneath my feet, I stepped outside to see what the day would be like. Instead, I saw the smoke of the fourth fire. A dark gray wash, almost black, swirled through the crape myrtles in my front yard, pushed by a stronger-than-usual early morning breeze. It wasn't leaf-burning season yet. I headed back inside for the phone, just in case this fire wasn't what had prompted Reebok's call.

"Thank you for calling," the 911 Operator told me, "but we've already received several reports, and the Martinsville fire department is on the scene."

She wouldn't tell me where the scene was, though.

"The smoke's coming from the direction of my library," I said. "Is the library on fire?"

"Stay where you are, ma'am. They don't need unnecessary bystanders getting in the way."

Unnecessary bystanders? What made her think I was unnecessary? Especially if it was the Martinsville Library—my library—on fire. I picked the receiver back up. I'd call the station. Bob or Reebok would be there. They'd know what was going on.

Softfoot is near the fire. I can feel him inside my head.

Marmalade purred her loud rumble and rubbed against my ankle. *She's so soft.*

Thank you.

Reebok answered on the first ring. "Martinsville Police. Deputy Garner speaking."

"What's going on Reebok? I called 911, but they wouldn't tell me anything."

"Good morning, Miss Biscuit. There was a fire."

"I know. That must be why you called Bob so early. Is it the library?"

"No, ma'am."

"Where is it?"

"On Willow Street."

"It wasn't Margaret's house, was it?"

"No." Bob's normally garrulous deputy—he insisted on

that title; he must have watched a lot of Westerns growing up—was singularly taciturn this morning. I waited for him to go on, but there was an ominous silence.

"Is it Monica's house? Lorna Jean's? Easton's?"

"No."

I was in no mood to keep guessing all the people who lived on Willow. "Whose house?"

"Nobody's house."

"Reebok," I said, my voice lower than usual, "would you please give me some details?"

"The shed beside Connie Cartwright's house caught fire."

"Shed?" It was hardly a shed, more like a house, but without a bathroom. At least forty-five feet on a side, with built-in workbenches, electric outlets every four feet, and all the paraphernalia she needed for her work and her classes. I didn't know the names of half those gadgets. "Her glass-blowing studio?"

"Yes," he said with a singular lack of chattiness.

"Is Connie okay?"

Silence.

"Reebok? Answer me."

"Don't worry ma'am, I'm sure it will be all right."

"Reebok! What on earth is wrong?"

The pause went on way too long.

"Answer me!"

"They can't find her."

~~~~~

Paula watched her brother gulp down yet another cup of coffee. Margo should have left the pot on the table.

She raised her glass of water in the final routine they'd spoken every September for almost four decades. The last twenty-five or so had been right here at the Delicious. "Here's to Sherry," she said. "Thirty-seven years."

"To Sherry." He touched his glass to hers. "Thirty-seven years."

They met, usually for lunch, once every other month or so. Hard to get together any more than that with their work schedules the way they were. And with his kids and all their soccer games and high school orchestra rehearsals, sometimes they'd go three months without seeing each other.

But they never missed this day. Always the same day. Always here, although there wasn't any particular reason for that except that they both liked the food.

They always ate out. No family gatherings at his house. His wife didn't want their children to talk with Paula. Too many questions about her job. Paula didn't understand that. She was sorry that her work was necessary, but she was proud of what she did.

Margo interrupted her thoughts. "Phone call, Captain. From fire headquarters. You can take it by the cash register."

Paula sprang to her feet. An early morning call could mean only one thing.

~~~~~

Reebok hung up the phone. He sure hoped Miss Biscuit wasn't as mad as she sounded. He knew he'd made a mistake not answering her right away, but then he couldn't figure out how to get out of the situation. Maybe he should call her back and apologize. No. She'd be on her way to the fire scene. He was sure of that. He set the phone back down. He'd heard a lot about those new cell phones. Too bad they didn't work in Keagan County. If he'd had one of those, he could go anywhere in town, anywhere in the valley, and people would be able to reach him. He could be at the fire scene and still be able to answer Miss Biscuit's phone call. *Or anybody else's* he reminded himself. That was his job.

He looked around the small office. This was a great place to work. He had the Chief as a boss. And all the nice townspeople to talk with any time they called. And Miss Biscuit—Reebok reined in that thought. Miss Biscuit was the Chief's wife. Miss Biscuit was a lady. Miss Biscuit wouldn't really be interested in someone like him.

He hadn't wanted to worry her, and now she was mad at him. The more he thought about it, the more he wanted to kick himself.

He kicked a desk leg instead and sat down. He opened a brand new package of 3x5 cards. He had a feeling he was going to need a lot of them.

It was good to stay busy. He'd call his mother so she wouldn't worry about him, and then he'd head down to Connie Cartwright's house in about fifteen minutes. After all, the Chief might need him.

And Miss Biscuit would be there.

~~~~~

The fourth fire. Bob looked around at the crowd beginning to assemble; it had grown steadily from a small clump of people in the predawn standing back from the fire engine. Now it was a congregation spread out behind the tape he and Hoss Cartwright had strung from stanchions they placed in the middle of the street. People would not stay back otherwise. And more were still arriving.

He looked for his wife. She didn't seem to be there yet, but he knew Biscuit. She'd show up. Especially since this was Connie's place. Captain Corrigan stood beside him, waiting until enough water had cooled the scene. It didn't seem to be cooling as fast as it should be.

The two of them had already done a walk-around, checking out the fire from all sides. Well, from three sides. The studio, like so many of the houses along this side of Willow, was backed up close to the cliff that formed the southern border of Martinsville. The captain made brief notations in a bright lime green notebook. He'd asked her about it once. The answer? Lime green was easier to spot than yellow or red. Captain Corrigan had even proposed that all the emergency vehicles in the county be re-painted that color, but tradition was a hard thing to overcome.

All of them—Bob, the Captain, and the firefighters—had carefully avoided stepping on the swath of burned grass that led from the street to the building. Accelerant. They all knew it. Which was the main reason they'd called for the Captain, who'd been close by having breakfast at the Delicious.

Why the glass studio? Why not the house? Was this just a prank that got out of hand? No, it couldn't be. The fire in the garbage bin behind the IGA could have been a prank, but three more fires put paid to that theory. Why would someone set four fires? For revenge? No. The targets—a garbage bin, a garden shed, a car, and Connie's studio—were too diverse. For attention? No again. The person would have to admit to it before any attention came his way. Gang activity? No. There weren't any gangs around here. Keagan County was such a small county, most people in Georgia had never even heard of it. And this dead end valley was hard to find. Why would there be gangs here? And if there were, every police officer in the county would know about it.

Somewhere in that crowd, he thought, the creep who started this fire was watching, probably thrilled by the results of his handiwork. If only that person would stand out, carrying guilt like a shawl around his shoulders. He thought briefly of the way Marmalade draped like a shawl around Biscuit's shoulders whenever she sat knitting on their couch. He almost smiled. But this was no laughing matter.

Who did this? Who poured the gas? Who lit the match? Which one in that crowd was the guilty one? He looked for any piece of the scene that was slightly off center, slightly out of place. The person feigning too much nonchalance. The person too fascinated by what was happening. The person with avid eyes bugging out. But heck, everybody here was interested. It was fun watching firefighters at work. Fires were inherently exciting. Maybe the mood would have been different if this had been a house on fire—a dwelling with the possibility of people trapped inside. But this was only a studio. It meant a lot to Connie Cartwright, of course, but nobody else in that crowd would have had a vested interest in it. So they were excited rather than apprehensive.

He'd have to check Connie's insurance records. Did she stand to make much money on this? Was there anyone else who would benefit if Connie's shed was gone? Was there someone looking to buy this acre and a half? He knew Connie had bought this lot and her house at the same time. It was hard to keep a secret in a small town. Not that there was anything secret about a land sale.

He stepped away from the Captain, turned around, and looked up at the cliff. If he were starting a fire, he would have dropped a rock through the studio skylight, then poured gasoline from up there and flung a flaming torch of some sort through the hole. That way, he would have been able to get clear away without leaving a trail of ruined grass, and without as much risk of being seen. He could have run back across the extensive kenaf fields. The harvest was over, the fields were clear. Once he hit the county road, he'd be gone, and nobody would be any wiser. Then he could pull into town a few hours later and feign surprise. He was glad this fire starter hadn't thought of that. Still, there were precious few clues. This trail of burnt grass wasn't enough to learn anything from.

He thought back to that building inspection he'd made. Something didn't fit. What was it?

~~~~~

Reebok told me to stay put. Fat chance. I'd spent my entire school career, from first grade up until I graduated from college, being a good girl, obeying instructions, following directions. It was no fun at all. Even when I was married to Sol, I lived a fairly boring life. After his death, I'd gone against all common sense, all good advice, and moved here to be the Martinsville librarian. And met Bob. So, following good advice wasn't always the best thing to do. Anyway, Reebok wasn't much older than my youngest, my son Scott, so I didn't have to listen to him.

I waited only long enough to hang up the phone, throw on a sweater, and check the crockpot; it had been on all night. I love slow-cooked soups.

By the time Marmalade and I got outside, a faint acrid tang hung in the air, but the smoke had dissipated. They must have gotten the fire out. I was glad it wasn't Connie's house, but she'd be very upset if all her glass-blowing supplies were ruined. It was like my shed—her tools had to be as important to her as my garden implements were to me. Maybe more so. I didn't make my living from gardening, but this studio housed what she needed to make money. I was hurt, but I wasn't ruined.

You and Softfoot were not hurt.

They couldn't find her. She had to be okay. She had to.

Connie was fairly new to Martinsville. I liked her because almost the first thing she did when she moved to town was to get a library card. Anybody who used my library on a regular basis had to have something going for them. And don't tell me that even serial killers have library cards. If they do, I don't want to know about it.

Marmalade scooted outside ahead of me and turned left when she got to the mailbox. That was the way I was headed. I wondered if she would have reversed her course if I'd turned the other way.

You are following me.

But this was the way I wanted to go. Nothing wrong with walking past the library just to be sure it was still standing. I wasn't sure I wanted Marmy near the scene of a fire, but she was pretty smart most of the time.

Excuse me? Most of the time?

She always looked both ways before crossing the street, but I don't think she'd ever been around a fire. Still, the smell would probably keep her away. She walked ahead of me, almost as if she knew where we were going ...

Oh, please. I heard everything you said, and I am following the scent.

... and she rumbled away as if she were answering me.

Mouse droppings!

Connie not only was a reader, but she'd joined our tap dance class, too. I didn't particularly like her way of always putting an X-rated spin on every comment anyone made at our gabfests after class every

Tuesday. Despite that, though, she was a fun addition, and a pretty good dancer—far better at learning the steps than I was. Of course, everyone in the class fit that category.

Marmalade paused at the corner and looked back uphill. I glanced around to see what she was looking at. A car rounded from Third Street onto Beechnut Lane. The butterfly magnet on the door of my sister's Civic glowed in the morning light. I waved.

~~~~~~

Mary Fleming hardly even acknowledged Lorna Jean as she joined the other woman, heading down Magnolia and picking up her pace before they reached Second Street. The first run of the day always felt good. There was a cast of smoke in the air. Mary gave a tentative sniff, but it wasn't heavy enough to interfere with her breathing. Sometimes she wondered if she overdid the running. Lorna Jean never ran more than once a day, but Mary sometimes felt incomplete if she didn't get in at least one more short run in the evening. Today would be a good day for two runs, the one now and another long one in the late afternoon. Her husband had said he planned to be home all day. The two of them had grown more and more distant over the past few months; sometimes she wished he'd go away and never come back. Or maybe she should be the one to leave.

He wasn't fun anymore. Wasn't supportive in the way he used to be. *Sort of* used to be. Come to think of it, he'd never really supported her in anything except moving to Martinsville. She'd have to think more about this. Mary liked to plan things out ahead of time, and leaving would take a good deal of planning. She had time, though. Lots of time.

Next to her, Lorna Jean raised a hand and pointed to the right. "Smoke," she said. That was all she needed to say. Mary nodded and veered right onto Second Street. If Lorna Jean was curious, they'd go; but deep down, all Mary wanted to do was run.

Chapter 12

9 Years Earlier:

SHE'D NEVER BEEN GOOD ENOUGH for him, except in that one way. Even her first big oil painting, a bright and lovely scene of wildflowers in a mountain meadow, wasn't good enough. It had shown the marks of an amateur—she admitted that—but he didn't have to sneer at it. "You overdid it on the color, didn't you," he'd said, not even a question in his voice. No encouragement, no word of approval, no word of love, of course. She'd never heard him use the L word.

But he was so tall, so sure of himself; his smile blinded her; his touch soothed her. So why couldn't he have praised her, even a little?

The second oil she took to him, a stark black and white winter landscape, garnered half a glance. "No color?"

Even when she added a bright red cardinal to the topmost pine branch, it still wasn't good enough.

All he wanted from her was what he always wanted. And it had nothing to do with painting.

She knew what the title had to be.

Chapter 13

So, if I get in, I'll be called
Number 4
you-know-who is Number 1
of course.
I think I've decided.
Tomorrow night.
I'll do my ~~innishi~~ thing.
I want my friends to like me.

~~~~~~

YOU'RE OUT EARLY," MY SISTER called through the open window as she drew alongside.

So are you.

"Good morning, Glaze. Hey there, Maddy," I said to her housemate in the passenger seat.

I couldn't see if Dee was in the back seat because of the reflection on the window, but it rolled down and Gracie, the homeless dog Glaze had adopted a few months before, poked her head out, tongue lolling. Marmalade jumped through the open front window, over Glaze, and across the console to Maddy.

Hello CurlUp.

From behind Gracie, Dee called out, "Where you goin'?"

We are going to the place that smells burnt.

Marmy let out a yowl before I could answer, so Dee amended her question. "Where are you *two* going?" I would have laughed, but couldn't when I thought about what was at the end of the street.

"The fire," I said. "Surely you smelled it. It's Connie's studio."

"We did," Maddy said, "but we couldn't tell where the stink was coming from."

"We'll take you there." Glaze's face looked grim.

Dee pulled Gracie onto her lap as I hopped in. Marmalade stood on Maddy's lap with her front feet planted on the dashboard, as if she were riding shotgun.

I get a better view this way.

She should have been in a cat carrier, but I'd let her get away with it this once. Since I didn't happen to have a carrier with me. "Where were you three headed?"

"We've had an application for some M-Money to refurbish the old Keagan Hotel to be used as a retreat center," Glaze said, "and we're meeting the new owner there to look it over."

"This early?"

She laughed. "Some people have strange schedules."

"The appointment's not *that* early," Dee said.

Maddy swiveled in her seat, and I saw Marmy shift to a new position on Maddy's legs, one of which was curled on the seat beneath her. She always sat that way.

That is why I call her CurlUp.

"The Butterfly Brigade always accommodates," Maddy said. "You want to come along with us?"

"No," I said. "I'd better stick around here. You can tell me all about it when you get back. But why are you headed *this* way? The Keagan's back the other direction."

Dee piped up from beside me. "We know. We were actually headed to the Delicious for breakfast first—the new hotel owner isn't *that* much of an early bird."

Glaze slowed down at the intersection where Second crossed Juniper at a deep angle. We really did need four-way stop signs there. Not that anybody drove very fast in Martinsville. Maddy looked out to the right. "All clear."

"Thanks, Mad."

It was funny how I could often tell my sister's mood just from hearing one or two words. And this morning she sounded happy. It had been a long time, come to think of it, since she hadn't.

It was so good to see her truly content after all those years of depression. My sister had blossomed even more than I'd thought possible after she took on the job of managing Margaret Casperson's money. Well, not all of it by any means. Margaret was rich as Midas but had never been miserly about it. She'd designated a percentage of her income to be used for the benefit of the town and the Martinsville residents—her definition of the fund's purpose was a little vague—but she trusted Glaze to manage it well. Glaze's staffing budget for the "Martinsville Foundation" was ample, so she'd hired Madeleine Ames (the woman with whom she shared the rental of Bob's old house on Upper Sweetgum Street) and Dee Sheffield (my husband's ex-sister-in-law) to help her. They called themselves the Butterfly Brigade because—

We are near the fire. I smell it.

Marmalade meowed and brought me back to the present. My tendency to veer off on little mental detours makes me miss an awful lot of what people say.

"… wasn't hurt, was she?"

This was easy to figure out, so I jumped back into the conversation. "They don't know," I said. "Reebok said nobody seems to know where she is."

The moment of disbelieving silence that followed my comment held for a second or two before all three of them exploded in questions.

"Where is she?" "She's okay, isn't she?" "What do you mean, nobody knows?"

"I don't know any more than you do at this point."

Glaze pulled to the curb under a wide-branched maple. Even though it was well past summer, the sun could still warm a car way too much to leave a dog in there.

Or a cat.

Ahead of us, a throng of pedestrians gathered behind the fire engine. She rolled all the windows up, leaving a five-inch gap. Enough for Gracie to get air, but not enough for her to get her head caught.

"Stay," Glaze said. Gracie lay down on the back seat.

"Wait here," I told them. "I'll find Bob. He'll know what's going on." I pushed my way through the crowd, aware of a faint smell of gas, but as soon as I rounded the corner of the fire engine, an arm shot out and blocked my way.

"You can't go in there, ma'am." Hoss stepped in front of me, his bulk blocking most of the scene from my sight.

"I just want to see Bob," I said, pointing across the lawn to where he stood facing the ruins of Connie's studio. A reasonable request. Nearby, three firefighters clustered beside the rubble, peering into the blackened mess. A black trail of scorched grass about a foot wide led from the street to what was left of the building. A steady trickle of water ran along the gutter. It must have come from the fire hoses. Connie's house and studio were both slightly uphill from the road. The cliff towered behind.

Cartwright shook his head. "He's talking to the Corgi, ma'am, and I don't know if you know it or not, but the Corgi gets pretty grumpy when she's interrupted."

"What's she doing here?" I asked. "Doesn't she only show up when there are suspicious signs?" I inhaled strongly. "It's arson, isn't it? I can smell—"

"You've been watching too much TV, ma'am," Hoss said.

"Bob and I don't have a TV," I snapped. "Anybody with a nose can smell gasoline. That's why *she's* here, isn't it?"

He turned to stop someone else from stepping too close. You'd think they'd pay attention to the yellow tape. The fact that I'd been about to scoot around it when Hoss stopped me didn't seem to apply. I looked up the street. Connie's car wasn't parked along the curb. That meant she had left. She was safe. She was going to be royally ticked off when she saw this mess. I pictured her sturdy body and her strong hands, hoping Bob found whoever did this before Connie did. Nonsense. Connie wasn't violent.

I liked Connie well enough, but I thought her brother was the real salt-of-the-earth type. All our firefighters were trained as paramedics, and he'd driven the Martinsville ambulance the night I was rescued from the flood. I'd felt a close connection to him ever since. Plus, he was a regular library patron. That counted for a great deal.

Bob thoughtfully stepped to his right at that moment, giving me a clear look at the Keagan County Fire Marshall and Arson Investigator. Captain Paula Corrigan was something of a legend in this county. Bob had talked about her often, but I'd never met her. Her diminutive body apparently housed a formidable intellect.

No wonder they called her the Corgi. She certainly looked like one. She wore a thick white turtleneck, too heavy, I thought, for this mild weather. Her light chestnut hair, almost a golden brown, sported a white streak that at the moment fell over her forehead. A Corgi indeed. All she needed was pointy ears atop her head. I could almost see Queen Elizabeth in her wake. Or Tasha Tudor. The effect was somewhat ruined by a pair of sturdy black boots and the heavy beige firefighter pants she'd drawn over her civilian clothes. And the matching jacket with its stripes of reflective tape. But the turtleneck still showed. She jotted down something and flipped her notebook closed. Even this far away the bright lime green of the cover stood out against her protective jacket. It looked incongruous and a bit silly.

A puff of smoke—or maybe it was steam, because the fire looked like it was pretty much out—blew outward toward her, and for a second or two, she was a fiend stepping forth from the flaming pit. I half expected to see snakes writhing around her head. No, wrong mythological character. That was Medusa, and the fiend was—*oh good grief, Biscuit McKee, get a grip.*

"... sure you're all right, ma'am?"

Cartwright looked a bit concerned. I think he wasn't used to my habit of zoning out.

"I'm fine," I said. "How did she get here so quickly? I thought her office was in Garner Creek."

"It is. She came down to have breakfast with her brother at the Deli. Luckily, she always tells someone in her office where she'll be, so when we called this in, they knew where to find her."

The DeliSchuss was something of a landmark here in Keagan County. Even though Martinsville's at the bottom end of a dead-end valley, people come from miles around for their wonderful breakfasts. And lunches, too. "She must carry her work clothes in her trunk," I said.

Hoss looked at me as if he thought I'd missed a point somewhere. "Of course she does," he said. "She never knows when arson's going to show up."

I nodded, watching Marmalade, who had apparently skirted around the crowd. She approached Bob. I was afraid for a moment that someone would step on her ...

I know how to watch out for people's feet. Softfoot never steps on me.

... but she oozed away from him at the last moment and sat a yard or two away. She curled her gorgeous orange tail around her front feet.

Thank you. I agree; it is lovely.

"... knew it was arson the minute we arrived on scene."

"Huh? Oh, yes. The smell of gas? The burnt strip of grass?"

He nodded his big square head. "and the black smoke."

"What do you mean?"

"Normal smoke from burning wood is gray." He gestured toward the ruins. "It's black only if there's an oil product—like gasoline."

There was a deep furrow between his brows, a furrow new to his usually carefree face. "Hoss? Have they found your sister, yet?"

The skin around his eyes tightened. "No. Not yet, ma'am."

"Her car's not here. She's probably gone on an errand without telling anyone where she was headed."

"Yes, ma'am. That's right." He smiled, a little ruefully I thought, and said, "I'm gonna give her what for when we find her, what with worrying us so much." His voice was light, but there was a tension in it that I'd never heard before.

I tried to imagine what it would be like to lose a sister. Ghastly thought, but there was no reason at all to think that Connie might have been in that shed when the fire started. I nodded to him and walked back toward where Glaze and her friends stood.

Maddy started asking questions even before I reached them. "What did you find out? Is she okay?"

I lifted my hands in the universal sign for *who knows?* "Nobody's seen her."

"This isn't getting us anywhere." Dee headed toward the crowd. "I want to see what's going on."

"You'll never get close enough," Maddy said, but Dee ignored her.

Without a word, the three of us followed her, Maddy and Glaze as anxious as Dee to see the fire scene. What was it about a fire that drew people to it?

Over Dee's shoulder I could see Lorna Jean Hagstrom's distinctive head, with her hair piled high. How did it ever stay up there? It added a good three or four inches to her height. Still, she was one of those truly pleasant women that it was hard not to like. Not that I had any reason to dislike her. Why hadn't I invited her to join our tap dance class? Now was certainly not the time to ask. She was busy talking to the woman next to her, someone I'd seen Lorna Jean jogging with on a regular basis. They must have put miles under their feet every morning. I tried to recall the other woman's name. Linda? Sue? Mary? Something like that. I'd met her in the IGA once. She'd been wearing the cutest pink socks. If she'd had a library card, though, I would have remembered her name, wouldn't I? Now, all I could remember was that every time I saw her jogging around town, her ankles flashed bubblegum pink. Or fuchsia.

The people just behind them parted for a moment, and I got a good look at the lower halves of Lorna Jean and her friend. Sure enough, the friend had on even brighter pink socks than usual. Above the neon socks was a set of cast iron muscles. On both of them. Calves like that only came from serious exercise. Both of them wore close-fitting pant legs that stopped just below their knees. If I invited the two of them to join our tap dance class, they'd probably dance rings around the rest of us, and I'd still be the slowest one in the group.

Someone pushed past us toward the front of the crowd. Rude.

I'd never seen him before. Martinsville was small enough that even if I didn't know someone's name, I could certainly recognize everybody by sight. I veered a bit to my left so I could get a better look at him. A weasel. That's what he looked like. A bald weasel. His pointy nose jutted out beneath an eye—the only one I could see from this angle— that looked dark. He had no eyelashes, and practically no eyebrows. Cancer? Something shifted inside me. Maybe he'd lost all his hair to chemo treatments. He had a large pack slung over one shoulder and a camera in one hand.

Before I could speculate further, Dee grimaced, and a murmur ran through the crowd. "Look." She pointed toward the cluster of firefighters. "Something's happening."

I peered over Ralph Peterson's shoulder—the crowd had swollen considerably just since I'd arrived. Captain Corrigan and Bob strode toward the three men gathered on the edge of the black ruins. The crowd was making too much noise for me to hear, but her abrupt gestures said *move back, move back.* The greenish-yellow reflective tape that spelled out her name on the back of the jacket seemed to waver as another tentacle of smoke—steam?—drifted around her.

Hoss lifted the yellow tape, and the hairless man stepped under it, his sturdy work boots squelching in the water that swirled along the gutter. He raised his camera, took a few pictures—it looked like he was photographing the trail of burnt grass—and strode across to the Corgi. Bob nodded at him, and Corrigan said something in a low tone as the man pulled a different camera from his pack.

Someone in the crowd, someone with a querulous voice, asked, "What's all the bother about a stupid shed?"

"It's arson," somebody else answered. "Can't you smell the gas?"

Ida looked back over her shoulder. "Just like our garbage bin."

I saw Lorna Jean Hagstrom nod her head. So did the woman beside her.

"Yeah," I said. "And I'll bet my garden shed, too, although there weren't any signs of arson. Not that they mentioned." Then there was the car, definitely a case of arson. But Bob hadn't said there was anything suspicious about the first two fires. Well, suspicious, maybe, in that we were sure there was some slug of a person responsible for them. But he would have told me, wouldn't he, if there were anything I needed to be concerned about?

Still, having four fires in one week was enough cause for concern, period. But why would anyone have set my shed on fire?

Chapter 14

9 Years Earlier

THEY ALL GATHERED EARLY FOR one last drink together before the Lara Curzon Gallery opened its doors. It was only one cramped room in a back corner of the gallery. Ron's dad had promised them room for a show, and she'd imagined the airy, high-ceilinged front room, but this negligible space could never be impressive.

The self-important gallery assistant—why had Ron's dad ever hired her? She was such a dud—bustled over. "We'll be opening the doors in just a moment, as soon as I check the refreshment table one more time."

At least her portrait, even larger than "The Picnic," which Charles had thrown together sometime in the last two weeks—his paint was barely dry—her masterpiece, signed with a flourishing *La Degasa*, hung in the most prominent place. Anyone walking through the arched doorway—a pathetically small arch, unfortunately—would see her painting first.

Just to make sure it hung straight, she walked to the arch and turned to see the impact "I Hated Him" would make. Yes. It was exactly right.

She couldn't wait to read the reviews.

She approached her painting and inspected the discreet card to the right of it. Just the perfect balance of fact (title/size/price) and hype ("La Degasa is a rising star in the Atlanta Art Scene"). She wished for a moment that she had used her real name. But it was too late to change anything. And there was still one person who might make the connection.

Miss Importanta Assistant herself did the checking, straightened a wine bottle, moved the dish of chocolate-covered strawberries an inch to the right, and glided to unlock the front door.

Chapter 15

So, I'm pretty sure nobody saw me
And I'm pretty sure nobody got hurt
Pretty sure
I thought I picked pretty well, but
they weren't ~~empres~~ impressed
but maybe that was just a show
they think they have to look tough
I wish I looked tough

~~~~

REEBOK SHOWED UP A FEW minutes later, his badge twinkling in the early morning sunshine. I watched him trundle across the lawn and confer briefly with Bob. He nodded vigorously and turned back toward the crowd. "Time for everybody to go on home now." His arms waved people back. His eyes roamed the watchers until he found me. He headed my way, and I walked back toward the fire engine to meet him halfway.

"I'm sorry I was so uncommunicative when you called, ma'am," he said.

"Connie's a friend of mine." I didn't mean to sound accusatory, but really now, what difference would it have made if he'd told me right away instead of pussyfooting around?

He ducked his head, for all the world like a little boy caught with his hand in the cookie jar. "Yes'm. I know that. I didn't want to be the one to give you bad news."

"Reebok." My exasperation showed. "Just because you can't find her doesn't mean she was in that shed when it burned." I thought about the time so recently when my sister had gone missing. We thought she'd been kidnapped, but she wasn't the one they'd taken. I pulled myself up short. No need to go there. "Connie's just fine," I added. "Just fine."

Obviously looking for an excuse to get away, Reebok mumbled something and headed toward a lingering group of bystanders. "Let's break it up, folks. We need to do some cleanup work here, and you'll just get covered with ash if you stick around." His voice faded as he walked farther up the street. Maybe I shouldn't have been quite so curt with him. It was rather like hitting a puppy.

You would not do that.

I heard Marmalade's distinct yowl and checked to be sure she wasn't hurt. She wasn't. She was just sitting there near Bob doing nothing.

I am not doing nothing. I am listening to GrowlVoice and SoftFoot. And I am watching.

One of the firefighters helped Hoss gather the hose back onto the engine. I knew enough not to call it a fire truck. Trucks had ladders on them. Engines didn't. Once when I visited the station with a big pot of soup, and told everyone how clean and shiny the fire truck looked, they'd corrected me. Politely.

I looked past them and caught Bob's eye. I blew him a kiss, but he didn't wink at me the way he usually did. The ghost of a smile played across his lips, but disappeared in a heartbeat. What was wrong?

"Hoss," I said. "Something's not right. What is it?"

He took a quick look around, but the crowd had pretty much dispersed, thanks to Reebok's urging. Of the people who were left, nobody was close enough to hear us. Glaze and her crew stood talking beside the car, and Gracie had her fuzzy brown head sticking out the back window. Glaze waved at me and pointed at her watch. "We have to leave," she called. "See you later."

I waved back and turned my attention to the burly firefighter beside me.

"Connie's not here," he said. "But …" His voice trailed off and he glanced back at the ruins of Connie's studio.

"Are you saying she was in…in there?"

He looked so miserable, no wonder he didn't answer my question directly. "They don't want me over there," he said, "when they go in. That's why the Lieutenant assigned me to stay with the engine."

It made sense. It was bad enough that he thought his sister's body might be there, but to *see* it? I couldn't imagine anything worse.

Beyond us, the voices of firefighters, Bob, and Captain Corrigan mingled in waves of soft tones. I could tell Bob's voice, of course, and the Captain's voice sounded like a truck grinding its gears on a steep hill. I couldn't distinguish any words, but I wasn't sure I wanted to. The glass studio was nothing but a tangle of charred junk. Half a dozen blackened studs still stood, an eerie echo of how the building used to look. What used to be the concrete floor of the building—she'd given our tap dance class a tour one evening—was covered by a mound of fallen joists, shingles, and God only knew what else.

Connie was a glassblower whose artistic creations were featured in several high-end galleries—New York, San Francisco, Chicago. Martinsville seemed to have become a haven for artists. Judy Smith, well known for her art quilts. Lorna Jean, a famous writer. Out of fairness, and because she was my friend, I added Maddy to the list. She hadn't been published yet, but had great hopes for her rather gory thrillers.

"… why we used way more water than we would have ordinarily."

Uh-oh. Hoss had been talking to me. "More water?"

"Yes ma'am. To drown out the heat so we—so the Corgi—could get in there faster. Sometimes we do that when we know there's a recovery to be done."

A recovery. He meant pulling a dead body out of the charred ruins. If there was a live person who could be saved, it was called a rescue. "I'm so sorry, Hoss. But maybe it's not your sister. Maybe she just drove somewhere. Her car's not here," I added brightly. My voice sounded fake.

"Yes ma'am, but it's *somebody* in there. I have to check the …" His voice faded as he turned abruptly away from me.

Poor Hoss.

He is very sad.

Marmalade rubbed against my shin, meowing softly. I bent to pick her up. I couldn't stand the thought that something might have happened to Connie. This was all just a horrible mistake. It had to be. There was no way they could be sure someone—or what was left of someone—was in that tangled mess.

But if there *were* a person … a body in there … I swiveled to my right and looked up the street. Turning a slow half-circle, I looked at every house within sight range. Somebody must have seen Connie when she left—I was sure she had left. She wasn't the one in the burned-out studio. But if it wasn't Connie—who was it?

I watched for a bit longer, but eventually Hoss came back. "I need to ask you to leave now, ma'am. The Corgi doesn't like people hanging around when she's going in."

Going in. Into the crumpled mess to investigate. To look at what might be a person. A person who might be all that was left of Connie.

"Why is she going…in there? Doesn't she have to wait for the medical examiner?" I knew that from listening to Bob talk about police work.

"She's supposed to confirm that it's a person before we call the dea..."

He stopped in mid word. Death investigator. That was what the ME was called sometimes. I couldn't blame him for not wanting to say it. Not if he thought it was Connie to be investigated.

"The Captain won't touch the ..."

I wondered how much longer he could go on with incomplete sentences.

"We have to stay ... There's nothing we can ..."

Apparently quite a bit longer unless I intervened. "I'm sure it's going to be all right, Hoss." Who was I kidding? It might not be Connie, but it was somebody, and there would be a grieving family left behind.

You are very sad, Widelap. We could go home and get some tuna. That would help.

I went home, cradling Marmalade against my heart. And even though I wasn't particularly hungry, I made myself a little tuna sandwich, with only one slice of bread. It seemed vaguely comforting. Or maybe the comfort came from Marmalade purring in my lap.

~~~~~

The Captain's guttural voice wasn't easy to listen to. Bob knew there had to have been some sort of damage to her throat, and he wondered what had happened. She'd spoken like that for as long as he'd known her. The myth commonly spread among firefighters and police in the valley—she belonged to both forces—was that she'd tangled with a bear. She'd tangled with something; that was for sure.

Bob's mind strayed. He wondered what Biscuit was talking with Hoss about. It had been a long conversation, unusual for the laconic firefighter. Maybe they were talking about Connie. Biscuit would know what to say to keep Hoss' spirits up. If only they knew for sure whether or not the body in there was Connie. They had a mess on their hands. As with any crime, he wanted to clear this up fast—but the more he found out, the less he seemed to know.

He checked his watch again. The medical examiner should have been here by now. Captain Corrigan had been so sure, she'd had one of the firefighters call it in immediately. He took another quick look. Fortunately, the people in the crowd couldn't possibly see over one particular pile of debris. Behind it, the unmistakable shape of a big bone, probably a femur, stuck out in plain view. No wonder she was sure. No wonder they were keeping Hoss away from this scene. *Let's get this over with.* He checked that thought. The agony was just getting started for the family of whoever the unfortunate body had been, particularly since somebody in that family might have been responsible for the fire. Bob couldn't believe how often spouses killed each other.

~~~~~

The steeple was all Henry could see of his church. It soared above the trees that bordered the lawn outside his and Irene's bedroom window. What am I going to do about this? He yawned as he thought. It seemed like he had barely made it back from his two to four a.m. prayer stint at St. Theresa's Catholic Church, something he'd long ago volunteered to do to help his friend, Father John Ames, and here it was time to be up and out again. He'd promised his daughter he'd pick her up at the signboard in—he glanced at his watch—in just a few minutes. Was he making a mistake?

He turned his back to the window and studied his wife's somnolent form. Irene was a good woman. She hadn't thought it was a mistake. She'd agreed that this was the right thing to do. To give his daughter a chance. But was it the best way? Should he back out of it this morning?

Well, they were having breakfast at the Delicious. He'd steer his daughter to that back booth, the one he and John favored. They could talk privately there; nobody would hear them. He hoped she wouldn't make a scene.

Who was he kidding? Of course she'd make a scene if he tried to wiggle out of this. "You promised," she'd say in that loud carrying voice of hers. He was stuck.

It *was* her money, her inheritance from her grandmother, her mother's mother. And she had the verbal support of her mother. Henry had no right to counsel Susan otherwise. All he could do was buy her breakfast and go with her to offer his support. And his signature on a dotted line. He owed her that much.

~~~~~

Glaze watched Maddy fork in a huge bite of pancake. Where did a little slip of a woman like her find such an appetite?

"This S. Porchinsky, whoever he is," Maddy paused to swallow, "better be impressive if he thinks we're going to hand over such a huge amount of money."

"Yeah." Dee thumbed through the four-page application. "I wonder why he wouldn't list a town sponsor?"

Every M-Money project had to have the backing of another Martinsville citizen. Glaze had instituted that policy, and she was still convinced it was a good one. It helped eliminate a few of the more crackpot ideas before they made it to the Butterfly Brigade's hands. She smiled. "Remember when Larry talked Mr. Orrin into signing his application—"

"To build a pond," Dee took up the litany, "next to the gazebo…"

Maddy made a face. "And stock it with those fancy fish that fight each other to the death."

Glaze gestured to the app Dee held. "How do we even know this S. Porchinsky lives here? Could this be some scheme from developers in Atlanta?"

"Not likely." Maddy shoved her glasses higher on the bridge of her nose. "Nobody in Atlanta knows where this whole county is, much less a little bitty town like Martinsville."

Glaze set down her fork and picked up her vanilla milkshake. Milkshakes for breakfast. Great idea. She felt stuffed, but it was so tempting to lick the plate clean and slurp up every drop in the tall sculpted glass. The DeliSchuss wasn't called the Delicious for no reason. "Still, somebody's going to extreme lengths to keep us from knowing who he is."

"You're right," Dee said. "I'm not sure why we even accepted the application in the first place. Half of it isn't filled out." She pointed to the bottom of the first page. "Just this note that says *when we meet, I will fill in all the particulars.*

Maddy swallowed before she spoke. "The handwriting is really strong. He must be a very decisive person."

Dee scanned all the empty lines. "He may be decisive, but he's not good at following directions. I still don't see why we agreed to meet with him."

Maddy poured a bit more syrup. "You know darn well why we're doing this. Sheer curiosity."

"You're right," Glaze said. "None of us has seen the inside of the old hotel, and this gives us a perfect chance."

Maddy glanced at her watch. "Still time for a cinnamon roll, Dee."

"Well, maybe just one." She lifted her hand. Margot was there within moments, cinnamon roll on a plate. "How'd you know I was going to order one?"

"Don't you always?"

Glaze took the application from Dee and looked it over one more time. S. Porchinsky. Who the heck was he?

The bell over the front door jingled. Glaze didn't usually pay much attention to the comings and goings of the myriad customers attracted by this marvelous food, but she took notice of these two. The Reverend and his daughter, that Susan person. Glaze shuddered. The woman might have hair like a silken waterfall, but that was about all she had going for her.

~~~~~

Paula Corrigan almost never saw one of her fires in progress. Usually firefighters or cops saw, heard, or smelled something that made them think arson. Then they'd call her. By the time she got to the scene, the fire was usually out cold. Everything was wet. Everything was finished.

Of course, she'd seen plenty of fires throughout her training and her twenty-three years as an arson investigator, and she could chase a fire engine with the best of them, so she'd been in on a number of live fires, but with arson, she always wished she could see the fire active and alive. She thought that somehow the fire might tell her something.

Now, here was her chance to test that theory. She'd had a feeling in her gut from the moment she arrived that something else was going on here. Something other than just a fire. Which may have been why she was looking for that telltale mound. Why she wasn't surprised when the black smoke cleared a bit and she spotted the femur sticking out like an obscene third finger.

Catch him. Catch the one who did this. As an arson investigator, she wore two badges. She was not only trained as a fire fighter but had gone through the police academy as well. She had authority to arrest. Whether she put the cuffs on this creep or Sheffield did—that didn't matter.

She'd never seen a one-story building like this take so long to cool down. Put the wet stuff on the red stuff, the firefighters always said. While they did their work, she'd wait and think.

She turned away from the fire to study the group of onlookers clustered near the engine. One of them, she thought. One of them.

Chapter 16

9 Years Earlier

IT TOOK A FEW MINUTES for the guests to reach the back room of the gallery. She could see them stopping to admire a painting here, a sculpture there. But then a wave of their friends—drinking buddies, most of them—swept in and headed for the food table. And the free wine. Once their plates and their glasses were full, they said complimentary things about all the pieces.

Barb and Tommy and Sal all told her that her portrait was the very best in the show.

"So much power," Barb said.

"Such a stunning composition," Sal added.

"And ooh, it just oozes ..." Tommy glanced at the title on the card, "... hatred, doesn't it?"

Ron stood beside her, his hand occasionally straying downward from the small of her back.

She happened to be looking toward the archway when a short, unimpressive woman—the kind she'd never usually notice—paused to survey the scene. She noticed this time, though, for the woman held a notebook. A critic? The press at least? Ron's dad said they might get a review—he'd sent invitations, or so his stuck-up assistant had said, but nobody in the gallery had sounded like they thought it would actually happen.

She looked in vain for someone with a camera. No such luck. It would have to be the dumpy lady with the notebook. She sure hoped the woman knew what compelling art was all about.

Chapter 17

So, I don't think about Mr. Latham anymore
But I woke up last night
he was talking to me in my ~~dream~~
nightmare
like he didn't like me anymore

~~~~~

I HAD TO OPEN THE LIBRARY. It was early yet, but with Peachie coming in a couple of hours—she'd said she'd be here for lunch—I needed to be sure everything was flowing smoothly so I'd feel comfortable taking the rest of the day off. Not that I was worried. My Petunias, the three elderly library volunteers who had worked with me ever since I moved to Martinsville, kept everything in order with hardly any input from me. When they found out that Peachie was coming for a visit, they'd instructed me to take as much time as I wanted.

"It's not every day a friend drives such a long way to visit," Rebecca Jo had told me.

"And friends are important," Sadie added. She'd sounded wistful. No wonder. At her age, friends she'd grown up with had begun to die on a regular basis.

I needed to remember to put them on my gratitude list. They were so dependable. Still, I'd feel better making an appearance at the library.

Marmalade and I took a long detour first, though, walking along Third down to Willow Street. I figured I could check with Bob and still make it to the library on time. Martinsville was laid out in a surprisingly logical pattern. First Street, which we usually called Main Street despite the green street signs, ran along the Metoochie River. The streets numbered Second through Fifth paralleled Main, each street a block higher on the gently—and sometimes steeply—sloping land. The streets that led uphill away from the Metoochie all had tree names. Bob and I lived on Beechnut Lane between Second and Third Streets. Glaze and Maddy were on Upper Sweetgum. Sadie lived on the corner of Pine and Fourth. And so on.

Thinking of the map of Martinsville, and the wonderful people who lived here, kept me occupied the three blocks to Willow. My mind did head off in a couple of other directions when I thought about a few of our less savory characters, such as Larry, the barber, but I tried not to dwell on the people I didn't like. Maybe Larry set all the fires. I skewered him in my mind, but had to admit that arson wasn't his style. It would be fun to string him up by his toes, though.

Ouch!

Marmalade sneezed, and I pulled myself up short. Biscuit McKee, whatever are you thinking about?

I certainly cannot understand you.

When Marmalade and I reached the fire scene, nothing much had changed except that someone, probably Reebok, had extended the barriers and blocked off the streets. Did he think there would be that much car traffic? Still, I couldn't get anywhere near what was left of Connie's studio without ducking under yellow tape. Bob still stood on the perimeter of the scorched earth; the firefighters stood around—Hoss had joined the others by this time—and Captain Corrigan was bent over something—oh my God—some*one* in the middle of the mess.

Bob must have spotted me. He walked toward me with an unusually heavy tread. "What are you doing back here?"

"I wanted to see if you'd found out anything. Is it Connie?"

He closed his eyes and opened them. "There's ... there's no way to tell. The Captain is just officially confirming that it's a person, although she put in a call for the medical examiner as soon as she saw the bo ..." He stopped.

"The what? What's a boh?"

He flicked his fingers, almost as if he were trying to brush away a noxious thought. "They'll transport the body to the lab at Decatur. Maybe then we'll have a better idea of what happened. And who it isn't."

"Don't you mean who it *is*?"

He brushed my shoulder with the tips of his fingers, as if he had to make contact with some part of life. "No. I said what I meant. There's not a lot left, but they'll be able to tell whether the body is male or female. If it's male, then it isn't Connie."

"And if it's female?"

He bent to kiss my forehead. "We'll deal with that if we have to, Bisque. In the meantime, there's nothing you can do. Go home, sweetheart."

My real name was Bisque. It had transformed into Biscuit before I went to kindergarten. Usually Bob called me *Woman,* or *honey.* The only time he called me Bisque or sweetheart was when he was really worried. This time he'd used both names in fewer than six seconds. He must really be concerned.

Widelap is afraid.

Marmalade wound between Bob's legs, purring loud enough to wake the … purring loudly. It wasn't Connie. It couldn't be.

You are afraid also.

~~~~~

Glaze set down her milkshake and looked across the booth at her friend. "Maddy, I swear you'll end up like a pretzel if you keep curling up like that every time you sit."

Dee snorted, making Glaze think of an old episode of Wild Planet she'd seen. "What do you mean *end up?* She's already a pretzel."

"I can sit any way I want to." Maddy stuffed in another bite of pancake. "I happen to think it's comfortable like this."

Don't talk with your mouth full, Glaze thought. Then she looked at Maddy's bouncy curls and happy face and decided it didn't matter.

"We should have chosen a table instead of a booth." Dee gathered the scattered papers they'd been discussing. "Then you'd have to sit straight."

"I can curl up on anything."

"Can it, you two." Glaze took one last bite of scrambled egg. "We've been sitting here way too long. We need to finish up and get going. I want to be at the old hotel before our client shows up."

"Yeah," Dee said. "So you can snoop through the place."

"I won't be able to. The realtor has the key."

Maddy sat up straight. "I thought our client had bought the place already."

Dee waved the application from S. Porchinsky in Maddy's face. "You should have read the fine print."

"What fine print?"

"Mr. Porchinsky added it to the last page."

Glaze thought Dee sounded patronizing. That wasn't good.

Dee spread the papers and quoted. *"Purchase of hotel is dependent on approval of Martinsville Foundation grant.* Didn't you read the whole grant application?"

"Nope. That's for you two." Maddy ducked as Dee threw a napkin at her.

"You're not holding up your end." Dee waved the papers in the air.

Dee was making a habit of that disgusting sound. Glaze would have to talk to her about it. Diplomatically. She couldn't help but notice that Susan had risen to leave. Susan and Henry.

"And," Maddy said, raising her voice one more decibel level, "quit snorting at me like that, Dee. You sound like a wild hog."

So much for diplomacy.

Glaze motioned to Maddy to lower her voice. Susan was staring. Everybody in the Delicious was staring. Everybody except Henry. He was pointedly ignoring them. Ministerial diplomacy. She was surprised he didn't walk over and offer a session of counseling.

"Time to earn our salaries, my friends." Glaze raised her arm for the check. This was a business meeting, right?

~~~~~~

With Bob's kiss still warming my forehead, I headed down to Second Street and went to work with a heavy feeling in my heart. What if that really *was* Connie's body in there? I was seriously considering lynching somebody—whoever had done this to her. I was so engrossed in thoughts of retribution, I walked right past Sadie Masters. She called to me as she crawled out of the high front seat of her bright yellow 1956 Chevy. She was so short her husband had ordered special pedals when they bought the car right off the factory floor. Wallace even installed a seat booster, too, so she could see over the steering wheel.

"I'm sorry I'm a bit late this morning," she said, adjusting her lemon-colored sweater set.

"You're not late."

"Well. I'm usually early, so getting here on time feels like I'm late."

"What held you up?"

"I was getting dressed and had a sudden urge to call Connie, but she didn't answer her phone, even though I called four or five times. It's not like her to be out this early. She always works late and then stays in her pajamas until noon. Do you think I should drive by there and be sure she's all right?"

I took a deep breath. "Let's stay at the library, Sadie. There's been…something's happened…"

Sadie grabbed my arm to stop my dithering. "What's happened to Connie?" Her soft, wrinkled old face peered up at me with unblinking eyes. I guess she'd seen a lot of tragedy in her 80-some-odd years.

"There was a fire," I said. "Last night. Her glass studio. Nobody can find her."

"Well," Sadie said with pioneer practicality, "Is her car there?"

"I didn't see it."

"That's settled. She's out of town and didn't tell anybody. I've a mind to spank her when she gets back."

The thought of Sadie, barely five feet tall, spanking the sturdily built, heavily muscular Connie, made me smile. Until I remembered the as yet unidentified body in the rubble. I waited until we were inside. "Let's make a cup of tea," I suggested.

She plopped her purse on the wooden bench under the community bulletin board and looked me up and down. "Forget tea. Out with it. What's wrong?"

"Hoss told me there was a body in the building." Sadie sat down abruptly. "We should know soon." I hoped she wasn't going to faint on me. She looked awfully pale. "Captain Corrigan is here inspecting the scene, and the medical examiner should be here soon."

Rebecca Sheffield, my mother-in-law and Head Petunia, breezed in through the heavy old front door. She blurted out, "Did you hear the news?"

"I just told Sadie," I said.

Rebecca patted her steel-gray hair, although not a strand was out of place. "I can't imagine why anybody wouldn't slow down on that curve."

"What curve?"

Sadie echoed me. "What curve are you talking about?"

Rebecca looked at us as if she thought we'd lost our marbles. "The. Curve. The big steep one just up the valley? What else would we be talking about?"

"I thought you were talking about Connie."

"What does Connie have to do with a tractor hitting the guardrail?"

It took a few more moments to get our stories straightened out.

She'd caught a radio announcement about the wreck while she was starting the coffee pot, but then she turned off the radio to get dressed, so had missed any mention of the fire. "Three deer ran across the road right in front of Jonas Pudley's John Deere," she told us. "He was hauling a load down from his upper field and decided there wouldn't be any traffic, so he'd take the easy way on the public road. The fields have been extremely muddy recently."

"Right," I said, wondering where this was leading.

"Jonas swerved, although how anybody can swerve in a lumbering old tractor is more than I can figure out. The back end jackknifed and he jammed the front end of the tractor into the guardrail and spilled a full load of hay all over the road, blocking traffic both ways. He was stuck there for over an hour."

"It's a good thing Captain Corrigan was already in town then," I said.

"Why?"

I told her, and then there were two of my Petunias sitting on the bench, fighting to hold back their tears.

Chapter 18

9 Years Earlier

THEY ALL GATHERED AT RON'S apartment to celebrate after the show, because six of them, the majority of the group, lived there already. Of course there was the inevitable hoopla of drinking and self-congratulation. Everybody stayed all night, sleeping in piles here and there.

The next morning, she slipped out early so she could buy the first edition of the *Atlanta Journal-Constitution*.

Her thought had been to read the review—if there was one—first, but when she checked the listing for the page number, her nerve failed her, so she simply clutched the paper to her chest and ran the block back to Ron's.

Barb grabbed it from her and paraded around the room, stepping over outstretched legs. "Who gets the honor of reading it out loud?"

"Me," the showoff Charles said, but Sal slapped his arm.

The vote, when they finally got around to taking one, was unanimous. "La Degasa! La Degasa!"

Ron pulled out the proper section and handed it to her. "Qu-qu-quiet, every-b-b-body," he yelled. "We have t-t-to l-l-listen real h-h-hard!" While she searched, he dumped the rest of the AJC on top of an overflowing trash basket.

"Here it is!" She mouthed the first three words, then, without a sound, skimmed the four short paragraphs. They were tucked between two glowing reviews of other shows.

She reread the review silently, unwilling to believe such vitriol. The other pages fell to her feet as she ran from the room.

Chapter 19

So, I have one sniffle
and she makes me
stay home from school
like I'm a baby

~~~~~

IT SEEMED HEARTLESS SIMPLY TO leave Sadie and Rebecca like that and go home, but I had to be there when Peachie arrived, and I still had a loaf of bread to bake to go with the split pea soup I'd started in the crockpot. "Are you sure you'll be okay," I said yet again as I opened the heavy front door. I don't know why I was so worried. They'd worked here often without me. The week I was on my honeymoon, for instance. But that was shortly after the library had opened and we didn't have the computers back then.

"Don't worry about us." Rebecca must have read my mind. "We've weathered heavier storms than this one."

I do not feel a storm.

Sadie smiled at Marmalade, picked up her purse, moved it to the shelf beneath the checkout station, and patted the monitor absentmindedly. Our new computers were functioning fairly well, but there were still occasional blips. I wasn't sure how comfortable the two of them would be if something went wrong. I closed the door and took a step toward the desk.

Almost as if she'd read my mind, Sadie said, "Go home, dear. If we need help with this thing, we can always call you."

That was true.

I reached for the doorknob again, but Lorna Jean Hagstrom breezed in, without even a hello to any of us. "Did you hear the news?"

This sounded like a re-run from a few days ago. Hadn't she asked that very same question on Wednesday? I took a step backwards and closed the door.

In out in out. You are confused today, Widelap.

"They think there's a body in the rubble ..."

There is. I heard the people in the funny suits talking.

"... and I sure hope it isn't Connie."

Lorna Jean's words sounded gossipy, but that was not her intent. I could tell she was as worried as we were. After all, she lived across the street from Connie. They were friends, or so I'd heard. I bent down to pat Marmalade, who was being exceptionally noisy.

Excuse me? Noisy?

Sadie nodded, and a wide strand of her white hair fell down over her eyes. They were still red-rimmed. "We know." She turned away from Lorna Jean. "Biscuit, you go on now. We'll be fine."

This time, when I closed the door, it stayed shut behind me. I headed for home, but Marmalade made a beeline in the other direction.

I am going to listen to Softfoot.

Peachie would be here soon. I needed to hurry.

~~~~~

Reebok studied the card in his hand.

This Tim Haversham could have done it.

But why would he? That one stumped him. He might have wanted the insurance on his car, but there wasn't any connection that Reebok knew of to make him burn down Connie Cartwright's studio.

Still, he had the information logged, so he wouldn't forget. He'd put Mr. Haversham on the list of suspects, and his wife, too. She was another possibility, although Reebok couldn't imagine her carting a gas can around town after dark. Still, he'd seen her coming out of that glass studio late at night several times in the last few months. He'd have to look up her other cards to see when those dates had been.

He might come up with the connection later, and then he could write it on the correct card and show it to the Chief.

~~~~~

Bob tried to concentrate on Captain Corrigan's raspy voice, but a vision of Bisque trapped in a burning building kept intruding, shredding his concentration. There was no indication that the fires would escalate to houses, but wasn't that what often happened? Someone got away with two or three crimes—or four in this case—and then it was that much easier to go on to another, bigger than the previous ones. Certainly these fires had shown a pattern of escalation.

The garbage bin at the IGA. Not much damage done there, but it could have spread to the grocery store itself. There were scorch marks up the back wall. Then the garden shed. Biscuit was pretty upset about it, but really, the loss hadn't been that great. Tools mostly. They could be replaced. Luckily, it was too far from the house—or from his beehives—to spread, and there hadn't been a wind that night. Then, the car. That was too big a jump. It was almost like the guy who'd done that had changed his own rules.

He was going to have to go back to re-interview the Havershams, the couple who owned the burnt car. The woman was a nice old lady. She'd been pretty incensed to begin with, and rightly so. But then she said she could almost see something funny in it. "It's insured," she'd told him. "We just might get a brand new car out of this. I've been thinking of driving to my sister's next week. It would be nice to do it in a new car."

Her husband had shaken his head at that. "Maybe a nice used one," he'd said. "Insurance only goes just so far."

Even though her words sounded like a motive for burning her own car, Bob didn't believe that for even one moment. Especially when she started crying after that brave new-car statement. It was like she was trying to keep something at bay.

He'd have to think about it some more. There was something he needed to ask them. Something he'd forgotten. Maybe he should read Reebok's cards.

Maybe he was wrong, but he was pretty sure she and her husband were decent, law-abiding people. He'd met them soon after they moved here. He liked them a lot.

Was there anything that connected Ralph and Ida, who owned the IGA, with Biscuit and her shed, and with the Havershams and their car? Three such different events. And now, Connie Cartwright's studio. He'd been in it once, for the required safety inspection when she built it—being one of only two police officers in town meant that the job was varied. Very varied. He and Reebok did everything. It was time to hire another officer. Maybe just part time.

Connie's studio had been well organized. More than that, though. The outer walls, the basic structure of the building, had been made of wood to make it blend into the neighborhood from the outside, but three walls of the studio inside had been lined with corrugated metal sheets, the back and half of each side. Too big a chance of an all-wooden building catching on fire. The wooden worktables were near the front door, well away from the back end of the building where the furnace was, where she melted the glass. Even the ceiling above that back end of the building was lined with metal. Connie hadn't taken any chances. The flooring was poured concrete. No chance of flammability there. *That* was what had bothered him from the first. There was no way a simple splash of gas could have turned into such a big blaze. So, how had such a conflagration been fueled?

Metal and concrete anywhere the molten glass might have splashed or spilled. Connie was exceedingly safety conscious. With a job like that, playing with what seemed to Bob like liquid fire, she'd have to be careful.

Bob rubbed his hand over his mustache, smoothing it down. You could be the most careful person in the world, but if somebody had it out for you, all that care might not be enough.

~~~~~

Henry followed his daughter out of the DeliSchuss into bright sunshine. He hoped they weren't going to be late for their appointment. Even if half the parties were late—and it looked like they would be—he didn't want to worry about it. Susan said she'd arranged everything, but he had no idea how she'd been raised. Was she organized? Was she scatterbrained? He glanced sideways at her rather stern profile. No. This was not a flippant young woman. And Irene liked her. That counted for a lot.

He opened the passenger side door for her. She thanked him, which pleased him inordinately. He thought of Holly. His and Irene's daughter. He had to be sure not to slight Holly, particularly after the fit she'd thrown the first time she met Susan.

"… should get there early enough."

"Right." He drove around the block, easier than turning around on Main Street, and headed for the old Keagan Hotel.

~~~~~

Paula wasn't liking the look of this one. Not that she ever enjoyed dealing with a fire scene where there was a body. But this building—

and possibly this body—was connected to one of her comrades, one of her firefighter brothers. The body might be his sister's. She didn't like anybody to die this way, but anyone who put her colleagues or their families at risk, was somebody Paula Corrigan wanted to see strung out to dry. Fast. People who set fires always left clues. She would find them.

She'd been the one to spot the telltale mound and the exposed femur, just before half the roof collapsed, and she hadn't needed to look closely before she was sure. But the ME wouldn't come if there were a good chance it was a big dog or just a pile of debris. She'd confirmed, and now it was just a matter of waiting. The breeze had been steadily mounting the whole time she'd been here. If it blew much harder, what was left of the roof was liable to fall.

As if the building had listened to her and decided to take her suggestion, the remaining part of the roof subsided with a whoosh as the back left corner of the building collapsed, burying the base of the glass-melting furnace under a heavy layer of corrugated metal. The chimney still stood, stark against the gray cliff face. The fallen sheets of metal from the ceiling were nowhere near the body, thank goodness. The mound lay about ten feet in from where the extra-wide door had been. It was partially covered by roof debris and fallen charred studs from the front of the building. Ash, of course. For reasons she hadn't understood until Sheffield explained them to her, the back half of the building was all metal-lined, but the front was built of wood. She knew precious little about glass blowing.

Paula was thankful there was no insulation in the building. Made for a cleaner fire scene. She hated it when gobs of sticky pink fiberglass clotted around her boots.

She took a quick glance at the tall man beside her. Thank goodness this town cop was not a chatterbox. She'd dealt with ones like that before, and they made it hard for her to keep her concentration. She'd end up asking—or telling—the officer to zip his mouth, and there'd be hard feelings. Just because she looked like a cute little dog— she knew exactly what they called her—they expected her to behave like one. Until they'd crossed her once. And then they'd either shape up or turn into snappy little dogs themselves, ready to bite at every imagined slight.

Sheffield was one of the good ones, and she was grateful for his silence. There were too many variables in an arson case, and she had to be aware of every single one of them. When there was a body, it made the job twenty times, a hundred times more complicated, because she'd almost always be called to testify. She hated courtroom appearances, but she had to do everything she possibly could to put these—she squelched one word and substituted another—these criminals away.

She would never have become an arson investigator if it hadn't been for Sherry. She wouldn't be here today if Sherry hadn't ... dense smoke ... raging roaring flames ... wax myrtle ... screams ... the most awful way imaginable ... couldn't help. She closed her eyes for an instant, willing those images away. They could fuel her determination, but she would not, *could* not let them ruin her concentration. She'd worked through her feelings of guilt a long time ago, but it still could trip her up at moments like this one. She shook her hands and wiggled her fingers vigorously. Sometimes that helped bring her back to the present.

The smell of gasoline, usually more noticeable after the fire was out, hung in the air. Whoever did this must have splashed gas not only over the body but also on most of the wood surfaces of the building. Had it been luck or skill that the spread had been thin enough for the fumes to ignite quickly? Most amateurs didn't know that too much gasoline wouldn't ignite efficiently. It had to be thin enough so the highly combustible fumes would catch fire.

She had already surveyed the scene as much as she could without moving anything, and Sheffield had given her the rundown about the metal lining on three of the inside walls, all the way across the back behind the brick glass-melting furnace and along the back half of each side wall. That would be about twenty-five feet, she estimated. The studs the metal was attached to and the wooden siding on the outside were all that had held the metal sheets in place. Once those were gone, the metal collapsed.

These firefighters were trained to disturb as little as possible when arson was suspected, and even more so when there was even a hint of suspicion that a recovery might be necessary. It was hard, though, to keep a tidy fire scene. All those hoses. All that water. All the equipment they had to have on hand just in case.

She wished they'd used the fog nozzle, which would have dispersed the water in a softer stream—almost like a mist. It was still forceful, but it would have done less damage than a concentrated stream of water at 50 or more psi. The body might have been moved by that amount of pressure if the stream hit it directly. She wanted to know where it was exactly when the fire started, but that might not be possible.

She certainly didn't blame the firefighters. They'd done their job admirably. Get the fire out. *Save lives and protect property* was the motto of a lot of fire and emergency services. Saving lives came first, but they hadn't known there was a person in there. They couldn't have known.

Usually, the firefighters would have rolled up their hoses and been long gone by this time, but with the possibility that the body might be Cartwright's sister, well, she couldn't blame them for hanging around.

Sometimes the body in a fire was the arsonist himself, caught in his own trap, so to speak. Some people were stupid enough to create a spark immediately after sprinkling the gas around. But here, with that burned trail through the grass, she was pretty sure that wasn't the case. No. Whoever the body was, it wasn't the arsonist.

Times like this, she itched to get in there before the medical examiner showed up. She knew she couldn't. No rooting around through the rubble. All she could do was verify that it was a human body so they could pacify the M.E. But she was primed and ready to go as soon as they hauled the body out. She'd sift the rubble a quarter of a cup at a time if necessary. She'd find … find something to nail this guy.

~~~~~

Baking bread has always been a relaxing occupation, although I was a bit frazzled, since I should have started the batch hours ago. There was no way it would be finished before noon. I stepped to the other counter and pulled open the breadbox. Half a loaf. That would be enough for Peachie and me. If I toasted it, it wouldn't feel stale. We could have the fresh bread this afternoon for a snack. Nothing like fresh bread with creamy butter and with honey from Bob's beehives.

Bob and I had a long-standing tradition of eating at CT's, Tom's restaurant, every Friday. We'd been planning on taking Peachie there this evening. I knew she'd love it. But with this latest fire—and the dead body—I doubted Bob would make it home by then. In fact, I was sure he wouldn't, so Peachie and I would only need a table for two.

Marmalade came in through her cat door, purring as usual. I wondered where she had been.

I went to see the place that smells so much.

I'd mixed all the ingredients and was turning the lump of soft dough over to oil all its surfaces when Marmalade walked away from me meowing gently, and I heard the front door open. Bob, I thought, with a smile.

It is not Softfoot. It is GoodCook.

I turned the dough one last time and covered it with a clean kitchen towel. I hadn't expected Bob home, not in the middle of what was probably going to be a nasty investigation, what with a dead body. That body was *not* Connie, I reminded myself. I wiped my hands and set the bowl to one side so the dough could rise.

Good morning, GoodCook.

Marmalade meowed at Bob, so I walked to the doorway and stuck my head around the corner. But it wasn't Bob.

I told you it was not.

My friend Melissa Tarkington stood there, halfway through the door, poised on one foot as if she'd been frozen in the act of almost taking a step. It was nice to feel comfortable enough with our friendship that we could walk into each other's houses, but she usually knocked or at least called out to me.

Why was she here, though? *Azalea House,* her B&B, was jam packed with a group of geologists who'd traveled here from all over the country to explore the caves across the Metoochie River. I knew they'd ordered an evening meal each day as well as breakfast and Melissa's special box lunches to take with them to the caves, so she should have been in her kitchen cooking instead of in my doorway. She made a boatload of money on groups that wanted two, or three, meals a day—somehow or other they were always happy to pay the outrageous prices she charged.

"Hey," she told me once, with a grin the size of Lake Lanier, "if I have to slave over the stove most of the day, they're going to make it worth my while."

And I'd said, "Good for you."

But she wasn't grinning now.

"What's wrong, Melissa?"

"Is Bob here?"

"Of course not. He's either at the fire scene or at the station. With these fires, he'll practically be living there for ages. Or at least until they catch the guy."

"I think I saw something, but I'm not sure about it, and I don't want to make an official report or anything. When's he going to be back?"

"Aren't you listening to me? He camps out at the station when there's something major going on. I never know when he'll be home." He'd been talking about hiring another officer – there was just too much work for two people. Although Reebok seemed to live at the station. Still, when something like this happened, they needed more manpower. Maybe he could hire somebody part-time.

"…can and he had a dark hood pulled down over his eyes."

"Huh?"

Melissa took a step backwards, which put her fully outside on the porch. "I'm usually very patient with this habit of yours, but today is not the day I want to deal with it. If you ever see Bob, ask him to come to my house."

"You saw something?"

"Forget it." And she stomped away toward the street.

She feels very angry and very confused.

Should I run after her and apologize? She didn't usually get in a snit like this. "I'm sorry, Melissa," I called out, and without turning around, she lifted a hand. It could have been a wave, or it could have been something ruder, but I didn't think Melissa would do that.

What do you mean?

"Hush, Marmy. I've already fed you."

Mouse droppings!

She sneezed, and followed me out the back door to the garden. I'd stop by *Azalea House* tomorrow. Maybe I could take Peachie over there to introduce her. Meanwhile I needed a big bunch of fresh parsley, some thyme, and a little bit of basil. The season was almost over, but this garden was so prolific, I was still getting plenty of green stuff. I should harvest some of the herbs to dry, though, enough to get me through the winter. That meant I'd need a lot, considering how often I made a big pot of soup, and how many loaves of herb-laced bread I baked. There was nothing like fresh dill bread. My stomach growled.

You are hungry.

I gazed around the garden. I'd waited too long. I could never get enough in time to dry them. Of course, I could always buy dried herbs at the herb shop.

I'd just stood up, thyme and parsley in hand, when Marmalade let out a yowl.

She is here.

I heard the doorbell. Peachie?

Or somebody else, the way I was going this morning. Maybe Melissa came back to apologize. Wait, she didn't need to apologize. I did. The doorbell rang again. Too early for Peachie. Maybe it was Connie? The basil could wait. I headed inside.

Chapter 20

9 Years Earlier

THE ATLANTA JOURNAL CONSTITUTION
Art Review

Seldom have I wasted as much time on a show as on one I visited recently at the Lara Cruzon Gallery. Ordinarily, the Cruzon presents the best of art, beautifully displayed. Not this time.

If the ringleader of the show group had not been the son of the owner, we would never have been subjected to such drivel.

At least "The Picnic," painted by someone who called himself "Seumouse" had a decent balance of colors, although little else can be said for it. The centerpiece of the show, ineptly titled "I Hated Him," was the most lukewarm example of hatred this reviewer has ever seen in the art world, as if two colors (black and—need I even say it—white) had been flung at the canvas by a dyslexic puppy.

Pass this one up. You won't miss a thing. Next time, Mr. Fleming, give us real artists.

Chapter 21

So, he says the reason she's like this
is cause she's worried
I know that
but I'm not my dad
and I can't drive anyway
so nothing like that can happen.
but plenty other stuff can.
she's worrying for
all the wrong reasons
this is all my fault

~~~~~

I WOULD HAVE RECOGNIZED PEACHIE Rose anywhere. She'd put on a few pounds, and her hair was considerably lighter than I remembered, but she still had that same wide, bright smile, and her eyes still twinkled.

"Biscuit!" She dropped her purse on the floor—it landed with a decided *thunk*—and threw her arms around me, trapping my arms in front of me. "I'm early. I couldn't wait to get here."

I leaned my head against her right ear for a moment. Although I cringed just a bit at the faint miasma of hairspray—I can't stand the way that stuff makes hair sticky, to say nothing of the smell—I relished the warmth. This was just what I needed. I was going to enjoy my guest. I was *not* going to think about Connie. And of course, with that thought, I pulled away from Peachie. "I think we squashed the parsley and the thyme."

"Squashed the parsley?" Without missing a beat, she quipped, "That reminds me of the words of ancient Chinese philosopher, Lah Tsa Phun: squashing parsley far easier than parsing squashly; vegetables so hard to conjugate." Her voice rose and fell in comic parody.

What does that mean?

"That wasn't very good—but," she pointed at the other herb in

111

my hand, "I'd need a little thyme to think of a better one."

After all these years, she hadn't lost her style. "Come on in. Marmalade and I were just brewing a pot of tea."

We were?

With all the excitement, I flat forgot about Melissa.

But I didn't forget about Connie.

"… your house. It's so cozy."

"Huh? Oh. Yes. It's kind of a rambling old house, with way too many bedrooms, and a kitchen table that could seat an army—certainly too big for just Bob and me, but I really like it. I'll give you a tour later if you like."

She bent to retrieve her purse and plopped it down on the drop leaf table across from the front door. I love this large entrance hall.

Hello.

Marmalade meowed, and Peachie looked at her. "I know who this is. I've heard so much about you in your mommy's letters, I know all about you."

No. You do not. You are friendly, but you do not understand cats.

Peachie settled into the breakfast nook and gazed out at my spacious back yard. "Great garden, and those trees back there are huge."

"They're one of the best things about the house. That grove has been there for hundreds of years. It fills about three-quarters of this entire block."

"I thought the early settlers always clear cut the land." She moved the vase of asters and goldenrod back closer to the window to make room for the teapot. "What kind?"

"Lapsang Souchong."

"You remembered," she crowed in absolute delight. "I discovered it our senior year when we rented that funny little apartment, remember?"

I remembered. "And you used to try to get the rest of us to drink it."

"If I recall right, you made it through about two sips of the first cup."

"That would be not only the first cup, but the only cup I ever tried, and it was one sip, not two. You may recall that I spit it out in the sink. It was like drinking a burnt cigar."

"It was not. This is an absolutely luscious tea."

I raised my *I Love My Library* mug. "I've already started on licorice root tea, so you can have the whole pot of …" I wrinkled my nose, "… that stuff."

"Thank you. I'll appreciate it." She paused to sniff the air; the heady aroma of split pea and ham made my mouth water. "Smells like you've improved. You used to make the most gosh-awful pots of soup, always throwing in beans and leeks and other strange things."

" I'll have you know my soups were really good. You used to practically lick the bowl."

"That reminds me of another thing Lah Tsa Phun said seven or eight hundred years ago."

"What's that?"

"You is full of bah loh nee."

We settled in for a long chat, pulling more old times out of our memories, dredging up old conversations and situations, all of it punctuated by Peachie's acerbic comments. She left me gasping at some of her more outrageous word acrobatics. Lah Tsa Phun played a big part in our conversation.

She drained the last of her tea and picked up the pot for a refill. "Have you seen Mary Cotton lately?"

"Mary?" I hadn't thought about her in years. Our freshman year, she'd hovered around the periphery of our group, never quite seeming to fit. I could barely recall her face. She was nice enough, I suppose, but tended to be sort of invisible. "No. Of course I haven't seen her. Why would I?"

"She moved to Martinsville a little more than a year ago. Didn't you know?"

"You're kidding. Really?" Peachie nodded. I thought of all the Mary's I knew in town. Nobody with a distinctive last name like Cotton. That was for sure. "She must not have taken out a library card, or I'd have known she was here."

"She's here, all right," Peachie said. "I kept track of her."

"How could you do that?"

Peachie smirked. "Don't you read the newsletters that come out once a quarter?"

"You've got to be kidding. Nobody reads college newsletters." Although, I admit I do tend to read the *In Memoriam* lists. So far nobody in the class of 1970 had died.

"I do." Peachie raised her mug in a salute. "Your wedding to Bob was in there."

"It couldn't have been. I never notified that stupid newsletter."

"I thought you might not have, so I did."

"Peachie Rose, you are on my ..." I made a downward gesture with my thumb, "... list." Although, come to think of it, it was kind of nice that old classmates might have seen my name and remembered some of the good times. Hopefully they didn't remember some of the dumber things I'd done in my twenties. I'd always been one to follow the rules. But there was that one time when I'd skipped medieval history class to go get doughnuts. I was scared the whole time that somebody would recognize me and ask why I wasn't in class. At the time, it wasn't worth the terror, but now I thought about how silly I'd been to think that skipping one class would bring about dire consequences. Boy, was I dumb back then. Not dumb. Innocent. No, I was right the first time. Dumb.

"... because something about Mary Cotton is in almost every issue." I came back to the present day. Peachie didn't seem to have noticed. Not like Melissa. "She wins a lot of awards."

"Awards? For what?"

"Her art. Didn't you know she was world famous?"

"Mary? I don't think so. She was too quiet, too self-effacing to ever be famous. Anyway, I think I saw some of her paintings back then. If I remember right, they weren't anything to brag about." Uh-oh. That wasn't a very nice thing to say. I had to pinch myself again.

"Well, people change. Maybe she's gotten better over the years."

Unlikely, I thought.

Peachie stood. "Point me toward the loo / because I need to poo."

"Too much info, Peach." I led her to the little blue and white powder room. "Once you're done, I'll give you a tour of the house."

Closing the door behind her, she said, "Mary's art really must have improved. She wouldn't be famous otherwise."

I could see the possibility of an argument there, but I let it pass.

"Maybe we could have lunch with her while I'm here." The suggestion floated through the closed door. I didn't like the idea. This was supposed to be time for Peachie and me, time for us to catch up on everything we hadn't been able to express in letters over the years. Sometimes I wished I could write letters like Abigail Adams. Letters that summed up the time she lived in, the people she met, the faces she saw. The revolutionary war and the founding of our country came alive through her letters.

But I couldn't write like that—was it maybe because we didn't live in such turbulent times, so there was less to write about? Regardless of the reason, Peachie and I had a lot of talking to do. Why bring a third person into the equation? Especially someone so painfully shy, unless that had changed as much as her art.

I walked back to the kitchen.

~~~~~

Peachie scratched the awful itch and took a good long look at herself in the mirror. Had coming here been a mistake? It was good to see Biscuit again. She hadn't changed much. But Mary? Peachie wasn't sure that was such a good idea. It was hard to tell from occasional letters, the few she'd had from Mary, but maybe the woman really had changed. It wouldn't hurt to find out for sure.

"Maybe we could have lunch with her while I'm here," she called out, but there wasn't an answer, so maybe they wouldn't have to. Stupid suggestion anyway. She could write to Mary when she got home next week and tell her the trip plans had been changed. That she hadn't made it to Martinsville.

No, that wouldn't work. This was way too small a town. Mary would see her for sure. She wondered, though, if they'd recognize each other. The shape of a face couldn't change that much. Bones were bones. Then again, maybe Mary had put on a lot more weight. She was way too heavy all through college. Or maybe she'd lost a lot of that excess. Either one of those could change a person's looks.

Too bad people didn't wear nametags. Or have their names tattooed across their foreheads.

Name changes, tattoo not, La Tsa Phun said in her ear. *Except to fade and wrinkle.* He was right. Who cared what Mary looked like? Just meet the woman and get on with it.

~~~~~

Melissa slapped at an errant mosquito. With all those bats living in the caves across the Metoochie, you'd think a mosquito wouldn't have a chance. There weren't that many around, but the ones who survived the evening bat swarms were real survivors. If the bats ate all the mosquitoes, though, would the bats end up starving?

Oh, who cared? She cracked her knuckles, a bad habit she tried to avoid doing around other people, particularly if they were paying guests. Like all these geologists. How could they possibly afford to stay at her B&B? *Azalea House* wasn't cheap.

She'd charged way too little when she first started the business, desperate to keep her clients. But then one day, one of her regulars mentioned what he paid when he and his wife went to the Berkshires. "You should charge a lot more," he'd said. "This place is too much of a bargain."

So she'd raised her rates, and he and his wife had never come back. She sighed.

The good news was that plenty of other people—many of them regulars—hadn't even blinked at the new prices. "Inflation," one of them said. "This place is worth it."

She slapped at yet another flying bug. By then, she was fast approaching *Azalea House*. She'd been practically running—well, a very fast walk—without even realizing it. It wasn't just that she was upset with Biscuit. She was frightened. What if she said something and the person turned out to be totally innocent? What if the guilty one went free just because she'd had the wrong person arrested? Could she be sued for—what would you call it—wrongful accusation?

And it was a young person. She was pretty sure of that. If she was wrong, though, she could ruin the whole rest of this kid's life.

But she wasn't accusing anyone. Not really. All she was doing was giving information. She just needed to talk it over with Bob.

She stomped up her front steps. Biscuit with half her brain off in la-la land wasn't the issue. It was kind of funny, she had to admit, how Biscuit wandered in and out of conversations. What she'd give to have a look inside that woman's head.

She paused with her hand on the doorknob. Should she go back and apologize?

The door pulled inward abruptly, catching her off balance.

"Oh, sorry," said one of the geologists, the tall gangly one with the scroungy mustache. She couldn't remember his name. She really ought to take a photo of her guests as they signed in so she could put the names with the right faces. There was probably some privacy law against it, though. She'd have to get them to sign a release form.

She creased her forehead. Maybe she'd give everyone a complimentary photo of them on the *Azalea House* front porch swing. Then she wouldn't have to have them sign…

"… so I tootled back for it. That footbridge is really handy."

Oh phooey! How could she be upset with Biscuit when here she was doing it herself?

"Yes," she told him. "It's a very handy little bridge."

He galloped down the walk, past the spreading Japanese maple. He hadn't noticed a thing. She hoped.

Fat chance, she thought as another kamikaze bug zoomed in for a bite. She swatted it with more vigor than she'd intended. With her luck, she'd get a big red handprint on her neck.

~~~~~

Christian kindness was overrated, Henry thought, at least as far as this real estate sales fellow was concerned. Henry had hated him on sight, and the limp clammy handshake hadn't helped any. The guy used both hands to try wiggling the porch railing. When it didn't give, he leaned back against it. "Can't be too careful," he said. "Now, Henry, are you sure you don't want to look through the old place while we wait for the others to get here?"

He should have known better than to ask Henry. It was Susan's purchase. She was the one who'd looked at the place already. Henry had to admit he was curious about the old hotel, but he didn't want to step on Susan's toes.

"He doesn't need to," she said. "I already have the floor plan memorized."

Memorized? Well, if I were planning to pay cash for a defunct hotel, Henry thought, I'd probably have checked it over pretty thoroughly.

The broker's bray sounded like a demented donkey. What was there to laugh about?

"I guess you should have it memorized," he said. "This is what? Your eighth visit here?"

"Ninth." Susan's voice was flat. Even Henry, who didn't know his daughter all that well yet, could tell that the real estate guy should shut up while he was ahead.

She must want the place really bad, he thought, to put up with such an … Henry reined in that thought. Who was he to judge? Still, he would have called somebody local. Ellen Montgomery was a realtor. She could have handled it without all the sleaze. And she didn't have a clammy handshake. If only Susan had asked for his advice. She must have found this joker in the yellow pages.

The whine of a car engine laboring up the steep slope interrupted his thoughts. Finally.

~~~~~

"You've got to be kidding me," Dee said from the back seat.

"What?" Glaze was so intent on maneuvering her Civic between the ruts of the long-abandoned driveway, she hadn't looked at the people on the front porch.

"See for yourself."

"We might as well turn around right now," Maddy proclaimed.

Glaze looked up and swore under her breath. Susan. Susan of the long hair. Susan, whose last name nobody seemed to know.

Maddy and Dee must have come to the same conclusion.

"S. Porchinsky." Dee said.

"She lied to us," Maddy said. "If she'd filled out the whole form..."

"If she'd been honest ..."

"... we never would have agreed to meet with her."

Glaze pulled into the weed-littered parking lot. "Stop ping-ponging back and forth, you two. We're here. We have an appointment. Let's act like the professionals we are." She thought briefly of the napkin thrown across the breakfast table. "Let's try to act like professionals."

Dee opened the back door, and Gracie bounded straight up the stairs to Henry.

Glaze put the inevitable two and two together. Henry was Susan's father. Henry was going to vouch for Susan. She groaned. That was going to make it harder to say no.

"Well, well, well," exclaimed the rather sleazy-looking real estate broker with his hand extended. "Here we all are!"

Where did Susan ever pick him up, Glaze wondered.

She avoided the handshake and introduced her two colleagues. When he started to gush yet again, she put up a hand. "We may not need to go in the hotel. Could you excuse us for a while?"

"That's not necessary. I need to be ready in case you change your mind. I won't be one bit in the way."

"Yes," said Glaze. "You will."

She saw the briefest glimmer of appreciation in Susan's eyes.

Chapter 22

9 Years Earlier

THE PHONE BOOK HAD BEEN no help. Too many people with that last name. Too many suburbs where that woman could live.

She paused on the corner, checked behind her, as if she might recognize whether someone followed her, and decided she'd be safer sitting in her car. Less conspicuous that way. She still had a clear view of the edifice that housed the offices of the *Atlanta Journal-Constitution*.

She didn't have to wait long. That woman filed out behind several dozen other people and turned to her left. Out of the car. Merge into the crowd. Easy to follow.

The woman chatted with a young man walking beside her, and waved when he turned left at the next corner. Another four blocks, five, six. Would the woman never get wherever she was going?

Finally, the woman turned into an inconspicuous restaurant on a narrow side street.

She watched through the window as a man, who looked vaguely like a movie star, rose from his seat and gave the woman an enthusiastic hug. The woman looked happy.

How dare she?

Another couple joined them a few minutes later, and she had to watch while they ordered and ate and laughed and—once—even sang along with the piano player in the corner.

Eventually, it was dark enough that she could stand closer to the window without fear of being seen. The other couple left early, and she took a moment to waylay them, asking in a breathless voice, "Was that really Michael Douglas you were eating with? I admire his work so much!"

"I'm afraid not," the man said. "That was Timothy Haversham."

"Tim does look a little like Michael Douglas," his wife said.

She had a first name. Now all she had to do was look in the phone book for an address.

Chapter 23

So, they didn't hear me sneak out of the house
we all went out after it was good and dark
and gathered in that ~~gazebo gazebo~~
band stand place in the park
I thought we ought to wait till later
but #3 said no it had to be then
he wouldn't tell us
where he was going to do it
he made us wait there until he got back
then we waited for a long time
and nothing happened.
they said they were going to
follow the fire truck
when it came
but I had to get back home

~~~~~

I THOUGHT YOU COULD SLEEP here. I hope you'll like it." I ushered Peachie into one of the numerous small bedrooms on the second floor, the legacy of the man—he probably had fourteen children—who built this old house so many years ago, and a boon to the generations of large families who'd lived here since. Bob and I never used these rooms, and sometimes I wondered why we'd bought such a spacious house to begin with. The attic held layers of junk stored by previous owners. Some day I'd tackle cleaning it out—but definitely not now. I walked to the window and looked out over the back yard. That yard was one of the biggest reasons why I'd voted for this house. The lush growth of the garden; the trees standing behind the fence like a line of sentinels protecting us; the sun brightening the late summer blossoms of the butterfly-friendly vines that twined around the—

"Biscuit?" Peachie poked my elbow. "Are you still with us?"

"Sorry, Peachie. I get carried away sometimes."

She nodded. "It must be our age. I enjoy those little side trips in my mind, too. No luggage, no hotel reservations. So far, cross my fingers, I've always found my way back."

Nudging me aside, she surveyed the luscious part of the yard, and then glanced to the right. "Whatever happened there? Did you zap an alien spacecraft?"

"Don't I wish? I'm feeling uncharitable thoughts toward whoever burned down my garden shed."

"Arson? Hmm." Her mouth skewed to one side in a parody of contemplation. "You think there's a dead body in there?"

Connie. No. Connie had to be alive.

"What did I say? Are you okay, Biscuit?"

"I'm fine." Fine. That typical Georgia cover-all that Southerners say whether they're truly dandy or they just developed a ruptured hernia. "It's just that there's been a series of fires over the past week or so, and they *did* find a body in the last one."

"Not in your garden shed?"

"No. No. In a glass-art studio across town."

"Who died?"

"That's the trouble. We don't know. They just found a burned body in the ruins, but it hasn't been identified yet."

For once her quip-meter seemed to have failed. She raked her eyes over me from head to foot and shook her head slightly. Had I forgotten to button something?

~~~~~

Peachie looked her old friend up and down. That was sad about the dead body, but it certainly wasn't any concern of hers. She turned her thoughts to more cogent matters. How could anybody manage to put on so little weight in the past twenty years? Biscuit looked awful good, doggone her. Funny how little some people change. Peachie pressed a hand into the curve of her lower back and slid it downward.

Biscuit moved forward, concern on her face. "Do you need to lie down for a little bit? We can always eat later."

"No," Peachie said. "I was just wondering how it would feel to be caught in a fire." *And wondering how I'd ever take off forty pounds.* "It's awful to think that someone's setting fires in such a quiet, peaceful little town."

Well, Peachie thought, *peaceful* was something of a misnomer if an arsonist was running wild. But why set fires? And why kill somebody?

She pulled herself up short. There was no indication that the person had been killed. Just that there was a body in the burned down building. Still. Sounded like murder to her.

It looked like Biscuit was studying her, raising her eyebrows like that.

Peachie wondered if she had something stuck between her front teeth.

~~~~~

Why on earth had Peachie decided to visit me after all these years? A nasty trickle of suspicion wandered through my not-quite-*un*conscious. Had she really come to Martinsville to meet me? Or was I just an excuse so she could get here to see Mary Cotton? "Well," I said, "let's go get your suitcase out of the car. And then, after we eat, if you don't want a nap, we can take a little tour around town. I'll show you the sights."

"I'm not sure I want to get back into a car after all the driving I've already done today."

"Who said anything about driving? Martinsville is so small, everybody walks everywhere."

The look in Peachie's eyes was halfway between panic and disbelief. "Everybody? Everywhere?"

Sadie Masters and her yellow Chevy came to mind. "Just about."

"Can we see the fire scene? Where the body was?"

The Peachie I used to know—the Peachie I thought I knew—would have wanted to avoid such a place. Funny how much people can change. "Let's get your bag and eat first. Then we can decide."

~~~~~

Reebok shifted from one foot to the other. Surveillance was not an easy job. He patted his shirt pocket. He still had plenty of 3x5 cards.

About an hour before, once most of the crowd had wandered away—after all, nothing much seemed to be happening over there—the Chief had entrusted him with the job of listing all the people who came and lingered. "An arsonist will often return to the scene a number of times," the Chief had told him. "I want you to list the names."

"Should I interrogate them, Sir?"

"No Garner," the Chief had said, sounding weary for some reason that Reebok couldn't fathom. "Just give me a list."

He took one step farther back into the deep shade, until he was almost against the trunk of the tree and pulled his hat more firmly in place. The wide brim shadowed his face. Thank goodness his uniform was a deep navy. Easier to stay inconspicuous. He pulled one of the index cards from his shirt pocket, and wrote the date in the upper right-hand corner, just to double-check that his pen worked. It was important to be ready. Just in case.

~~~~~

While Peachie powdered her nose and unpacked a few things, Marmalade and I scooted out to the garden for the basil I'd forgotten to gather earlier. My argument—I guess I could call it that—with Melissa weighed heavily on my heart.

Your have a good heart.

Why couldn't we just purr our way through this the way Marmalade did?

Humans can not purr.

Will having Peachie here keep me from patching it up?

What is a paachingidup?

When Marmalade answered me—well, it sounded like an answer—I wondered if I'd been talking out loud. Thank goodness we had no close neighbors. Was I going crazy?

No.

I broke off a couple of stalks of basil—too lazy to harvest just the leaves, and headed back inside with my questions unanswered.

Excuse me? I answered you.

~~~~~

Glaze tossed her purse on the kitchen counter. "You might as well make some coffee, Maddy."

"Cinnamon rolls?" Dee always wanted cinnamon rolls.

Glaze's stomach rumbled, even though she'd finished that enormous breakfast just a couple of hours ago. "I guess. This may take a while."

"It won't take any time at all," Maddy snapped. "I vote no."

Gracie swished her tail back and forth a few times. She sat in front of Maddy and raised a hopeful paw. Maddy's voice softened. "Not now, sweetie. You've been fed."

Dee plopped down in her usual place. "Why did she lie on the application?" She pulled it out of her briefcase and spread the pages on the table.

"She didn't lie," Glaze pointed out. They'd been hashing this over all the way home, but nobody seemed to be listening to her. "She didn't. Not really. See?" She pointed. "All she did was use her first initial. And here? It's not lying when you leave questions unanswered."

Dee shrugged. "We just assumed she was a man."

"If we'd spoken with her," Glaze said, "we would have known. But," she turned to the final page and pointed "she asked to meet us at the hotel ..."

Maddy broke in. "And she specified the day ..."

"And the time," Dee finished.

"We know all that," Maddy said.

"Yes, we do." Glaze ran a hand through her silver hair. "I just hope we learned something from all this."

"Yeah," Dee said. "Never accept an incomplete application."

Maddy readjusted her glasses. "Look at the bright side. We wanted to see the inside of the old hotel. If we'd received an app like this for any other project, we would have turned it down flat." She puttered with the coffee maker. "You really put that realtor in his place, Glaze."

"Thank you. I was pretty proud of myself."

"You scored points with Susan, too." Dee lifted the glass cake plate cover and snagged a roll. "Anybody else want one?"

"Like you have to ask." Maddy sat across from Dee. "I still vote no."

"Let's think it through, though." Glaze snitched a twist of Dee's cinnamon roll that threatened to fall off. "I don't like her any more than you do Maddy—or you either, Dee. But she has a hefty amount to put toward the purchase ..."

"Then she doesn't need our money," Dee muttered.

"Margaret's money," Glaze said without being deflected from her argument. "That old place needs a lot of refurbishing."

Maddy waved her fork in the air. "It's going to take a minor fortune just to bring it up to code," Maddy said.

"You can say that again," Dee said.

"My point exactly." Glaze stared at each of them in turn. "It's been run down for years, and nobody's even thought of buying it till now. If we don't approve these funds, she won't buy it ..."

"And the place will gradually fall down," Dee finished for her.

"Right."

It took a full pot of coffee, four more cinnamon rolls, and another hour of arguing, but the Butterfly Brigade eventually approved S. Porchinsky's application.

"At least we know her last name now," Maddy said as Glaze signed the form.

Chapter 24

9 Years Earlier

HOW DARE HER MOTHER GET sick at such an inconvenient time?

"You're all I have left. You're all I've had ever since your father … since your father … I can't talk about it. Come home. Come home and help me. You owe it to me. You went away to college and then you never came to visit me when I moved here. You owe it to me."

It wasn't her job to nurse anybody through something like this, but she had to. She wasn't prepared to enjoy it, though. In fact, she planned to hate every minute she was there. The funeral couldn't come fast enough. Too bad she couldn't think of a foolproof way to speed things up.

It was as bad as she thought it was going to be. She hated staying there month after month, for more than two years. She had work to do in Atlanta.

But it would wait.

There would be time.

She spent the days and nights beside her mother's bed planning. Planning.

Chapter 25

So, I wish I could have followed
the fire truck
but she said she wanted me
home early
but this doesn't feel like home yet

I was afraid they'd catch me gone
I didn't want to give them
one more reason to hate me

~~~~~

LORNA JEAN HUNG UP THE phone and straightened her papers. She'd deal with these changes later. What a shame that her editor wanted her to change the title. Nervy Nineteen was a great name, and the next one could be Terror-Stricken Twenty. If only her editor would agree.

She pulled back one of the thick gold curtains and watched that young police officer skulking underneath the oak just downhill from Connie's ruined studio. What on earth was he doing? As she watched, he patted his shirt pocket, pulled out something—a notebook? a card? a pack of cigarettes?—no, not cigarettes; he looked like he was writing something down.

Lorna Jean leaned against the wall of the narrow dormer. She was truly worried. She'd heard the rumor that there was a body in there. People thought it might be Connie. She was almost certain it wasn't. She didn't want to think it was.

She didn't really know anything for sure. Not really.

When she'd asked her husband about it, he'd said there was nothing between them, and he'd said he'd make sure nothing happened. Whoever the body was, Connie or one of the other women in the class, Lorna Jean was dreadfully afraid that Mark might have "made sure nothing would happen." Just how well did she know the man she'd married? If this was a mid-life crisis—well, she'd heard that men could do outrageous things at that time of life.

The street had been empty for a moment there, but now three people walked down Willow and stopped in front of her house.

The first pedestrian was a man with a funny hitch in his gait. She thought he might be Mr. Orrin, the lonely old man who lived up on Fifth Street, but she wasn't sure. He planted his feet on the sidewalk, right next to Lorna Jean's rosebush. Nobody could get near the fire scene. There was still all that yellow tape. That woman in the white turtleneck was still hanging around. Weren't they supposed to take away the body? Or had they taken it while Lorna Jean wasn't watching? If so, why didn't that investigator leave?

Most of the crowd who'd been there earlier had dissipated— well, she herself had been there, too, and she'd come home, hadn't she? If Mr. Orrin had known anything about how the fire started, he would have gone to the police, wouldn't he? Mr. Orrin was a responsible citizen. As if she could tell. But why had he come back? She could see him shake his head slightly. Or maybe he just had a tremor. He was old enough for that, with his white hair and his very thick glasses.

A young person shuffled along in the gutter, and Lorna Jean wanted to tell him how lazy he looked—or was *he* a *she*? They could be so androgynous at that age. *Why don't you put your shoulders back and walk tall*, she wanted to say to the youngster on the street. There was no telling how he'd react to such advice though, and she didn't think it worth the possible danger. So many young people could be violent, she thought, remembering what Emma had told her about the gang that tore up their house in Atlanta. She wondered briefly why she hadn't seen Emma at the fire, but the crowd had grown quickly after she and Mary arrived. And Emma wasn't that tall. Maybe Emma stayed away from the fire because any death reminded her of her son's tragic end.

The young man in the street—she was pretty sure now; it was a male—took off his ball cap and ran a hand through his hair. Why wasn't he in school? He walked on down the street and Lorna Jean lost sight of him as the thick branches of a maple tree blocked her view.

A woman, one of the many women who jogged around town a lot, paused on the sidewalk well up the street from the limping man, facing away from Lorna Jean, looking at the charred mess. Did that woman know what had happened there? Her body looked tense. But what did Lorna Jean know? She was imagining guilt in everyone she saw. The woman—Lorna Jean thought her name was Linda, or something like that—swiveled her head, seeming to check out the man inspecting the fire scene. She's as suspicious as I am, Lorna Jean thought. Were we all going to start doubting our friends and neighbors? Not that these three were friends; she didn't even know their names for sure. But still, the thought was disturbing.

The policeman under the oak tree seemed to be taking notes. And trying to act as if he weren't doing anything at all. What was he writing, though? She shook her head and turned away, brushing her fingers over the frayed golden fabric of the curtain. She hated that color. That was the trouble with buying a furnished house after somebody died in it. Well, she'd died down in the river, but still, no matter where they died, you were stuck with that person's crummy taste. This house had been a really good deal, though, so what else could they have done? She heaved a sigh. She could measure the windows and go to that store up in Russell Gap, that's what she could do. She'd put up with these ugly curtains for too long. Maybe she could get her sister and her niece to go shopping with her. There wasn't any school on Saturday. She nodded once, looked back out at the now-bare street, and let the ugly curtains fall into place. She'd take them down tomorrow.

Meanwhile, she had some serious running to do.

~~~~~

Reebok shifted one more time and looked uphill across the street. That woman who lived over there had peered out of that second-floor window again. The window in the left-hand dormer. That was definitely suspicious. He already had one index card on Lorna Jean Hagstrom, from when he'd interviewed her after the fire at Miss Biscuit's shed. She was one of the runners who had tried to jog past and who'd pretended they weren't looking. Two of the women had berated him for stopping them. "Don't you know our calves can cramp if we stop suddenly," one of the women had asked, but it hadn't sounded like a question. More like a complaint.

"Keep bouncing on your toes, Sue," one of the other women had said, and then Reebok had been forced to interview those six women while they were all jiggling up and down, bouncing to their hearts' content. It was unnerving.

Now here was one of them skulking behind her curtains. Well, now he'd have another card on her.

Surveillance was kind of fun.

He tucked the cards on the last two people into his jacket pocket, and eased a blank one out of his shirt pocket. It was important to keep them separate. He noted her name and a description of her actions. She stood there a long time, just watching, but from behind the curtain like she didn't want to be seen.

He took out three more cards for the next three watchers. They seemed to be showing up in groups of three. From here in the shadow of this big old oak tree, he was invisible to those people in the bright sunshine as they peered at what was left of Connie Cartwright's shed.

A nondescript station wagon pulled up to the yellow tape. Reebok recognized the medical examiner. He watched as the man approached the mound of charred debris. He'd much rather be up there than here under this tree. Surveillance was a drag.

~~~~~

I love it when people like my soups. Peachie ate three bowls. I do so little cooking—breads and soups—that's about it, so when someone appreciates the effort, I find myself preening.

"Is the newsletter the only way you know about Mary?" I tried to sound casual, but Peachie skewered me with one of those looks.

One of what looks?

"I just wondered," I said. "Or do you ever write back and forth?" This was getting ridiculous. I had no reason to be so suspicious. "Do you ever call her?" Shut up Biscuit. It's no big deal.

What are you talking about?

I bent to stroke Marmalade. Was she in pain? Her little yawps sounded strangled.

Excuse me? Strangled?

"There are a lot of articles about her in the newsletter," Peachie said, wiping her mouth. "This soup is delicious. Do you give out the recipe?"

"What recipe? I just dump stuff in the crockpot and turn it on." Actually, I took a bit more care than that, but I was somewhat ticked off that Peachie wouldn't come clean about Mary.

She smells clean to me.

"I'll be ready for that walk soon," she said. "As soon as I have one more slice of that dill bread. It's really good."

Of course it was good. I made it.

I toasted the heel for her, since that was all that was left. "Do you know Mary's phone number?"

"Um," she said, slathering butter on the browned heel.

"We could call her." Not that I wanted to, but I was definitely curious as to whether Peachie had brought the number along with her.

She munched away with great gusto.

Fine with me. She could deflect my questions as much as she wanted to, but I was determined to find out what was going on.

If I knew what you were talking about, I would be willing to help you.

~~~~~~

Lorna Jean went through her usual quick warm-up routine and then jogged slowly around the block to Mary's house. She could have just as easily cut directly from her back yard into Mary's, but she liked to take the longer route as a way of completing her warm-up. Up Willow she kept the pace slow. When she turned right onto Third Street, she picked up her pace. By the time she rounded the corner onto Magnolia, she was running at about three-quarters of her regular speed. She saw Mary doing jumping jacks on the front sidewalk and called out to her.

Without discussion, they veered into the street and ran down the rest of the block. Lorna Jean loved living in a town with no traffic to speak of. At Second Street they turned left onto the wide sidewalk. When they took this route, they usually ran up as far as Pine Street, up past St. Teresa's, right on Third to Axelrod's Funeral home, and then on up Lower Sweetgum to Fifth Street. From there it was a straight shot—as straight as streets in Martinsville got, which meant a lot of ups and down and twists—back home.

Sometimes they did the whole route twice, but today Lorna Jean was too conscious of her deadline. She planned to drop out after the first go-around. She was already sweating, and they hadn't even reached Beechnut Lane yet. Ahead of them, she saw two women round the corner.

Chapter 26

7 Years Earlier

AT LONG LAST.

Mother was dead and she was free.

She could spread her dark wings and fly to Atlanta like an angel.

An avenging angel.

The time had come.

The first thing to do was check the phone book.

The next thing to do was reconnaissance.

The final thing to do would be revenge.

Chapter 27

So, all the guys threw pebbles
at my window this morning to wake me up.
I snuck out of the house.
When I found out where we were going
I got really mad at Ke #3
my garbage bin didn't hurt anyone's feelings.
he didn't have to go do that
she's a nice person
I like the library
but I can't talk to her
not now
at least I helped them clean up some
and it wasn't just for the hot chocolate
then I had to go
to church afterwards
that minister was worse than
the nightmares about Mr. Latham
he talked all about
personal responsibility
it's Ð #2's turn now.
I wonder what he's going to do?
it's not my fault, is it, Mr. Latham?

~~~~~

I OPENED THE FRONT DOOR, AND Peachie picked up her purse. "Put that down," I told her. "You won't need it where we're going."

She glanced around. "Where should I put it?"

"Just leave it there on the drop leaf table."

She looked dubious. "Even with the door locked, that doesn't sound safe."

"Don't worry. It'll be fine." I neglected to mention that I had no intention of locking the door. This was Martinsville after all, but Peachie might not appreciate its finer points. Oh, there had been some problems from time to time, but I had no reason to think somebody might walk into my house to steal Peachie's purse in broad daylight.

She looked around and tucked her purse out of sight behind the tall umbrella bucket I'd bought at an estate sale the previous week. Her purse handle drooped to one side and would be perfectly visible to any burglar, but I didn't think I needed to point that out to Peachie.

Marmalade slipped through the door in front of us. I couldn't imagine a walk without her.

We walk together well.

Glaze sure enjoyed walking Gracie. I toyed idly, and not too seriously, with the idea of getting a dog …

Excuse me?

… but only as far as our mailbox. I decided I'd much rather stick to Marmalade, with her cute little yawps and gurgles.

I do not believe this.

Ahead of me, Marmalade turned left onto the sidewalk and shook her head. I hoped she wasn't coming down with ear mites. I'd have to check her thoroughly this evening.

The day was overcast. Not the kind that portends rain. Just the kind that gives everybody a chance to relax a bit from unrelenting sunshine. With my vitiligo, I always appreciated a day like this.

I headed straight toward the library. Might as well show Peachie all the important stuff first. Maybe we'd stop at *Azalea House* later so she could meet Melissa. No. Melissa was mad at me. So, instead of *Azalea House*, we could circle up to the cliff above 5th Street and then down to the Delicious for some hot tea. I doubted they had Lapsang Souchong, though.

As the three of us turned right onto Second Street, Lorna Jean and that woman she always jogged with ran toward us. The other woman, the one wearing bright pink socks, veered to her right, vaulted over the daylilies by the curb, and sailed across the street. She was very graceful, but it was a good thing Sadie Masters wasn't driving by, or we would have had a squashed jogger. I love Sadie dearly, but she's a menace in that 1956 Chevy of hers, although I had to admit I'd never heard of her running over anyone.

Peachie turned to watch her. "Who was that?"

She stepped on my tail once.

"I can't remember her name," I said as Marmalade let out a squawk, "but she always wears pink socks."

Lorna Jean pulled to a stop—well, as much of a stop as a jogger ever did. Her legs kept pumping up and down. "Hey there, Biscuit."

"Meet my old college friend. This is Peachie Rose. Lorna Jean Hagstrom."

"I'm not *that* old." Peachie stuck out her hand.

Lorna Jean demurred. "I'm too sweaty to shake hands with anybody but a fish."

Fish do not have hands.

Peachie jerked her thumb back over her shoulder toward Lorna Jean's running mate. "Who's your uncommunicative friend?"

"Oh, that's just Mary Fleming. She's kind of shy. We jog together most mornings."

This is not morning.

I bent to lift Marmalade into my arms. She always purred and squawked a lot...

Excuse me? I do not squawk.

... but today she was even more vocal than usual. "Mary. Yes. That's her name. I knew it was either that or Linda. Or Sue."

Lorna Jean wagged her head up and down. I couldn't tell if she was agreeing with me or was just stretching her neck. "I must have met five women with the name of Mary in this town. And three or four Sues."

I thought briefly of Henry's daughter, Susan. The one with the long black hair. I wondered if anyone ever called her Sue. Probably not. She looked like someone who would insist on her full name. I sure hoped she'd leave town soon.

"... Linda." Peachie laughed, and brought me back to the conversation.

"At least five, maybe six," Lorna Jean said. So they were still talking about name frequency.

"I met her in the IGA a couple of months ago," I said. "She doesn't have a library card." Even I could hear the faint tinge of disapproval in my voice.

Peachie chuckled. "That's how you separate the world? The haves and have-nots?"

I thought of objecting, saying that I didn't worry about people being rich or poor, but then I got what she meant. "Well, I'm happy to say that most of the people in Martinsville are *haves*. I see practically everybody in the library."

"I have to get back to my morning run." Lorna Jean raised her hand in farewell.

Peachie tapped her wrist, although I could see there wasn't a watch there. "You're a little late for a morning run, aren't you?"

"The fire," Lorna Jean said. "We got so caught up in watching it, and then I had to be home at nine for a phone call from my editor."

"Lorna Jean's a writer," I told Peachie. "This will be her 19th book. Can't wait to read it."

"If I can ever get the rewrites done to satisfy my editor."

"Nineteen books? I don't think I know your name, and I read a lot."

"She writes under a pen name," I said.

"My first editor said they'd never get Lorna Jean Hagstrom to fit on the cover. So I picked another moniker. The funny thing is…" She stopped her bouncing for a moment and leaned closer to us, "…it's only three letters shorter."

I told Peachie the name, and her jaw dropped noticeably.

"I love your books! I have every single one of them!" It was the most excited I'd seen her since she arrived.

After a bit more gushing from Peachie, Lorna Jean took off at a trot. She'd never catch up, unless her jogging partner was waiting for her around a corner somewhere.

As we strolled on at a sedate pace through town, Peachie exclaimed delightedly at all the right places. She admired the late-blooming daylilies lining the street and loved the town's gazebo, which we saw through the shade of the massive old trees that dotted the park. She oohed and aahed over my stone lions that flanked the library's massive front steps. The heavy oak door brought approving comments, and both Sadie and Rebecca Joe were judged as 'absolute jewels.' I couldn't introduce her to Esther, because the children's afternoon activity session was in full swing. Something from Dr. Seuss.

I much preferred dealing with children who were a bit older. A lot older. Old enough to discuss ideas. Old enough to love reading. Of course, I knew it started at this age.

Esther's voice rang out from behind the low bookshelves that separated the children's section from the rest of the main floor. "An elephant's faithful …" and the throats of many children proclaimed, "ONE HUNDRED PERCENT!"

Maybe that was how Genevieve Russell, one of my favorite young readers in town, started out. She devoured books. Even with all her school work, she was in here at least twice a week. We'd discussed the story flow from one generation to the next in Lois Lowry's *The*

Giver series, and the …

"Biscuit! Yoo-hoo! Don't you agree?"

"Sure." I reconsidered. "With what?"

Peachie grinned, an expression precisely mirrored on Sadie's wrinkled visage. "Never fails, does it? She was like this back in college, too."

"Go ahead and tease. I was thinking about our young readers."

Sadie glanced at the group who had reached "*My egg! shouted Horton. My egg! Why it's hatching!*" Full volume.

I do not see an egg.

"Not that young. More like twelve or thirteen. Genevieve."

Sadie nodded. She'll probably solve all the world's problems before she's thirty."

That would be easier if everyone acted like a cat.

Marmy gave another of her funny little gurgles, and headed toward the door.

I know you are ready to leave.

We took the hint.

At the end of the block, we crossed the street to talk with Nathan Young, the town doctor, outside the front door to his medical office. "Just catching a few rays of sunshine," he said, after I'd introduced them. "I try to step outside four or five times each day." His face crinkled in an irresistible grin. "Vitamin D, you know."

Hello, GoodHands.

Marmalade skirted around him, purring loudly, and touched noses with KorsaCat, the office greeter.

Hello, GrayGuy.

Korsi paid no attention whatsoever to people who were healthy, which was why he'd always pretty much ignored me, except for that time my nose was broken, but he was an invaluable comforter to Doc Nathan's patients, the ones who were sick or injured. If someone came in for just a routine checkup though, Korsi was politely unavailable.

The gray cat pulled away from Marmalade, walked between Nathan's legs, and put a paw up on Peachie's knee. She looked delighted, and bent to pat the cat; Korsi snuggled his head against the palm of her hand.

She did not pat me when she met me.

I looked at Doc. He studied Peachie's bent back for a moment as she stroked KorsaCat's thick, luscious gray fur. He turned his head and lifted an interrogatory eyebrow. I raised my shoulders and shook my head. I thought Peachie looked terrific. So why had Korsi greeted her?

"What a lovely cat you have." Peachie straightened with a groan and put a hand to the middle of her back. "I'm sure not as flexible as I used to be."

I expected Doc to say something about exercise or good eating habits, but he reached out to take Peachie's hand. "I hope you have a lovely visit," he said. "If you need a checkup while you're here, you know where to find us."

She laughed. "Only if the cat will be here."

"Oh, he will be," Doc said. "You can count on it."

As we reached the end of his walk, I turned briefly. Doc was shaking his head. He looked baffled. He looked worried.

I dithered for a while wondering how to broach the subject. I doubted I could say *Doc's cat thinks you're sick.*

Finally I decided there was no need to skirt the issue. "How's your health been, Peachie?"

She waved an airy hand. "Couldn't be better."

I would have said something else, but by then we'd arrived at the fire scene. The fire engine was gone, but yellow tape still ringed the area, and the Corgi—I shouldn't call her that—Captain Paula Corrigan still rummaged through the ruins. Why was she still here? Wouldn't she have been done hours ago? I couldn't imagine what was taking her so long.

Peachie clutched at my arm. "Is the body still in there?"

"No," I said. "Bob said they'd take it to Decatur for identification." Surely the medical examiner had gotten here already.

She looked at me with her head tilted to one side. Like an inquisitive puppy. "Why not just ask around town to see who's missing?"

"Well, that's the trouble. There *is* somebody missing—the woman who owned the burnt building—but I can't believe it's her. It has to be some stranger who came to town."

"And just happened to wander into a burning building?"

When she put it that way… No. I didn't want to consider that it might be Connie. Why couldn't I just be like Marmalade and not know anything about any of these problems?

Excuse me?

Just walk around town all day mooching food and … and whatever else cats did. "Let's head on up Willow to Fifth Street," I said.

We really need to have a conversation.

That's what cats did, I thought as Marmy let out a long grumbly sound. They meowed and mooched all day long. I waved to Bob, but he must not have seen me, so I waved to Reebok. He turned his head, as if searching for whomever I was waving at. Did he really think I couldn't see him under that tree?

~~~~~

This walk was all very well, but Peachie's feet had started to hurt after the first three blocks. She half-listened to Biscuit's travelogue, wondering all the time about how soon she could find a convenient bench. She'd been getting tired an awful lot lately and couldn't figure out why. Of course, she'd done a lot of driving to get here. No chance to stretch her legs. And this walk had been awfully long. That explained it.

She wanted desperately to scratch scratch scratch that itchy spot she hadn't been able to get rid of. She'd read once—maybe in one of Biscuit's letters—that home was where you could scratch anywhere it itched. A public street in Martinsville was not home. No scratching here. Well, she thought, maybe the walk was almost over. They'd seen the library and where the fire was. Not very exciting. Just some people poking around among blackened two by fours. She wondered where all the burned material would go. And who would take it there.

Biscuit waved to a policeman skulking under a big tree. Shouldn't he be working? Peachie turned away. She wanted to get this over with.

Chapter 28

7 Years Earlier

IT HADN'T BEEN THAT HARD, really.

All she had to do was wait for them to leave and then wait for it to get a little bit darker. Mid-December. Dark early.

Their next-door neighbors picked them up at the end of the driveway. She could see they were all dressed up for an evening out. She had plenty of time.

Easy to break a pane in the back door.

He had an antique tool collection, housed behind the glass doors of what looked like a specially built cabinet. Well, wasn't that just dandy?

Just what she needed, a specialty hammer with an unusual head. She wondered vaguely what it might be for. But she didn't wonder for long. After all, she knew exactly what it was for.

She slammed it into the fancy kitchen stove first, then stood back and admired the pattern it made. A four-pointed star. She'd been meant to be a star, but that woman had ruined her chances.

Appropriate, then.

Chapter 29

So, I really, really want to go home
only it's not there any more

~~~~~

REEBOK WAS PRETTY SURE HE didn't have to fill out a card on Miss Biscuit, but whoever was with her might be a suspect. He'd have to ask a few discreet questions to find out just who that woman was.

He wrote *female, about 5 ft. 4 in.(?)* He took a guess at her weight, too. He wondered if there was some course he could take on how to figure out how much people weighed. He made a note of that on another card, then went back to writing *light brown slacks, yellow blouse with big flowers, dark brown shoes, no handbag. Seen with Miss Biscuit at—*he looked at his watch and noted the time. *Walks funny, like her shoes are too tight.* He used to have an aunt who walked that very same way. Why hadn't she just bought larger shoes?

On the next card he wrote, *Miss Biscuit (with unknown female).*

No need to note Miss Biscuit's height or weight. He'd remember those details forever. But it was important to note that she'd been there. The Chief wanted a list, after all.

She waved in his direction. He was invisible, though, here under the heavy branches—the shade was so dark he almost had to squint to see what he was writing. He turned, thinking perhaps she'd seen someone off to one side. That was poor police work on his part. He should have been aware of someone sneaking up on him.

But nobody was there. By the time he turned back to look at Miss Biscuit, she and the other woman had started up the street.

~~~~~

At the top of Willow, we swung right over to Magnolia and on up to Fifth Street. Just past the Peterson's house I stopped to show her the cliff where Diane Marie had plunged to her death such a short time ago. I'd written Peachie about it, but I knew she couldn't have imagined the sheer size of the cliff face.

"This looks just like a cliff where we picnicked in the Tetons a few years ago," she said.

So much for not being able to imagine something.

"It must have been awful for you," she added, "seeing her fall like that."

I blinked back the tears that threatened. I nodded, unwilling, unable to speak for a few moments. I led Peachie to one of the comfortable wooden benches that Margaret's husband Sam installed the year after Diane Marie died. A brass plate simply listed Diane Marie's full name and two dates.

Peachie plopped down without even looking at the dedicatory plate. Had I been too enthusiastic about Martinsville and all that went on in this little town? I watched her for a moment. After just this short walk, she looked awfully pale, almost haggard, and her breathing sounded ragged. Of course, I was used to walking these steep hilly streets every day, and she wasn't. Living in the Midwest, she probably never changed altitude more than ten feet up or down from one side of the city to the other. Feeling slightly chagrined, I sat beside her, and Marmalade jumped into my lap. I stroked her silky fur and wondered how people ever managed to get by without animal companions.

They would be lonely.

"Do you have pets, Peachie? I don't think you've ever mentioned any, but I never actually asked." Still I knew the answer before she spoke. She couldn't possibly have a cat or dog, or I would have heard about it—and I would have seen photos, too.

"No. It's too much bother."

Excuse me? I am not a bother.

Marmalade raised her head from my lap and meowed yet again, sounding for all the world like she was objecting, and we laughed.

"Sorry, little cat. I obviously didn't mean to include you in that category."

I am not that little, and yes you did.

Peachie raised one leg and then the other, twisting each foot at the ankle and exhaling loudly. "Do you walk this much all the time?"

"That's how we get around here." Ugh. That sounded so lame.

She lowered her head and looked at me from under her eyebrows. "And you don't provide mules for us visitors?"

~~~~~

Biscuit could talk all day about how good it was to walk so much, but she didn't have extra weight to carry around. With quick side-glances, Peachie looked Biscuit up and down. So, all right, she did have some extra weight. What was it Biscuit had said in one of her letters, that Bob called her a comfortable armful? Peachie thought that was sweet.

As casually as possible, she raised her left hand to the right side of her face, and rubbed along the jawline. In so doing, she dragged her forearm along the foremost curve of her body. It was the only way in public that she could scratch the almost irresistible itch she'd felt for some time. Her skin was just too dry. She remembered every day to moisturize her face; she'd just have to remember to add a little extra farther down on the left.

She really didn't want to move, but the sooner they left this bench, the sooner she'd be able to lie down for that little nap Biscuit had mentioned.

Sounded like a very good idea.

"I'm ready," she said, hauling herself to her feet and forcing energy into her voice. "Shall we head home now?"

~~~~~

Even though I was used to walking, it felt nice to sit for a few minutes. And then Peachie jumped up like a cheerleader after a first down. Where did I come up with a football analogy? I don't even like the game. But how could she be so wiped out one moment and so full of energy the next?

I took another good look at her, though, and saw that it wasn't energy. It was more like desperation. I needed to get her home and lying down. Maybe a nice warm tub bath would help? With Epsom salts. Yes. And some sort of energizing tea. Ginger maybe?

"It's mostly all downhill from here," I said, and her face brightened just a bit.

Maybe KorsaCat really did know something.

The rest of the walk was fairly quiet. I was increasingly aware of her labored breath, but I didn't know what to do about it. Should I offer to run home for the car? No. By this point we had only about three blocks to go. Thank goodness the day was so mild. I slowed my steps even more.

I've never been able to walk quietly without my mind heading off in a dozen different directions. Here was Peachie to worry about, even though I didn't know why I was worrying. And we had four fires, most likely all started by the same person, although the pattern made no sense—what pattern? There wasn't any at all. The garbage bin at the IGA, my shed, Emma's car, and now Connie's studio. And a dead body.

There wasn't a thing I could do about any of this.

I hate to feel so helpless. I hooked my arm through Peachie's. At least I might lend her a little support.

Chapter 30

7 Years Earlier

THE GLASSWARE CAME NEXT, AFTER the kitchen wall and those lovely star-shaped dents in the expensive stove. Why did they have so many wine glasses? She swept them off the fancy display shelves and crowed in delight at the sound they made. She'd worn work boots, so she was in no danger as she crunched through all those deliciously sharp shards.

Plates, platters, bowls. Measuring cups, canisters, cook books.

Milk, juice, leftovers. Flax seeds, pistachios, chocolate syrup.

Fish fillets, ham hock, great big roast.

Vases, statues, photo albums. Books, knick-knacks, pencils.

Towels, soaps, bath salts. Toothpaste, toothbrushes, floss.

Couch cushions, pillows, chairs. Tables, display cases, picture frames.

TV, radios, clocks.

Curtains, curtains, curtains.

And, of course, knotty pine paneling everywhere. Stars everywhere.

How to know when she was done?

What was enough to satisfy?

What would ever be enough?

Chapter 31

So, they told me if I ratted on them
they'd tell everybody all this was my idea.
I'm stuck

~~~~~

I RAN THE BATH FOR PEACHIE while she changed into the soft blue robe I kept hanging behind the door in the guest bedroom. I added two generous handfuls of Epsom salts and a dollop of geranium essential oil to help ease her tired muscles. I thought about duplicating the process for myself in my own bathroom, but decided I needed to finish baking that bread and work on a meal for the two of us. I planned to make extra and take it to the station for Bob and Reebok—and maybe Captain Corrigan as well?

For the meantime, though, I ran myself a cup of cold water from the sink and sat on the edge of the tub, sipping and watching the warm scented water swirl as it filled the tub.

I was glad I hadn't made a reservation at Tom's restaurant for tonight. It would have been nice to take Peachie there, but with her so shaky, a lot of my plans were going to have to change.

I'd planned also to invite her to go up the valley with me to that wonderful old hardware store in Garner Creek so I could replace my garden tools, but I wasn't sure she'd make it. Of course, I could drive right up close to the store. They had a parking lot and an entrance in back; that way she wouldn't have to walk too far. She'd barely made it up the stairs once we got home. I couldn't ask her to do anything strenuous.

As I pondered, she walked in. "Ancient philosopher Lah Tsa Phun reported to have said that sipping on side of tub better than slipping inside of tub."

"I'll keep that in mind. You enjoy your bath. I put this big bell here." I gave it a clang, and Peachie winced. "If you need anything, just ring it real loud."

I could see her wheels begin to turn, but Ancient Philosopher must have dried up for the moment. Peachie just nodded and began to untie the belt. I closed the door softly and wondered how I could possibly get her to go to Doctor Nathan. For the present, though, we weren't going anywhere else or doing anything even slightly active for the rest of the day. An early bedtime. That's what we needed.

I like bedtime.

"Shush, Marmalade. I'll feed you, but you have to be quiet and not disturb Peachie."

Marmalade made a grumbly sound and led the way to the kitchen. I wondered if I could leave Peachie alone long enough to run some food up to the station.

~~~~~

Paula Corrigan wanted to see that autopsy report. There was something funny about the head. The forehead. She'd bet her badge that it wasn't a falling joist that had made such a dent in the skull. She'd never seen anything like it. She'd mentioned it to the M.E., but all she got in reply was a noncommittal grunt.

She put in a call to the lab in Decatur, asking them to fax her the report as soon as it was ready. Then she buzzed the department secretary and requested a particular book from the county library. "If they have it, get John to run over there and pick it up."

She pulled out a blank report form and started sketching in details, referring to her lime-green notebook periodically, although that was hardly necessary. The scene was too fresh in her memory.

What would she need to nail this guy, whoever he was? Where were the inevitable clues that would point to just one person? She'd find them. She'd get him.

She laid her head in her hands for a moment, but backed quickly away from the smell on her fingers. Would she ever get used to it?

It didn't matter where she was—at a scene, here in her office, at home, having dinner with friends—the smell of char stayed with her. It didn't seem to matter how thoroughly she washed. Charred wood. Whenever there was a recovery, the smell was of charred flesh. She hadn't even touched this body, but that sweet, completely unique smell of burnt human flesh seemed to cling to her. She knew other arson investigators who smeared Vicks under their noses, just like some autopsy assistants did. But it didn't help. It just overlaid the miasma of burnt flesh with an aura of menthol. A part of her brain knew she didn't really carry the smell anywhere except in her mind, but she still tried to keep her hands away from her face.

How could anybody ever forget to check the batteries in their smoke alarms? They'd never forget if they saw even once what she saw all too often.

But she supposed there hadn't been any smoke alarms in that studio building. The Cartwright woman probably didn't think one would be needed. Or she might have thought it would be going off all the time with all the stuff she did in there. "I'm going to have to read up about glass-blowing" she muttered, "or glass-firing or whatever it's called."

Her secretary stuck her head around the door. "Did you call me?"

"No. Just talking to myself."

"Why am I not surprised?" She walked to the desk and dumped a thick manila envelope next to the inbox. "Here's that book you wanted. Hope it's worth the fee we'll have to pay the courier."

"John? He's charging a fee now?"

"Yep. He wants a full box of Krispy Kreme donuts."

"His price has gone up." Paula lifted the package and pulled it open. "Didn't I get away with half a dozen last time I sent him on an errand like this?"

"Inflation." She pointed to the package again. "It's because that thing's so gosh darn heavy."

"At least he was quick about it."

"Last time I looked, the county library was right next door." She gestured to the package. "Looks important."

"It will be if I can find one particular item in here. I needed the information this morning about nine o'clock."

"Good luck." The woman left, closing the door softly.

Paula extracted *The American Handbook of Specialty Tools*. She'd happened to notice it on the "new arrivals" shelf the last time she'd been in the county library. But she hadn't thought she'd need to refer to it so soon. I need to get a copy for myself, she thought. Starting at the back and moving forward page by page, she thumbed through the hefty tome, looking.

~~~~~

Even though the medical examiner always insisted on clearing the scene of any extraneous personnel while he did his inspection, Bob had managed this time to get close enough. Closer than he wanted to, really. Close enough to see what remained of the head. Practically no flesh left on it. A caved in section on the top of the skull and a dent—an imprint almost—in the middle of the forehead that was unlike anything he'd ever seen.

He called the Decatur lab and asked how soon the results might be in.

He was told, in more or less polite phrases, that he shouldn't hold his breath. He and everybody else who'd been asking would get the answers when the answers were ready.

All right, so they were busy there. One homicide in Martinsville probably didn't make much impact on a state crime lab. Still, this was his town. He wanted those answers. He wondered, though, whether the report would bring up more questions than it would answer.

Of course it would. Impatiently, he moved aside an In-box that had shown up on his desk out of nowhere. Maybe Melody, the town clerk, had thought he needed one. Nothing in it. He didn't need an In-box. He needed answers. He rested his face in his hands for a moment until he became aware of Reebok making an unearthly amount of noise playing with those index cards of his. Crazy. But maybe something would come of it.

~~~~~

Reebok watched the Chief slam down the phone. Maybe not slam it exactly, but he didn't usually hang up that noisily. It couldn't be good if the Chief was rattled.

He moved the cards around on his desk one more time. It reminded him of when he was a little boy and couldn't shuffle a deck. His dad told him it was okay just to slide them all over the table, as long as they really got mixed up.

There had to be a connection between at least one of these people and Connie Cartwright. Or, he corrected himself, whoever that body was. Somebody had to be angry about money. That was the usual reason.

Or love. Jealousy was a nasty emotion. He couldn't imagine anybody being in love with Connie Cartwright, but there were some strange combinations of couples in Martinsville. People you'd never think could possibly get along. Of course, somebody pretty obviously couldn't get along with whoever that dead person was.

Or it could have been revenge. That was a good motive. What did he really know about Connie Cartwright? What was her life like before she came to Martinsville? Was somebody out to get her?

Then again, power could have been the reason they had a corpse on their hands. What was the contest and who needed to be the winner?

Greed. Jealousy. Retribution. There always needed to be a winner in any of those situations. Who wanted to win bad enough to murder somebody? If he knew the answer to that one, he'd have his killer.

He splayed his fingers out and attacked the cards yet again. If he mixed them up enough, maybe he'd see the answer. It had to be here.

~~~~~

Lorna Jean's calves ached. She pushed back from her desk, crossed her left ankle over her right knee, and massaged her lower leg. She'd run faster than usual this afternoon, and then she'd had that pause in the middle when she ran into Biscuit and her friend. She'd tried to keep moving, but it was bad to break up a run like that. She never had caught up with Mary. Not that it mattered. Sometimes they ran together. Sometimes they ran separately. Or started out together and took different routes. She liked that about Mary. She was flexible. It was too bad Mary was so painfully shy; it was a wonder they'd ever become friends.

She looked at the wall to her right, as if she could see through from her office all the way across the house and over her back yard. Beyond the fence was Mary's yard. That was the reason they'd met. Lorna Jean had been out there in back for some reason, she couldn't remember what it was, and she'd seen Mary across the fence, stretching the same way Lorna Jean did after she'd put in a few miles.

"Are you a runner," Lorna Jean had called out.

Mary had started, looked up, and said something. At least Lorna Jean thought she'd said something. Her lips had moved, but what came out was just a whisper on the breeze.

Lorna Jean leaned her forearms on the gate in the chain link fence. "I usually run a mile or two each morning."

"Is that all?" The only way Lorna Jean could tell what the woman had said was that the lips were readable. Had she no volume whatsoever?

Fortunately, Mary'd inched over to the fence to introduce herself.

After that, they'd fallen into a schedule of running together. Sometimes.

Lorna Jean pushed back an errant wisp of hair that had fallen out of her topknot. It wasn't much of a schedule. Still, she didn't mind that. The only thing in her life that she was rigid about was her writing. Six and a half hours a day every single day here at her desk.

She'd think about it later. Right now she had other things to worry about. Like a deadline to meet on those rewrites her editor wanted. Like whether her husband had murdered Connie Cartwright.

~~~~~

There it was, on page 729. A mining tool called a Star Hammer. Paula read through the descriptive paragraph. Head two inches in diameter. Used by miners—and blacksmiths—to clean drill bits.

She'd been calling it a cross because the fracture on the skull was perfectly in line with the horizontal and vertical planes of the body. But she could see why it was called a Star Hammer. All you had to do was lengthen the bottom line and you'd have a perfect Star of Bethlehem. A four-pointed star.

Or change the angle 45 degrees and you'd have an X.

~~~~~

My Gratitude List for Friday

1. This has seemed like such a long day. It's hard to believe it's only Friday. Exactly a week since my shed was burned. I'm still grateful for the Martinsville firefighters. They're a good crew.

2. Patricia Jean / P. Jean / Peachie. No matter what everybody calls her, she's a good old friend, and it's nice to connect with her. It's been too many years. But I do wonder what she's doing here. STOP IT, BISCUIT!!!!! I sure hope she's okay. Maybe she just got overtired. I need to stop worrying.

3. Marmalade. I checked her for ear mites, and she seems to be fine, but she's still shaking her head a lot.

4. Doc. And KorsaCat. Now I'm worrying again.

5. Glaze and Dee and Maddy – and even the dog. At least Gracie doesn't jump on people.

and 6. I have to add Bob. I sure hope he finds that arsonist murderer soon.

I am grateful for
> *Widelap and Softfoot*
> *bugs*
> *catching the intruders in the book place*
> *good food*
> *this soft bed*
> *I do not need to add anything else*

~~~~~

I woke twice that night, restless and concerned. The first time, I tiptoed along the dark hallway to Peachie's doorway. It was faintly limned in light. The door obviously didn't fit as snugly as it should. Maybe Bob could adjust the hinges or something. There wasn't a full moon, and Martinsville didn't have streetlights—they wouldn't have shone into Peachie's windows anyway, since this bedroom was on the back of the house. She must have traveled with a nightlight. Was she afraid of the dark?

Two years ago I would have thought that was silly, but after having been shoved into the river on a dark and stormy night (shades of Snoopy on top of his doghouse with his typewriter rose into my head—or was that Linus with the typewriter? No, he had the piano. No, that was Schroeder). I shook my head at myself. After that terrifying experience, I'd been rather squeamish about late-night walks and dark rooms, but even so, I didn't need a night light in my own house.

This is not her house.

Marmalade wound her soft purring body around my ankles, and I felt inexpressible comfort. She was so sweet to get up with me.

Thank you. I keep watch.

I put my ear to Peachie's door. She wasn't a snorer; at least, she hadn't been in college, but she'd always had a loud breath, as if the air had to force its way up through a tightened esophagus. I could hear her breathing deeply, evenly. I was just going to have to assume that all was well.

She is not asleep.

And I was going to have to talk her into having a checkup. Soon.

GrayGuy is waiting for her.

I went back to bed, but woke to the sound of thunder an hour or so later. Well, I thought, Peachie will be delighted. Now we absolutely won't be able to go walking.

~~~~~

This old house had entirely too many creaks and groans for Peachie's taste. She was used to a nice modern apartment, where someone else took care of all the maintenance, and there was a crew to do the landscaping. She had to admit that Biscuit's front yard was most attractive, with all those shrubs and flowers, and the garden in the back yard looked extremely productive, but Peachie had no intention of ever putting herself into a situation where she had to do all that bending and bothering. Weeding. Watering. Fertilizing. No, she remembered from one of Biscuit's letters that she never used fertilizers. Compost, or something like that. Not that Peachie cared about such stuff.

She shifted from her right side to her left side and then back onto her right side again. She scratched at the itchy spot and then forced herself to slow her breathing and lie perfectly still. Sleep would come eventually. The bath had relaxed her. The evening meal had been quiet, even though she wasn't sure she wanted soup twice a day. The fresh bread had been tasty, though. She was glad Biscuit hadn't insisted on her company when she took the extra soup and bread to the police station for Bob and his assistant, the one with the funny name. Adidas? Something to do with shoes.

Speaking of which, she stretched her ankles one at a time. Not much more sore than usual. But she was glad she'd stayed here and let Biscuit do the running around. It hadn't taken her long to deliver the meal to the men, and then the two of them had just talked through the evening. She'd gone to bed early, but now here she lay, wide awake.

The night light, the one she always packed whenever she traveled, cast a soft glow. She heard the cat utter a soft meow outside her door, and then a few more several moments later. She was not going to let that creature into her room, no matter how much it begged. She had nothing against Marmalade personally—was it even possible to get personal with a cat?—and Peachie had to admit the cat was soft, and well-behaved, too. An occasional pat was all well and good, but Peachie simply couldn't understand how some people, who seemed otherwise sane, could devote so much of their lives to furry four-legged creatures. Biscuit wasted entirely too much time writing about the cat's antics, and had even claimed that Marmalade had saved her life when that madman attacked her on the cliff-top a couple of years ago. Ridiculous. Sheer coincidence.

She tossed for another hour or so, and then she heard the thunder. Good. No walking around tomorrow.

She slept.

Chapter 32

7 Years Earlier

SHE HID BEHIND A HEDGE across the street. She watched them come home. She watched the blue flashing lights appear.

But no one would ever catch her.

No way for them to know the avenging angel's identity.

She watched through binoculars. One policeman wrote in a notebook; one took photos. She should have brought a camera with her. It would be nice to have pictures of her work. But it wouldn't be safe to have them developed. Somebody might ask questions. That was okay. She had the hammer. A perfect souvenir.

What a spectacular view through the front window, where the curtains used to be. The curtains she'd torn down and slashed. That woman was crying. Her husband patted her shoulder, but she kept on bawling like a baby. Served her right. Now she'd know how it felt.

She had to retreat for a while when some of the neighbors came out to look at the police cars, whispering among themselves. She could hear them speculating as to what might be wrong. Even with all the noise she'd made, ripping and slashing her way through the house, none of them had heard anything. Fine bunch of neighbors they were, all closed up in their fancy houses, set back from the street, separated by their fancy brick walls. Now here they were flooding the street and wondering what had happened.

She slipped away and walked the few blocks back to where she'd left her car. Not good to risk being seen, so she drove around for a while. By the time she went back, all the lights were out. That was delicious. She'd left one bed untouched. Or so she was sure it would look to them. She'd slipped a few glass shards under the sheet at the foot of the bed. A little surprise. She'd worn gloves. She was safe.

She imagined them slipping into bed for some rest before they tackled the cleanup job they'd have ahead of them. By now there should be blood all over that woman's feet, ripped to shreds by the little secret present she'd left. Ripped to shreds. How appropriate.

Retribution felt wonderful. Somehow, though, it wasn't quite enough.

Chapter 33

> So, all during supper she cried
> and he got mad
> kids, gangs, he said
> and they both told me they were
> glad I wasn't like that
> if they knew
> would they get rid of me?
> So, later I snuck out and
> met up with the guys
> I told them I wanted out
> but #2 said he really didn't know
> whose car it was before he did it
> he just picked the one farthest out
> #3 gave him the signal
> when everybody came outside
> I think that's against the rules
> we're supposed to do it by ourselves
> this whole thing stinks

~~~~~

SATURDAY MORNING HARDLY DAWNED AT all. Doodle-Doo crowed as usual, but the sun apparently didn't listen to him. The rain that moved in overnight came with terrific thunder and kept us inside. Getting my garden tools replaced could wait. Anyway, I'd rather go with someone who shared my love of gardening—and if I couldn't find someone like that, I'd go with nobody but myself. Peachie just didn't seem too enthusiastic about a jaunt up the valley. In fact, she wasn't too enthusiastic about anything. Except Lorna Jean's bestselling books and Peachie's ancient philosopher. I had to admit he was entertaining. Parsing squashly.

I poured boiling water into the teapot, and the smell of burnt cigars wafted up. Disgusting stuff. What I did for my friends.

Peachie took a deep breath. "Lovely," she said.

The rain pounded so loud I could barely hear her across the little round table in the bay window alcove.

"So, you slept okay?"

No. She did not.

"Sure did."

I knew she was lying. Those circles under her eyes were the color of a summer dusk, darker than the blue bathrobe she wore. She looked awful. Pale. Pasty. Chalky. That was the word I was looking for. She hadn't looked this bad yesterday. Maybe we shouldn't have gone for that walk. But surely one little walk couldn't hurt anybody.

It was a very long walk.

"Peachie?"

"Yes?"

"Are you sure you're okay? You look a bit peaked."

"Peak-ed?" She emphasized both syllables. "That's a word straight out of a Victorian novel."

"Well, it's true. Was it the walk?"

"Wise old philosopher Lah Tsa Phun say, *dawn is streak-ed / I am peak-ed / bones they creak-ed / tears they leak-ed.*

I didn't laugh. I didn't even chuckle. "I know you're not going to believe me when I tell you this, Peachie—"

"Then why bother to tell me?"

"Because I think you need to hear it. All I'm asking is that you think about it."

I was right. She didn't believe it a bit. KorsaCat was just a cat, she said. "What could a cat possibly know about medical diagnosis? All she wanted was a scratch on the head."

"He," I corrected her. "He's never been wrong yet."

She gave me one of those *you've got to be kidding* looks. But then she rested her hand briefly on her heart. And then she rubbed her jaw. Was she going to turn out to have heart trouble? Jaw pain was one of the symptoms of a heart attack. What if she had a heart attack over the breakfast table?

That was okay. Well, it wasn't okay, but I'd taken a CPR refresher course. I was prepared.

~~~~~

Reebok ducked, dripping, onto the wide front porch, glad to be under cover for the moment. He looked back down Magnolia Street to where a bend blocked the view. Nobody from here could have seen the fire. Maybe the smoke, which had risen higher than the tops of all these big trees.

A light shone through the pebbled glass panel in the front door, a light that hadn't been on when he'd driven around town two hours ago. Somebody had to be up. He hoped it wouldn't be Mrs. Haversham in her pajamas. No. It was well past eight o'clock. Women with families always got up early, didn't they? His mother was always up, dressed, and drying the breakfast dishes by this time of the morning. Yesterday, he'd called her at six-thirty to tell her that the fire investigation was going to take a lot of effort. "Don't worry," he'd told her, "if I can't call you at the usual times."

He pulled his navy blue slicker back so his badge would be visible. It was always nice to reassure people right away that this wasn't a stranger at their door. It was a Police Officer. He stood a little straighter and rang the doorbell. It was exceptionally loud. The old man was partly deaf, Reebok knew. He had an index card that said so. Two hearing aids.

It was the grandson, though, who opened the door, his eyes widening at the sight of Reebok's uniform. The boy's Spiderman pajamas drooped on his gangly frame, exposing bony ankles and wrists. Reebok checked his mental card file. Thirteen years old. "Good morning, Jimmy. Could I speak with your grandparents?"

Jimmy lowered his head and stammered, "Grandpa's in the kitchen. I'll go get him."

But there was no need to do that. Mr. Haversham rounded a corner into the hallway. "Officer Garner, isn't it? My grandson will hang up your rain slicker. Come on back to the kitchen. I just made coffee." Reebok tried to steel his face, but Mr. Haversham seemed to be exceptionally alert to nuances. "Or there's some hot chocolate I made for Jimmy. Maybe you'd rather have some of that?"

He was on duty. Should he turn down a drink? No. Sharing something to drink might make the interviewees loosen up a bit. And the hot mug would feel good on his chilled fingers. "Thank you, sir. I'd like that."

There was no chance to interview the boy, though. He grabbed his hot chocolate. "May I be excused, Grandpa? I've got some…some homework."

"Sure thing, boy. Quiet on the stairs, though. Don't wake your grandma."

That answered that, Reebok thought. Mrs. Haversham certainly wasn't like his mother.

Maybe the boy was as quiet as a boy that age could be, but Reebok distinctly heard his steps clattering up the stairs.

"Is your wife sleeping in, sir?" He slipped into the chair Mr. Haversham indicated.

"I guess."

Reebok raised his eyebrows. "You guess? Don't you know, sir?"

Mr. Haversham glanced toward the stairs and lowered his voice. "My wife and I sleep in separate rooms, Garner." He rubbed the back of his neck. "I guess I snore like the dickens, and she threw me out years ago." He smiled as he said it, though. There didn't seem to be any rancor. "That's not what you came to see me about this early in the morning, though. What can I do for you? Do you need more information about the car fire? I'm pretty sure we told you everything we know."

"It's not that, sir." Reebok shifted his rear end around. This was the most uncomfortable kitchen chair he'd ever sat in. Why didn't they have padding? "I don't know if you've talked to anyone about this latest fire, the one down the street."

"Connie Cartwright's place, you mean?"

"That's right."

"I heard about it at the Delicious yesterday morning. I stopped by for a quick breakfast after the boy was off to school. Everybody was saying it was arson."

"Did you walk down to the fire scene?"

"No. I've had enough of ... crime scenes," he invested those two words with a strange venom that Reebok found disturbing, "to last me the rest of my life."

Reebok waited for him to go on, but the old man stayed silent. "Do you know if your wife saw the fire scene, sir?"

Mr. Haversham shook his head. "She'd be even less likely than I to look at something like that. The car fire was more than enough for her to handle."

Once again, he left the comment hanging.

"Did you talk with your wife about this fire?"

Mr. Haversham thought for a moment. "Can't say I did, but I know this; Emma's going to be pretty angry about that fire when she hears about it. She takes classes there, you know."

"Wouldn't she have heard about it already, sir? After all, the fire truck was there for a long time yesterday morning, and there was a lot of smoke."

"We don't get out much, Garner. Ever since our son and his wife were killed in a car accident—you did know about that, didn't you?"

Reebok nodded.

"Ever since then we've stayed pretty quiet. Except for the boy. He was cut up awful bad over his parents' death. We try to do things with him. I take him fishing most weekends. Emma gets him to help her bake cookies. Things like that."

"So you're saying your wife might not have heard about the fire yet?"

"No, I'm not saying that. I'm sure she's heard." He paused, and his face crinkled up on the sides. "She must have."

"You're sure you didn't talk about it?"

"I doubt we would have with the boy around."

"So you didn't," Reebok persisted.

"No. I went fishing most of the day, but I was back before the boy got home from school."

"What did your wife say then? Did she indicate she might have heard about the fire?"

Mr. Haversham pulled out one of his hearing aids and made a minor adjustment of some sort. Reebok had the distinct impression he was playing for time. "Now that I think about it, Emma wasn't here. In fact, she didn't make it home until late last night."

"What time did she come in?"

"I don't rightly know. I take off my hearing aids when I go to bed. Maybe that's why I don't wake myself up with my own snoring." He chuckled at his own little joke. "I can't hear a thing without these."

Reebok made a note on an index card. "What time did you go to bed?"

"Right after the eleven o'clock news."

"She wasn't back by then? Is that unusual?"

"Not really. Ever since she took that class of Connie's, she's worked at the glass studio pretty late some nights."

It took Reebok a moment or two to process this. It wasn't that he was slow. It was just that Mr. Haversham's comment seemed so logical. Several seconds passed before Reebok said, "But the glass studio wasn't there last night, sir."

~~~~~

Bob had another half-dozen houses to visit down Willow. Reebok had volunteered to take the upper blocks. There were a lot more houses up there than down here, Bob thought, but Reebok was like a puppy in obedience training. *Pant, pant, what else can I do to please you?* That wasn't fair. Reebok couldn't help it if being a policeman was the be-all and end-all of his life. He'd taken a big load off Bob's shoulders by being willing to take the night shift—and a lot of the day shift as well. Bob was convinced that Reebok had no other life.

Last night Biscuit, laden with a big pot of soup and a loaf of fresh-baked bread, had told him Melissa wanted to talk to him about something important. He might as well take care of that now. He could finish lower Willow later. He crossed the street and walked the short block along Second Street to *Azalea House*.

~~~~~

Melissa stared out the door at the pouring rain as the last of her geologists scooted down the path, the boxed lunches she'd prepared swinging next to their knapsacks, yellow slickers glistening in the wet. Better them than her. She heard the slow hiss of the furnace as it kicked in. Good. No sense letting the humidity get ahead of her. Mold was nothing funny to deal with. This valley had milder weather than most of the rest of Georgia, but even here you had to watch out for…for what? Where was her mind leading her?

She really ought to drop by Biscuit's and, not apologize exactly, but at least straighten things out between them. But Biscuit had company from out of town. Anyway, there was plenty of time; the geologists were eating out at Tom's restaurant this evening, so she had no meals to prepare, just the usual cleanup chores.

Biscuit had probably forgotten to say anything to Bob, so maybe she should run up to the police station and talk with him. She still felt she was in something of a quandary about whether to say anything. And about what to say, too.

She cleared the breakfast tables and washed dishes half-heartedly. She spread out fresh blue and white checked tablecloths. She was happy to have the business, but this particular group were exceedingly messy, dropping toast crumbs and odd bits of scrambled eggs off the sides of their plates and dripping maple syrup from pancake-laden forks as they got caught up in a discussion of fault lines and geophysical anomalies, whatever those were.

She peered through her fogging kitchen window, the one that looked out over her spacious lawn where visiting families often played croquet on mild evenings.

The wide-spreading branches of the Japanese maple bent even more than usual under the driving rain. It was definitely coming down harder than before. She'd pour herself a cup of coffee—there was plenty left, even after she'd filled thermoses for a couple of the geologists, the two who'd sworn they couldn't live without mucho java.

The apology could wait. So could Bob.

Deciding she'd rather have tea, she lifted her favorite mug from the rack and turned to fill the kettle. As if her thoughts had summoned him, Bob knocked on her door. She reached instead for a second mug and motioned him inside. "Hang your hat and slicker on a peg there and I'll pour us some coffee." She knew better than to offer him tea. "Have a seat." She waved at the side of the table nearest the door, but he chose a seat at the far end. Who was that gunslinger, she thought, who would never sit with his back to a door, always had to have a wall at his back?

"Biscuit said you needed to talk with me." It was a neutral statement, but Melissa thought she could detect a hint of question in there. Biscuit may have remembered to pass on the message, but she probably told him she didn't know what it was about. And of course she didn't; she'd been off in that la-la land of hers.

"… thought I'd stop by."

Whoops. Hopefully he hadn't noticed. Although, he was probably so used to Biscuit's meanderings, he might not think anything about hers.

"Does it have to do with these fires?"

"Isn't that what they call a leading question?" She placed cream and sugar on the table. He wouldn't use them, but she would. She couldn't stand black coffee.

"Suppose so, but I can't figure out what else you'd be wanting to talk about so mysteriously."

"It's just that I think I saw something that might be connected, but I don't know for sure."

"Why don't you tell me about it? I can't decide what matters if I don't know what you're talking about."

That made sense. Melissa poured the coffee. "It must have been Saturday."

"Last week?"

"Right. The night Biscuit's shed burned down."

Bob nodded and waited.

Melissa had been trying to craft this conversation for days. "The morning after, when I heard about the fire in the garden shed, I almost called you about it, but I'd hate to get somebody in trouble if he doesn't deserve it."

Bob raised an eyebrow.

"I know, I know. You'll be careful and responsible. But, Bob, it's kids we're talking about."

Something in the room, something indefinable, shifted.

"Kids? Can you be more specific?"

"The geologists—you do know I've got a group staying here for three weeks? They're doing some study project in the caves across the river."

"I know."

"Well, they'd all turned in for the night, and all the lights were out. But for some reason I couldn't settle down. My private apartment has a door," she gestured over her shoulder, "that opens here into the kitchen, so I came in here and just stood looking out the window."

"Any particular reason?"

"No, just standing still and letting my mind drift." She paused, letting what she'd seen coalesce again in her mind. "There were two of them. Kids. Boys, I'm pretty sure. They walked all gangly and hunched over. And one of them, the one farther away from me, was carrying something."

"Could you tell what it was?"

"Not really. I thought at the time it might be a book bag, the kind they all have for school now. But the more I think about it, it could have been a gas can."

Bob didn't say anything. He seemed to be waiting for her to continue. "I couldn't see faces or anything, but I'm sure they're boys from here. From Martinsville."

"Would you recognize them again if you saw them?"

Melissa thought about it, even though she'd been thinking of little else for the past week. "No. I don't think I could. They were just shapes in the dark."

"What were they wearing?"

"I don't know for sure, but I think they must have had on those hooded sweatshirts with the hoods pulled up over their heads. I couldn't see any hair, even though the full moon that night was bright enough to cast shadows."

Bob didn't say anything.

"I don't want to get anyone in trouble." She watched him over the rim of her coffee mug. She could almost see the wheels turning.

"You won't. If they're innocent, I'll find out. If they're guilty, I'll find that out, too." He took a swig of coffee and pulled out a small notebook. "Which direction did they come from, and where did they head?"

Melissa tilted her head over her left shoulder. "They came from the direction of Willow Street, and I watched them cross kitty corner through the intersection here. They walked along Second up past Doc Nathan's house, and I lost sight of them just beyond Tom's house."

"Could they have just been a couple of kids headed toward the park?"

"I suppose that's possible." Melissa's hands tightened on her mug. "Except for that gas can."

~~~~~

Bob knew of two families on lower Willow with boys old enough to be out by themselves at night. He remembered how he and Tommy and Sam used to roam all over the place when they were kids. That meant these boys could have come from anywhere in town. But it was more likely that they lived in the direction Melissa had seen them coming from. What were those names? One of them was the boy in the hospital. Dan Russell. The other one was Billy or Kenny or something like that.

This was when he needed Reebok's infernal index cards.

As if in answer to Bob's need, Reebok came pelting down the sidewalk. "There you are, Sir. I think there's something you need to know about." Reebok slid to a stop, then took a respectful step to one side and turned to keep pace with Bob's measured steps. "I interviewed Mr. Tim Haversham, the man whose car burned up Tuesday night."

"And?" Bob knew perfectly well who Tim Haversham was. He was going to have to talk to Reebok about getting to the point.

"He said his wife hadn't heard about the fire."

Bob turned his head sharply to his right, and the rain coursed in a new rivulet pattern off the brim of his hat and into his collar. "Just why is that important, Garner?"

"I thought it was something out of the ordinary, Sir. In a town this size, everybody hears about everything almost as soon as it happens.

And also he hasn't seen her."

"Hasn't seen her? What do you mean?"

"He told me she was out late a lot of nights working at the glass studio, but she couldn't have been there last night because the studio had already burned down."

"I see what you mean, Garner." But he didn't. Not really. Why should he care about these two elderly people who couldn't keep track of each other, when he needed to be finding a couple of kids who might be starting fires. The sooner he put a stop to that the better, before they did some real damage.

Bob shook his head. That made no sense. There had been a body in Connie's studio. A dead body. That didn't fit with a couple of young kids. One of the town boys was laid up in the Keagan County Hospital from a beating that would have killed anybody without the thick skull Daniel obviously had. There had to be a connection, but what was it? "We may be looking at a group of youngsters who are starting these fires. Ones who live on this street, possibly."

Bob could sense Reebok nodding beside him. He wasn't about to turn his head again to look.

"Mr. and Mrs. Haversham have a grandson who didn't want to talk to me."

Bob forgot and turned his head too fast. The rain wasn't cold, but coursing down the inside of his shirt, it sure was wet.

Chapter 34

7 Years Earlier

SHE WAITED, DAY AFTER DAY, hoping to see that woman come out from the AJC offices, but it was as if she'd never worked there.

Finally, in disgust bordering on desperation, she drove past the woman's house. It had been long enough. Nobody would be watching anymore to see if the angel would return to the scene of destruction.

For Sale and over it, a red banner proclaimed *SOLD*.

Damn her. Where had that woman gone?

Chapter 35

So, I heard #2 got beat up awful bad
I was pretty mad when he burned the car, but
not enough to beat him up like that.
the woman who found him
she called the ~~ambleance~~ ~~ambaluence~~
for help.
She said
it looked like a whole gang
had done this
but #1 saw it happen
he said it was only one person who did it
my question is, why didn't #1 help?
or at least call somebody

~~~~~~

I HATED TO SUGGEST IT, but decided I might as well get it out of the way. "Do you want to call Mary this morning? We could…" I was going to say we could have her over for lunch, but wasn't sure I wanted to go to that much trouble. "We could meet her at the Delicious."

Peachie looked dubious, so I added, "I'll drive us down there." It was barely two blocks, but I could see she wasn't up to walking anywhere.

"I suppose I could. Her number's in my purse." She gestured vaguely toward the front hall. "I think it's still behind the umbrella stand."

I finished my last bite of toast and honey butter. She didn't appear to be ready to move, so I stood. "I'll grab it for you."

"Thanks."

She rummaged for quite a while. The little address book she finally pulled to light was covered in lime green fabric. Rather like Captain Paula Corrigan's notebook, I thought. As if that had anything to do with the price of tea in China.

Where on earth did that saying come from? My grandmother

Martelson always used to say it. Auntie Blue used the phrase a lot, too.

"Biscuit? Come back to the land of the living."

"Oh, sorry."

"I was saying I'd found Mary's phone number. Do you think it's too early to call her?"

The rain still pounded down. "This is a day a lot of people would want to sleep in."

"I doubt Mary falls into that category. Don't you remember? She always took the early classes and never fell asleep in them."

"I don't remember that, but if you say so," I pointed. "There's the phone."

She hauled herself to her feet and I cleared the breakfast plates.

"Mary," she said a few moments later, "this is Peachie. Peachie Rose. Remember I told you I was coming to Martinsville?"

Told you. So she *did* talk to Mary. All she ever did was write to me. That wasn't true. She called me on my birthday most years. She forgot this past birthday, though. Not that I was keeping track.

"Yes. I'm staying with Biscuit. Remember Biscuit? Biscuit McKee?"

I would not be jealous. I would not. I would not. I scrubbed one plate and then the other.

"What? I can't hear you. ... No, she's not single. She's married, but she kept her maiden name."

Maiden name. What a quaint term. Why ever did we still use it? I picked up the dishtowel. "Birth name," I said, perhaps more loudly than I needed to. "I kept my birth name."

"How about meeting at the Delicious?" Peachie said. "Biscuit says the food is yummy."

It is, but I never said that. Not to you anyway.

"Eleven-thirty?"

Mary must have said yes, because Peachie beamed. "We'll see you then ... What? ... Oh, Bob Sheffield, the town cop. Do you know him?"

Go ahead, I thought as she prattled on. Tell my life story to just anyone. I pinched my arm and dried the other plate.

~~~~~

Peachie hung up the phone and gave a contented sigh. This was good. The three of them could have a nice long conversation about old times and all the fun they used to have together. Not that she could remember many such times, come to think of it. Had they ever done much together other than cook meals and drink tea? She and Biscuit had rented that apartment with those other girls. Linda and Sue and Jackie. She couldn't even remember their last names. Was this what they called a senior moment? No, she decided. Those other ones weren't all that memorable, which may have been why she hadn't kept in touch with them.

She sat back down at the little round table. Now, did she remember much about Mary? Well, yes. They'd taken several of the same classes, and Peachie could remember working on homework together. But maybe that had just been their junior and senior years. Mary had been so shy. Peachie couldn't remember her ever being in the middle of things. She always seemed to hang around on the periphery. She was nice enough, but with that quiet voice, she always seemed … Peachie thought for a moment. She always seemed fragile somehow.

College was fun. Especially her senior year when she dated Gus. He was quite a guy. She wondered whatever had happened to him. And she thought back to the donut shop where she'd met him toward the end of their junior year. It was raining that day, too. She'd blustered in off the street, her hair every which way. The place was crowded, but she saw Mary at a booth in the back, so she went over and asked if she could join them. It was the next day when Gus called her.

She could feel herself beginning to blush. She hoped Biscuit wouldn't notice. Biscuit. What was Biscuit like in college? Now that she thought about it, the two of them hadn't seemed to have much in common at the time. Biscuit didn't even like *Lapsang Souchong.* Peachie shook her head. Unbelievable.

~~~~~

Bob didn't care one way or another about the rain except that it put him at something of a disadvantage walking into someone's house, dripping on their carpet or puddling on their hardwood floors.

Mr. Haversham didn't seem disconcerted, however. He just pointed out the coat rack and led the way to the roomy kitchen. Then he pulled another mug out of a cabinet and poured another cup of coffee. He looked at Reebok. "Refill?"

Bob saw a mug rimmed with an unmistakable chocolate smear of dark brown. Reebok slipped onto the chair closest to it. "Thank you.

It's a good thing you didn't wash it already."

"I figured you'd be back."

Bob raised an interrogatory eyebrow.

"As soon as I told him I hadn't talked to my wife yet about the fire because she was out all day yesterday—and she didn't get home last night or the one before that until after I'd gone to bed—well, he lit out of here like a jackrabbit. I had a pretty good feeling he'd be bringing reinforcements."

Bob was more interested in the teenage grandson who hadn't wanted to talk to Reebok. He did not seriously consider Emma Haversham as a suspect, even if she had stayed out late two nights in a row. "Your grandson. Is he here?"

"Upstairs doing homework, or so he says."

Bob rearranged his butt. The chair was darned uncomfortable. "You don't believe him?"

"On a Saturday? I wasn't born yesterday. Nobody does homework on a Saturday morning."

"I always did."

Reebok's comment was one of those conversation stoppers. There just wasn't anything to say in response. Mr. Haversham looked as astonished as Bob felt, but Mr. Haversham managed to rise to the occasion. "Emma thinks he's writing love letters to some girl in school. He's at that age, you know."

"I remember," Bob said. Reebok looked a bit blank and buried his nose in his hot chocolate. At least he didn't say anything this time. Had he really never had a girlfriend? Not that Bob cared, but it might be a detriment in some interview situations. Like this one, Bob thought. If he could get the boy downstairs.

~~~~~

This rain was almost more than Lorna Jean could handle. She hated thunder. Hated it. So, why did she feel so guilty about calling Mary and begging out of their run this morning? Mary went running in any weather. Nothing ever stopped her. Lorna Jean felt a pang of jealousy. How could such a quiet person be so brave?

She cringed as an extra-loud thunderclap shook the old house. What if lightning hit a tree and it crashed through the roof? Luckily, Martinsville didn't seem to get too many bad storms. Maybe she and Mark could move to Antarctica. There wasn't any lightning down there, as far as she knew. And precious few other women.

You're being ridiculous, she told herself. Mark wasn't guilty and lightning wasn't all that bad. Except that she wasn't a hundred percent sure, and lightning *was* bad.

Naturally, when she peeked out the window to be sure all the trees still stood, she saw Mary run past. In the rain. She recognized the bright pink socks. The woman must have fourteen pairs of them. I need to get my thoughts back to a better place, she thought. She turned back to her desk. Writing always helped ease her mind. And she had a deadline to meet.

~~~~~

How did the Chief do it? All he said was, "I need to speak to the boy," and the grandfather went and ushered him downstairs. He'd done it quietly so as not to disturb Mrs. Haversham, but the result was still the same as if he'd hollered at the boy to get down here this instant. Reebok had heard other fathers do things like that to their sons. He didn't like those men very much.

Now, here the boy was, looking as nervous as a colt. It made sense he'd be nervous. Not many young people got questioned by the police. At least, not in this town.

"You've heard about the fires in town, son?" The Chief sounded kind.

"Yes sir." The answer was so muted, Reebok hardly heard it.

"Did you see any of them?"

The boy's eyes widened even more. "No sir."

The Chief leaned back in his chair. "You're welcome to think about that answer for a minute, son. In case you want to change it."

The boy gulped. "I really didn't see any of them. Uh, I mean I saw them afterwards. I…I helped clean up the mess when the garden shed burned."

"Yes you did. I remember you there."

How could one gangly kid look so miserable? Reebok thought the weight of the world was on the boy's shoulders. But then he remembered that the boy's parents had been killed in a car crash, and he was living with his grandparents. That must be hard. Hard on the boy and, in a leap of intuition, Reebok knew it was hard on the grandparents, too. He ought to call his grandmother more often.

"Is there anything more you'd like to talk with me about?"

This time the pause strung out for almost longer than Reebok could bear. "No sir." Such a small sound.

"Are you friends with Daniel?"

The old man spoke up. "You mean the boy in the hospital?"

Reebok could tell the Chief was irritated at the interruption because he never looked at Mr. Haversham. He kept his eyes on the boy.

"I know him from school."

Even the Chief couldn't get much more out of the boy. It was almost a relief when the youngster fled back upstairs.

~~~~~

Bob thought about the woman sleeping upstairs. Or maybe not sleeping. Maybe she had heard their voices and was staying apart, aloof. No. That didn't jibe with what he knew of her. The Emma Haversham he knew would march right downstairs and tell him what she thought. She'd seemed timid when they'd first moved to Martinsville, but maybe that was just an inborn shyness. The more he knew her, the more he liked her.

Each time he'd spoken with her, she had seemed bright, alert, eager to question anything she didn't understand. Just two weeks ago, they'd had a conversation about the probable reasons the early settlers of Martinsville had left such large stands of the original trees. "I love the feel of these trees," she'd told him, tilting her face up toward a low-hanging branch of one of the oldest oaks. "The very air tastes different here."

"This stretch of Fourth Street," Bob had said, "between Juniper and Dogwood, is one of my favorite places in Martinsville."

"Mine, too. We had some lovely trees where I used to live, but nothing like this."

"Atlanta?"

She nodded, and Bob could have sworn her face clouded for a moment, but maybe it was just the cloud, the real cloud, that passed over the face of the sun at that very moment.

He'd get Biscuit to invite the Havershams to lunch some weekend. They'd enjoy walking through the old woods behind the backyard fence. For now, though, he didn't want this hole in his investigation to hang on much longer. "I'd like to talk with your wife."

Tim Haversham's mouth set in a stubborn line. "I'm not waking her up. She needs her rest."

Bob made a point of looking at his watch. "I need to talk with her, Tim. Somebody died in that fire, and if Emma was out late, she might have seen somebody."

"She would have told you if she'd seen anything suspicious."

"She might not know. You said yourself that you haven't talked with her about the fire. There's an offhand chance she doesn't know about it." Slim chance, he thought. "Even if she does, she might not put two and two together if she saw somebody Thursday night." Thinking of Melissa's observation, he added, "Maybe somebody carrying a gas can."

~~~~~

Peachie set her mug of Lapsang Souchong—her third one of the morning so far—on the bedroom dresser and took a good long look at her face in the cheval mirror. Biscuit was right. She did look pale. Peaked. She untied the sash belt and let the blue robe drop to the floor. She could pick it up later. She undid the top six buttons of her old-fashioned nightgown and pushed it off her left shoulder.

She looked. Hard. The scaly patchy itchy area seemed bigger than it had been the last time she looked, but that could very well be her imagination. She was letting it run away with her. This was ridiculous. There wasn't any trace of illness in her family. Her mother, her aunts, they were all healthy as could be. Even her grandmother was still alive, cranky as ever, at ninety-nine.

This wasn't anything.

But the itching was driving her crazy.

Was it some kind of infection cropping up in just that one place?

Maybe she'd schedule a physical when she got back home. Maybe they could give her some sort of cream to stop the itch. In the meantime, she needed to moisturize more.

As she bent to retrieve the robe, she thought of that cat putting its paw on her knee.

Stupid.

What could a gray cat possibly know?

~~~~~

No matter how hard he and the Chief prodded, Mr. Haversham absolutely refused to fetch his wife. "She's under a lot of stress right now," he said.

The car fire, Reebok thought, but that was five days ago. She should be over it by now.

"I'm sure she is," the Chief said. "Why don't we come back in a couple of hours?"

"Nope. Not today. I'd like to be here when you talk to her. I'm taking my grandson fishing today, as soon as he finishes ..." he grinned and made quote marks out of two fingers on each hand, "his *homework*."

The Chief took in a big breath. "How long will you be fishing?"

"Late. So you'll have to wait until tomorrow," he said. "You can stop by after church."

For such a scrawny old man, he sure could be forceful.

Chapter 36

5 Years Earlier

ALL HER WILES HAD NOT been enough to unleash the information she needed. Where had they gone? Where were they now? She'd been looking for the past two years. Way too long. She needed to find that woman. She had unfinished business.

No matter who she asked, and even with the mail she stole, she couldn't find a single hint. Soon after she'd learned that woman's house was for sale, she'd found one envelope in the next door neighbor's mailbox, but there was no return address and the cancellation stamp was smudged. Somewhere in Georgia, she could tell. But that alone was no help at all. There was a stupid birthday card. Stupid knock knock joke. She hated those. The note stuffed inside was short and breezy, but there wasn't a single hint about where they lived. Small town. Big deal. No help. It did mention a son though. Tim Junior. Something to think about. Someone else to look for. Someone else to focus on. Until she could find the woman. And she would find her. She would.

The neighbors on the other side, the ones they'd gone to dinner with the night she broke in, had a PO box. She'd seen the return address on some outgoing letters. Unfortunately, none of those letters had been addressed to that woman, so she hadn't gotten any information there.

She considered breaking into their house to look for letters from her quarry, but that particular neighbor had a fancy-schmantzy alarm system.

Chapter 37

So, there's only one of us left to go
#1 said his was going to be spectakular
I didn't like the look in his eyes
when he said that
he said we'd know when it happened
I don't like this
#2's still in the hospital
maybe we should stop.
#1 said he saw
the cop at my house
he said I better watch out
or I'll be sorry
So, I'm back where I started
Mr. Latham still
sends me nightmares

~~~~~~

I CUPPED THE MUG OF hot chocolate in my hands. Even on a moderately warm day, having a mug of hot chocolate between my hands just made everything feel better. On a cool showery day like this, it felt like heaven, especially since the "Crock of Choc" the Delicious served was enormous, so it held the heat for a long time. I looked around the Delicious one more time. Nobody there looked even vaguely like how I remembered Mary. "I think we've been stood up."

"Maybe she just got the day wrong."

That was stretching it. I thought back to Peachie's last phone comment to her friend. *See you in a couple of hours.* Something like that would be hard to misinterpret.

Margo stopped, fresh coffee pot in her hand. "Want a warm up?"

Peachie nodded.

"You ready to order yet?"

We'd already waited half an hour. "It's noon. Let's go ahead and have lunch, Peachie. She may show up yet." I didn't believe that for a minute, but it seemed the right thing to say.

"Give us a few minutes, would you? I haven't looked at the menu yet."

Margo turned away as the bell over the door jangled. It's funny how everybody in the Delicious always looks up to see who's coming or going whenever that bell rings. We're like Pavlov's dogs.

Mr. Orrin limped in, followed closely by Mary of the pink socks. He took a table nearby. She looked around and headed our way.

"Peachie? Biscuit?"

"Mary?" Peachie stood up so fast her coffee splashed out of her cup. "I wouldn't have recognized you in a million years."

"Sorry I'm late. I went running and lost track of the time. Then I had to go home and dry off from all the rain."

Her voice was still as quiet as I remembered from college, but she must have lost seventy or eighty pounds. This wasn't the Mary I remembered.

"To think that we saw you running with Lorna yesterday ..."

"Lorna Jean," I said under my breath, too low for Peachie across the table to hear, but Mary must have registered what I said. She glanced my way for a split second.

"... and didn't even recognize you."

I scooted over and Mary slipped into the booth next to me.

"Maybe because I've lost some weight."

"I'll say! You didn't tell me in your letters that you'd gone on a diet."

Mary shrugged. "I lost a hundred and fifty-four pounds." When Peachie gasped, she added, "It took a while."

Probably a long while.

"You know who else in our class lost a lot of weight—"

Fortunately, Margo interrupted Peachie.

After we ordered, there was one of those silences where nobody knew much what to say. Mary fiddled with her paper napkin and I hid behind my hot chocolate. After all these years, I didn't know where to start.

Peachie broke the silence. "Lorna told us you were Mary Fleming."

Mary set the napkin down. "I got married a few years ago."

"And you never told me? I would have loved to come to your wedding."

Somehow I couldn't picture Mary wanting to be the focus of a bridal party.

"It was a very quiet ceremony. We just went to the county courthouse." Her voice kept getting quieter. For someone so shy, it must be excruciating to have to answer what must have seemed like an interrogation. But she knew us—well, she'd known us back in college. That felt like a lifetime ago. Surely she didn't need to feel so shy with Peachie and me.

"But I've mailed all my letters to Mary Cotton. I didn't know you had a new last name."

"They know both names at the Post Office."

"Of course they would," Peachie said without hesitation. "Because of your art. You use Cotton to sign all your famous paintings, don't you? Don't you like your husband's name?"

Now, how was Mary supposed to answer that? Luckily, she didn't have to because Margo began placing plates in front of us.

We tucked in for a while, murmuring comments about how good the food was, but really paying attention only to filling our stomachs. The toast and honey butter I'd eaten four hours ago hadn't lasted long. Even the enormous Crock o' Choc hadn't filled the void.

Mary ate with very little fanfare, as if she did it only because she had to.

Peachie ate with a real flair, fluttering her hands and laughing over the sheer deliciousness of it. "No wonder it's called The Delicious," she said.

I laughed. Mary smiled. I wondered what it must be like to be saddled with such a quiet voice. I wondered if everybody overlooked her the way I had to admit I'd done in college. She was just so ... so bland. No color to her at all. No life. No humor. Oh, rats! I pinched myself. I saw Mary's head turn just the slightest. She'd noticed. Luckily she didn't say anything. I would have had a hard time explaining I'd had to pinch myself because I was thinking unkind thoughts about her. Only they weren't really unkind. They were true. Sigh. I pinched again and lifted my napkin to cover the movement.

None of us had been very welcoming to her back in our college days. I remembered calling her a mouse once. She was so quiet. We were all laughing and horsing around, and Mary just stood up and left the room. "If I hadn't seen her leave I never would have known she was gone," I'd said to the others. "She's such a quiet little mouse." And we went around for days calling her Mousie behind her back.

I felt bad, remembering. I hoped she hadn't heard me. But even so, I pinched myself again for good measure.

Eventually, though, we slowed our chewing and went back to a real conversation.

"Did you see any of the fires, Mary?"

Mary shook her head, nodded, shrugged. I wondered which to believe. "I saw the aftermath. Not the one at the IGA, but," she glanced up at me with what looked like an apology, "the shed. I was there the day after. I'm sorry I didn't know it was yours, Biscuit."

"That's sweet of you, Mary, but there wasn't anything you could do."

"I could have helped with the cleanup."

"No way. The men had that covered. All I did was make coffee."

"Do you know who set the fire?"

Mary really needed to take voice lessons to get her volume up. While I was thinking about that, Peachie answered for me. "No, but that husband of hers is sure looking."

"I think he's more concerned about Connie's studio fire than about my shed."

"I'm sure that's true," Mary said, "but has he questioned the kids in town? These fires sound like the sort of pranks a kid would pull."

I wouldn't call them pranks, I thought. Not with a dead body in that fourth fire. "He's questioning everybody," I said. "I'm surprised he hasn't questioned you."

"He already did." Her voice sort of squeaked, and she took a drink of water. "Well, not him exactly. It was that young officer."

"Reebok?"

"Shoes?" Mary sounded puzzled.

"No. Reebok is his first name."

Peachie chuckled. "His parents were Adidas and Nike Saucony."

I stared at her, but Mary laughed. "I didn't know you knew much about running, Peachie."

"I don't. But I see plenty of ads."

Oh dear. Don't let them start talking about commercials. "Actually, he told me he was named for the antelope."

Peachie tented her fingertips. "Ancient philosopher ask *when did your aunt elope?*"

Mary and I looked at each other and groaned.

Margo walked up. "You ready for dessert?" She rattled off the possibilities.

"Peach cobbler for me," Peachie said. "Of course. Anything peachy."

"Margo's triple chocolate cake is fairly new to the menu," I told them, "but I've already had it three times. Might as well stick with success." I gave Margo a thumbs-up and turned to Mary. "What about you?"

"Could I just have half a serving of vanilla ice cream? I'm still pretty full from lunch."

Margo nodded, and Peachie pulled the conversation back on track. "Was Reebok the policeman hiding under the tree?"

"Yep. That was Reebok. He's always either taking notes or polishing his badge." As soon as I said it, I felt vaguely uneasy. Reebok tried so hard, and here I was hitting the puppy again. I pinched myself, determined to cut unkind words out of my conversation. Poor Reebok. He was so easy to make fun of. Sigh. I pinched myself again.

"…surely whoever is setting these fires left clues at all of them." Mary's soft voice faded away uncertainly.

Here was one conversation I could rejoin easily. "Not that I'm aware of. But, of course, Bob doesn't tell me everything about an ongoing investigation."

"Well," Peachie said, "I wouldn't worry about it. He's bound to catch the guy."

"Mary," I said over dessert, "I take tap dance classes on Tuesday evenings down at Miss Mary's. I'd love it if you could join the class. We usually head up to *Azalea House* after each class and talk our heads off. I think you'd fit right in. It's a great group of women."

Peachie grinned. "You didn't invite *me*."

Peachie? Tap dancing? Not hardly. Oh phooey! I pinched myself again. "Consider yourself invited. Now, all you have to do is move to Martinsville."

"Lordy, my feet would never take me through a tap dance. But what about you, Mary? Are you going to try it out?"

"Thanks for the invitation, but I have absolutely no sense of rhythm. Maybe that's why I enjoy running so much." Her voice was still so soft I had to lean closer to hear her, and Peachie cupped a hand behind her left ear. "Running is steady and regular and I can just sort of forget about everything else while my feet pound the pavement."

"It must be hard on your knees," Peachie said.

"I invest in good shoes."

"Well, that explains it." I leaned back against the padded seat. "All I need is a great pair of shoes and I could run the way you do."

For such a lame line, it got rather more of a laugh than I thought was necessary. I'm not that out of shape, am I?

You are perfect the way you are.

For some inexplicable reason I thought of Marmalade at home, probably curled up on the bed.

Yes I am.

I always felt so connected to her. I wondered why.

Because you are. You just do not know it.

~~~~~

Paula Corrigan needed to talk to that Connie Cartwright, the one who owned the burnt building. If only somebody knew where she was. There was a good chance she'd burned her own building. Insurance money. That was a prime motive. There'd been a lot of pricey equipment in there, and the woman must have poured a boatload of money into the building itself. The floor, a poured concrete slab, was the size of a small house, fifty-four feet from front to back and twenty-seven feet wide. But if Ms. Cartwright burned her own place down, who was the body? And why was it there?

She flipped open her lime green notebook and wrote a few more reminders. She added little square boxes next to them. She liked to check off tasks as she completed them. She'd drive back down to Martinsville tomorrow. Go through the ruins one more time. They'd sifted everything. They couldn't have missed anything.

But she knew, from previous experience, that sometimes there was one small clue, so charred it was almost unrecognizable. That was what she needed to find.

~~~~~

Margo's chocolate cake was even better this time than the last. If I stayed any longer, I'd ask for another serving. We'd been here long enough anyway. I raised my hand for the check. The rain had been alternating between gentle shower and relatively heavy downpour all day. Now, though, the sky was lightning-laced.

"I'll give you a ride home, Mary. No sense in your walking if the lightning's this heavy."

She began to shake her head, but her objection died as three quick flashes followed by booming thunder drowned out all conversation. "Thank you. That's a good idea."

As I backed out of the parking space, she gave me the address on Magnolia and said it was between Second and Third Streets. Half a block up the street from *Azalea House*, I thought. I wondered if I should stop in to see Melissa and patch things up. But the rain was too heavy. All I wanted to do was drop Mary off at her house and head home. Anyway, Peachie wouldn't want to listen to apologies. I hoped there'd be two of them. I'd apologize to Melissa, and she'd apologize right back at me.

"… always run in the rain? I should think it would be dangerous."

Peachie must have been chatting for five blocks. As I turned right from Main Street onto Magnolia, I asked, as casually as I could manage, "I haven't seen you in the library, Mary. I'd be happy to issue you a card if you'll just stop by sometime."

The muffled sound of a guffaw came from the passenger seat, but Peachie refrained from comment.

"I'm … I'm still trying to read all the books that came with the house. The living room has shelves from floor to ceiling, and they're absolutely packed."

"Really? I'd love to see them sometime." I'd never been in that particular house, and I was a bit surprised to hear it had so many books in it. Most of the Martinsville residents left all their books to the library when they died. Still, it wasn't a residence requirement, although for the life of me I couldn't figure out why it wasn't.

"How much longer will you be here, Peachie?"

There wasn't any thunder, which was the only reason I could hear her soft voice drifting over the back of my seat. I sensed Peachie's look. "I hope she'll stay for a nice long visit," I said. Maybe that way I could get her to Doc for a checkup.

~~~~~

Peachie and I watched Mary scoot up her walkway. Before she reached her door, it opened, flooding the front stoop with light, and a man I only vaguely recognized lifted a hand. Whether it was acknowledgment or dismissal, I couldn't tell. Mary squeezed past him, and he closed the door.

"Well, Peachie said, "I can see why she didn't invite us in."

"What do you mean?"

"That husband of hers doesn't look very friendly.

I was saved from answering by the rain, which chose that moment to increase in volume and noise level, like the canon and kettledrums at the end of the 1812 Overture. I turned the windshield wipers up higher, and wondered if he might be the fire starter. And the murderer.

What a ridiculous idea, I thought. Mary wouldn't have married a fiend like that. She was too quiet. But the image of him standing there, haloed by all that orange light from behind him kept reminding me of somebody stepping out from his own private hell. Was it possible?

No. I wasn't sure about the murder, but that rough student of Tom's—the one from Enders—could very easily have been the one who started the fire. I'd have to ask Bob about him.

~~~~~

That evening, once the thunder and lightning stopped for good, Lorna Jean lifted the phone to call Mary. They hadn't talked about their running schedule for next week, and she needed to get her writing times inked in on the calendar. If she didn't hit this deadline—it was only eleven days from now—her editor was going to raise a hissy fit.

Why, she wondered, as much as they ran together, hadn't they worked out a regular schedule by now? The only routine thing about it was that they ran every day, unless one of them was out of town. She had occasional book tours, of course, and never got any running done during those events. Mary had been out of town a couple of times the past year or two, just two or three days at a time. But Lorna Jean always ran by herself when Mary was gone. She had no idea whether or not Mary kept up with her running when she was on a trip. Probably.

Even if they were both here, they didn't always run together. And usually not on Sundays. At least, Lorna Jean didn't run on Sundays.

She dialed the first three numbers, but hung up as soon as she saw through the dining room window that Mary's house was lit up like a Christmas tree. Mary wasn't home.

It was that husband of hers. Mary had said he'd never in his life turned off a light bulb. If Mary wanted the lights out, she had to follow him around and turn them off. As she watched, lights began to darken in one room after another. Mary had come home, obviously. Lorna Jean laughed. What a pair they were.

She thought for a moment. Occasionally the house would stay lit up all night long, on those times when Mary was away on business. Not that Lorna Jean knew what sort of business Mary did. Consulting or something like that, Mary had mentioned to her once. Or maybe she'd heard wrong. It was easy to miss things around Mary, who never could speak above a whisper. How could he sleep with so much light?

Lorna Jean sucked in her breath. What if that need to leave the lights on was just a mask? What if he was the one sneaking out after dark and setting the fires? Was her friend, Mary, hooked up with a maniac?

Should she talk with somebody about this?

She'd been right yesterday when she wondered if these awful fires would set neighbor against neighbor. Surely Mary's husband couldn't be guilty.

Could he?

~~~~~

Late that evening, Paula stretched her arms up as high as she could reach and yawned mightily. It was way too late; she had to leave before she fell asleep on her desk. She locked her office door and almost stumbled—she was so tired—down the quiet hall. The fax machine started its insane clatter. She hated that thing.

She had to check it, though. Just in case.

Good thing she did. She ripped it out of the machine, took a quick look, and with no thought about exhaustion any more, headed back to her desk. She read the whole thing through. Then she leaned back in her chair and raised both fists high overhead in a victory sign. Yes!

She'd been right. The autopsy report said there were two fractures in the skull, and both came from a four-pointed star-shaped object. The first fracture was superficial. The second one had pierced the skull with enough force to push bone fragments into the brain. A minor hairline crack radiating from the more serious fracture stopped when it met one of the arms of the star on the forehead, proof that the superficial impact was the first. Probably just enough to knock the victim out, so the guy could slam into her for good the second time.

She flipped open the *American Handbook of Specialty Tools* to page 729, the one she'd marked with a jumbo paper clip. There it was. The only item in the entire catalog that could account for a four-pointed wound like that.

Paula shook her head and read the report again. It still said the same thing. Neither of those impacts had killed her. The ME's report was very clear; there was smoke in what little was left of the lungs, so she—it was a woman's body—had not been dead when the fire started.

She'd still been breathing, and some lunatic set her and the whole building on fire. Paula sure hoped the unknown victim was unconscious by that time.

Murder.

Paula had had a feeling this was a homicide when she first recognized the mound that turned out to be a body, but she'd learned over the years that many of her colleagues scoffed when she mentioned her hunches, her feelings. It was intuition. She figured it came from a deep-seated body of knowledge. Facts about fires. Facts about how things—including bodies—burned. Much of the processing of that knowledge was probably subconscious. Hence her intuition. It was a mindset that could recognize numerous signs, myriad symptoms, and put them all together before she consciously added up all the factors.

Part of it was twenty-plus years of experience, but she could remember this flash of *knowing* even at her very first arson scene. She never talked about it anymore—she'd learned the hard way that it was best not to mention it—and she tried not to consider this … this talent of hers as foolproof. But, dang it, it pretty much was.

She read all the way through the report a third time. The only part she didn't understand was the paragraph about the contents of the mouth. Newspaper? What was the woman doing eating newspaper? That made no sense. So, if she wasn't eating it, then whoever killed her must have stuffed it in there. Hoping to choke her? No. Again, it made no sense.

Sheffield needed to see this report and the page about the hammer. She grabbed up the tool handbook and headed for the copy machine. What was the law-enforcement world like before copiers and faxes?

She sure hoped he worked as late as she did.

~~~~~

Bob smoothed his mustache down with both hands, folded his copy of the autopsy report, and reached back to tuck it into the jacket that hung over the back of his chair. He'd been right. Murder. The report made that very clear. Some sort of heavy object "consistent with the size and weight of a hammer" had bashed in her skull. Or rather some guy on the other end of the hammer had done so. A tool never committed a murder. A person did that.

There were two fractures in the skull, just as he'd seen. The X-shaped wound happened first. Radiating lines from a second fracture would intersect, but not cross fracture lines from a prior wound. He knew that from his own reading; he didn't need it spelled out, but he thought it was interesting that there had been only one hairline crack that reached as far as the wound on the forehead.

He had no clue what could have caused such a wound. Whatever the weapon was, it had crashed into the woman's skull, twice, with enough force to stun the woman completely, but the fire was what had finished her off.

The newsprint that was jammed in her mouth had to be some kind of clue, but he sure couldn't see what good it could do. He pulled the report back out of his jacket and spread it on his desk. The ME had taken a photo of what they'd pulled from the back of the woman's throat. Bob examined the obviously enlarged photo. Between the woman's saliva and the ravages of the fire, few words were discernible. He could pick out a letter here, half a word there.

Like *NAL-Co*. What on earth did nal-Co refer to? Farther down, peeking from the sodden mess was one clear word: *Hated*. Half the final d was obscured by charring, but it couldn't be anything else. One line above it was the partial word *iece*. Piece, maybe, or niece? And the line below held *exa*—exam? example? Texas? Individual parts of words screamed at him, but he couldn't hear what they were trying to tell him: *zon G*—that looked like the end of one word, horizon maybe?—and the beginning of another; and *eming,*—could be seeming, deeming, teeming. But why was there a comma after it?

The fax machine started its robotic humming, and Reebok bounded across the room. Then he just had to stand there and wait while the machine spewed out a stream of paper.

"It's from Captain Corrigan, Sir," Reebok called out. He lifted the paper and peered more closely. "It looks like the autopsy report."

Bob refolded the papers and began shrugging into his jacket. "Just put it in that In-box on my desk. I've already read the thing twice." And you've probably read it three times, he thought.

"She must not have realized you were on the distribution list, Sir." Reebok read the first page. "She says she'd like to talk to you about this in person."

"Right. Give her a call, and tell her I'll drive up to her office," he looked at his watch, "tomorrow afternoon. We have to interview the Havershams after church."

"I know that, Sir."

There was only the mildest of criticism in Reebok's tone, but Bob heard it. He looked toward the window and saw, against the dark night outside, a reflection of his deputy standing at attention. "I'm going home, Garner." He patted his chest pocket. He'd look at the autopsy report again first thing in the morning. "Hold down the fort. Call me only if you absolutely have to." He sure hoped his deputy's definition of *absolutely* was the same as his.

As Bob left, the phone rang. "Mr. Orrin," he heard Reebok say. "What can I do for you?" He turned back, caught Reebok's attention, and said, "Call the Captain." He made a *hurry-up* motion with his hand and closed the door behind him. Did Reebok never sleep?

He thought again of the first sentence in the examination section of the autopsy report.

> The decedent is a white
> female, approximately 70
> years old, with an unknown
> hair color and length and
> unknown eye color.

Who the heck was this unknown woman, the one with a newspaper clipping shoved in her mouth? It sure wasn't Connie with an age like that. Biscuit would be glad to hear that much, but he wasn't going to share any of the other details with her.

He ran quickly over the women in town that he knew who were in their seventies, and just to be sure, he extended the range to late sixties and early eighties. He'd seen all of those women in the past few days. His own mother to begin with, and Myrtle Hoskins, Sadie Masters, Esther Anderson.

He started his car, and kept the list running in his head, but he simply couldn't think of anyone of that age who might be missing. Reebok and the index cards. He almost got out of the car to go back inside the station, but sanity prevailed. Reebok would read his own copy—how did police forces cope before copy machines came along? And Reebok would pull out his silly index cards and make his own list. No. They weren't silly. That was just the way Reebok thought.

At home, Biscuit was full of talk about another college friend she and Peachie had run into. Bob tried to be attentive, but the words of the autopsy report kept breaking into his concentration.

~~~~~

My Gratitude List for Saturday
> 1. Bob – thank goodness he made it home, even though I was already set for bed. I'm glad we had a chance to talk. He was awfully quiet, though.
> 2. Peachie – I hope she gets some sleep tonight. Maybe she's just extra tired. Maybe that's what KorsaCat was picking up on. I sure hope so.
> 3. Marmy of course
> 4. Hot chocolate and chocolate cake, both in one meal!
> 5. Rain, when it's gentle
> 6. And I need to add Mary. It was good to see her after all these years, even though I could barely hear what she said. Does she do that on purpose so everybody will have to lean toward her and pay extra attention to her? That woman needs voice lessons.

> Oh phooey!
> I pinched my arm again.

I am grateful for
> *Widelap*
> *SoftFoot*
> *naps*
> *being inside when it rains*
> *this soft bed*
> *I do not need to add anything. I am complete.*

~~~~~

I put my gratitude journal in the drawer of the bedside table and Marmalade shifted from my shoulders, where she so often draped herself, to the bed, about where my knees would bend when I got settled.
> *I know how you sleep.*
I snuggled close to Bob. He shifted his left arm to cradle my head. His stomach, under my palm, rose and fell in rhythm with my own breath. "Bob?"

"Hmm?"

I should let him sleep. He sounded exhausted, just in that one syllable. "Bob? You don't think it could have been one of Tom's students, do you?" His breath stilled for a moment, two moments.

"What makes you say that, Woman?" How could he do that—go from sagging sleepiness one minute to full alert the next?

"I don't know. It's just that some of them…some of them…" I groped for the words. "Some of them aren't from here. What about that boy from Enders?"

Bob stayed perfectly immobile for a second or two. "What about him?"

I had to admit I had a bias against Enders, the next town south of here, where the Metoochie poured out of the Gorge. It was outside of Keagan County, and it seemed outside of reality. I'd had dealings with several unsavory characters from there. Surely anybody from Enders would carry a taint.

What is a taynte?

That's ridiculous, Biscuit, I told myself. Had I forgotten about Cornelia with the unpronounceable last name and her grandson Hugh, the ones who had stopped to help me when my tire went flat that night I was so scared? And who rescued me from the flood and saved my life. They were from Enders.

Still, it was the Enders boy who'd attacked the tall one—I wished I could remember their names. He'd hit him from behind with that basketball.

They were playing, like kittens or puppies.

"Well, Woman? Have you decided what to say yet?"

"He's sneaky," I said. "He hit that tall boy, the one who served us two weeks ago, remember him? Such a nice kid."

"You mean the one who tripped over his own feet and almost spilled your spaghetti in your lap? That one?"

What is a spagehdi?

"He couldn't help it. But the one from Enders…"

"The one you don't like just because of where he's from?"

"Stop interrupting me. The one I don't like because he attacked that gentle boy from behind. Hit him so hard with that basketball, I thought he'd get a ruptured kidney."

"And just what did the poor victim do?" For some reason Bob had a smile in his voice.

"He turned around and pounced on the rat, and they tussled in the parking lot."

"Woman, woman, woman. When will you ever learn? That's what boys do."

I told you that.

Boys are nuts, I thought, but all I said was, "Humph, they're too old to act like…like a bunch of puppies."

"I'll talk to him tomorrow if that will make you feel any better."

"He was in the group watching our shed fire," I said.

"Well then, that'll be just fine. Reebok will have a little index card on him."

What is an endixcard?

We chuckled over that, and then our hands strayed a bit here and there, and we forgot about Enders and spaghetti mishaps and fires altogether.

And you ignored me completely.

Chapter 38

Eighteen Months Earlier

IT WAS TIME FOR HER to give it up. Sal and Charles and Barb told her she'd changed. She wasn't any fun anymore.

If only they knew, she thought.

Still, she had the hammer, and she had a feeling that someday, somehow, it would come in handy.

She'd seen an ad in one of those realtor magazines. Idyllic house to buy, small town, quiet, near a river.

Time to get away.

Ron had been talking about getting hitched. She didn't want that, but maybe it was time to go along. He had money, after all.

She wouldn't tell anybody where they were going. Well, maybe just one person.

Chapter 39

So, when I woke up this morning
she wasn't here again
he said she was sleeping late
but I don't believe that
there's no sound from her room
he took me to church
she wasn't there
he looked worried
where is she?
what did I do to make her leave?
did she find out?
I hear ~~Dan~~ #2's still got a broken arm and
this ~~humonngus~~ big bump
on his head and he can't tell anybody
what really happened
because he's not awake yet
~~Jake~~ #1 said the person who beat up #2
hit him with a big rock
What if that person
comes after me?

~~~~~~

HENRY STOOD AT HIS BEDROOm window and listened to Maggie Pontiac's rooster greet the day. The sound carried over the trees from a full block away. Many mornings he'd listened to that bird and envied it for its lungpower.

How could it be Sunday again? Surely it hadn't been seven days since his last sermon. He gazed across the early morning cloud-shadowed lawn toward the signboard. The arsonist—the murderer of that poor dead woman, whoever she was—still hadn't been caught. And here his sermon topic, THOU SHALT NOT KILL, splayed across the signboard as if he thought his preaching could prevent such crimes.

They must think I have an ego the size of Manhattan, he thought. No. Only one person in this town thought that. And that person, whoever it was, was probably laughing at him.

~~~~~

I couldn't help laughing at Marmalade's antics.

I like to chase my feather toy.

I waved the toy Bob had made for her, patterned after a fishing lure he'd tied last year—but without the hook—back and forth across the coffee table and she dove over, under, and around, trying to pin the elusive feather.

I do not intend to catch it. The game would be over.

Peachie didn't look impressed. "What time do we have to leave for church?"

"You don't sound too enthusiastic. Are you feeling any better, or do you need to rest some more?"

"No. I don't need to rest. You're driving us there, aren't you?"

I nodded. My old Buick was getting more mileage on it this week than it had seen in ages, but the increments had all been one and a half or two blocks at a time.

She flicked at her slacks. Probably a cat hair. Or two. "I'd like to hear what that preacher of yours has to say, especially since nobody's been caught yet."

I truly did not think she meant to imply criticism of Bob, but I bristled anyway. "It's only been two days. Most murders take longer than that to solve."

"Ancient philosopher say, *hold your fire or you get burned; hold your burn or you get fired.*"

What does that mean?

Marmalade skidded to a stop under the coffee table and looked up at Peachie.

Peachie waved an airy hand. "Did it ever occur to you that whoever did it might be sitting there in a pew listening to the reverend?"

No. It had to be a stranger. It had to. But something told me it wasn't.

"And no signboard in the world is going to stop a murderer," she added.

~~~~~

Glaze and Maddy made it to church early. Glaze wanted to be

seated long before Susan came in. She didn't want to risk running into that woman on the way up the walk. Susan would ask if they'd made a decision about funding the hotel renovation, and Glaze wasn't ready to tell her yet. Let her sweat it out a bit. Anyway, she thought, the Butterfly Brigade doesn't work on Sundays.

She placed her bulletin on the cushion beside her to save a place for Tom. Biscuit should be here soon, too, she thought. It's a pain, her having company for so long. No chance for them to talk, not really. She hadn't even told Biscuit that the S. Porchinsky on that strange application was really Susan. Susan Porchinsky.

Tom stepped past Maddy and started to settle in next to Glaze.

She grabbed the bulletin before he could sit on it and began to circle the errors. Thou shal tnot kill.

~~~~~

Bob steered Peachie and me into one of the back pews. I liked to sit halfway up on the left near Glaze, but his hand on my arm prevented it.

Mr. Haversham and his grandson Jimmy walked past us and settled into a pew about three rows ahead of us. Emma wasn't with them. I hoped she wasn't sick. I'd have to ask him after the service. I could tell Bob was studying them, but then he moved his head a fraction to focus on someone else. It was funny how I could track where he was looking. Was that because I was particularly astute, or just because I loved him and paid attention?

Glaze turned around as if she were looking for me, but Susan walked down the aisle right then and Glaze turned her head back so fast I thought she'd get a crick in her neck. I knew she didn't particularly like Susan, but the reaction seemed overly abrupt. With Peachie here, though, I couldn't have any of those heart-to-heart sister talks that Glaze and I had been increasingly used to ever since she moved to Martinsville, particularly ever since she almost died not too long ago.

I wondered how her Butterfly Brigade appointment had gone.

Bob might have been sitting in the Old Church next to me, but I had the feeling he wasn't listening to a thing Henry said. Every time I glanced up at him, his eyes were boring into the back of one of our friends, one of our neighbors. God bless him, I sure was glad I didn't have his job.

~~~~~

Doggone Emma, sleeping in again and leaving him to cook for the boy. Well, he wasn't going fishing today. He'd get this figured out.

Tim followed his grandson into their usual pew, about halfway down on the right. These two cops were going to stop by this afternoon, and Tim wanted to hear what she had to say about why she'd been—he held his breath for a moment—hiding out. What was she afraid of? That the scumbag who'd burned their car would come for her? Nonsense. He'd keep her safe. He just wished she'd talk to him.

He nodded to several of his neighbors and tapped Jimmy on the shoulder to remind him not to fidget. Emma would have remembered to bring along a quiet little game for him to play or a puzzle book for him to work on.

Tim wondered why she'd withdrawn so suddenly. It was like Atlanta all over again, only back then she'd pushed the world away and clung to him, and this time she was pushing *him* away. She'd refused even to talk to him when he tried to get her to come out. He didn't try when the boy was around, of course. Didn't want to worry the kid.

This morning, though, while the boy was in the shower, Tim had called to her to unlock her door, but she gave him the silent treatment.

He wasn't worried about her. Emma was healthy as a horse. But there was a little piece of him that wondered if that car fire had pushed her over the edge.

Well, he'd have his answer in a couple of hours. Once Sheffield and Garner showed up, she'd have to come downstairs.

~~~~~

Bob watched Tim Haversham and his grandson settle into the pew where they usually sat. Emma was in that seventies age range, but she couldn't be the missing woman or Tim would have raised the roof long before this.

Something was going on there, though. Why had Emma skipped church? The boy was far too skittish. And he'd swear the old man was hiding something. Tim had been too carefully casual; he'd adjusted those hearing aids of his too many times. Tim and Emma had probably had a fight, and they didn't want to wash their dirty laundry in public.

He wondered if Biscuit might be right, if Tom's students were behind these fires. They did seem awfully juvenile at times. He'd seen them romping around on the lawn behind the restaurant like overgrown puppies. But these puppies might have killed somebody. And it wasn't an accident either. He'd have to ask Tom about it, just to be thorough, but he didn't set much store by the idea. He looked around at the congregation. The church was almost full this morning. He sure hoped Henry's sermon was worth it.

Bob looked at his watch. Not too much longer. He *would* have answers. He patted the inside pocket of his jacket and felt the reassuring crinkle of the autopsy report. Reebok had called him disgustingly late last night to say he had a four o'clock appointment with Captain Corrigan. Biscuit hated it when he had to work on a Sunday, but finding a murderer couldn't wait for normal business hours. He'd have time for a quick lunch with her and Peachie, probably soup, he knew, and then he'd round up Garner and head to Tim Haversham's house. He sure hoped Emma had seen something worthwhile, something that would help him put this guy behind bars.

He'd flat forgotten to tell Biscuit the dead woman couldn't be Connie, but the Old Church was not the place to speak anything you didn't want the whole town to hear. The acoustics in this place were downright scary at times. Well, there would be time, later.

He reached out and took his wife's hand. From the other side of Biscuit, he heard a soft sigh from Peachie.

~~~~~~~

Mary and her husband were late getting to church, so they had to sit near the front. Mary felt … felt exposed. She didn't like that feeling. Maybe that was one reason she spent so much time turning off the lights her husband turned on. She felt less conspicuous in the dark.

At least she didn't know any of the people sitting nearby, so she didn't have to talk to anyone. Not that they'd be able to hear her with that infernal organ screeching so loud. She nodded to the woman on her left and lowered her head. Let them think she was praying.

She'd been curious to hear what the minister was going to say about the killing. She'd run past that signboard three out of the last four days. The other days she and Lorna Jean had taken a different route. Murder probably wasn't a usual sermon topic. She shivered.

Her husband looked sideways at her and raised an eyebrow.

"I'm okay," she mouthed.

He frowned.

She glanced around and saw Peachie and Biscuit way in the back. They must have come early, she thought, and felt like giggling. Come early and get a seat in the rear. That would make a good signboard saying. Maybe she'd mention it to Reverend Pursey. But no. If she did that, she would have to talk to him. It would be funny, though.

To calm herself, she looked through the bulletin. Thou shal tnot kill.

Tnot indeed.

~~~~~

Melissa wasn't far behind Biscuit and Bob. She thought seriously about joining them. If the seat beside Biscuit had been empty, she would have. But Peachie was there. Peachie, whose visit Biscuit had been so excited about after all those years. Melissa sighed. She shouldn't have flown off like that. But Biscuit should have listened better. She sighed again and the woman next to her glanced over and gave her a tentative smile.

They'd straighten this out eventually.

She'd chosen a seat well back on the left where she could study everyone. She missed a lot of the sermon because she was so busy looking at all the young people in the congregation, trying to imagine each of them in a dark hooded sweatshirt, bathed in stark moonlight. Whoever said moonlight was romantic was nuts. It bleached out all the color and cast eerie shadows.

Every one of the young people she examined looked guilty. But she couldn't pin an ID on any one of them.

She opened the bulletin when the service was almost over. Thou shal tnot kill. Kids with gas cans. Had they known there was a person in there when they burned down Connie's studio?

~~~~~

Once the service was over—it hadn't been one of Henry's better sermons, but naturally I didn't mention my opinion to him on my way out—I stopped outside to wait for Glaze so I could introduce her to Peachie. I'd seen Tom come in and sit next to her. Nothing unusual, they generally sat together in church. But I wanted them to GET together in church—whenever were they going to get married? I had my matron of honor dress all picked out, but those two weren't cooperating.

As we'd filed out, though, I'd seen her motion him to go on while she turned to talk to a woman I didn't know. It was probably another one of those M-Money clients of hers. She took the confidentiality of the position seriously, so I seldom heard anything specific from her—only silly things like Larry's request through Mr. Orrin to put in a pond for fighting fish. There was no way Margaret would want her millions to pay for something like that, but Margaret probably wouldn't have been able to turn them down. Glaze could do it without batting an eyelash.

Bob patted my shoulder briefly and walked away from us. He headed toward Tom. They'd been friends since childhood. Tom was a good man. Just like Bob. I saw him motion to Tom to step away from the throng of people. That was good. He was going to ask about that student from Enders.

Bob was going to be home for lunch, but he said he'd need to take off right after that to go interview the Havershams. The next time I saw Emma, I'd invite her over to see my back yard. She'd enjoy the trees out back, I thought. It would be good to get to know her better, too. Many of the older women in Martinsville had become special friends of mine. Women like my Three Petunias. They were marvelous role models. Maybe Emma and I could gradually become friends. Yes. I'd invite her for tea. I hoped she liked tea. I hoped she didn't like Lapsang Souchong.

Oh, phooey. There I went again, snipping about something that really, in the long scheme of things, didn't matter. So I pinched the soft skin of my inner arm. It hurt like the dickens. If it weren't already black and blue, it soon would be.

Peachie had been singularly quiet. I watched her for a moment. She was totally oblivious of my gaze. She stood there with her arms crossed and gnawed at her lower lip. What on earth was wrong?

Not knowing what to do, I looked away and watched the exiting crowd, expecting to see Glaze any minute.

Melissa came out first, though. She glanced at Bob and shook her head. Whatever was that about? I'd have to ask him later.

She extended her hand as she came up to us. "Is this the friend I've heard so much about?"

Peachie uncrossed her arms and beamed.

Melissa might be mad at me, but she hadn't lost her manners. I introduced the two of them, although that was hardly necessary. Both of them knew tons about each other, through the filter of my thoughts. I wondered if I'd presented each one fairly to the other.

~~~~~

Bob skirted a bevy of boys, who fell suddenly silent as he and Tom passed them. He stopped under one of the old oaks that shaded the cemetery fence. He leaned against the topmost rail and looked out across the gravestones. Some of them dated back to the founding of the town in 1745. He wondered how many fires there had been in Martinsville since then. "There's something I need to talk to you about, Tom."

"You already said that." Tom hooked a thumb back over his shoulder toward the front of the Old Church. "What do you want to talk about?" He leaned against the fence, his back to the graves, glanced once at his friend, and turned his head back toward the chattering crowd.

Bob saw the movement out of the corner of his eye. "I got to wondering if there's a chance one of your students—the one from Enders—might be involved in these fires."

Tom crossed his arms and was silent for a long time. "Why are you asking me?"

Such a simple question, but Bob heard the anger in it. "Just checking out all the possibilities, Tom."

"Oh?"

Bob pushed away from the fence and turned to face Tom. "Yeah."

"That boy is not a possibility, and you ought to know it. It's because he's from Enders, isn't it?"

That didn't sound like a question. More like a challenge. "No, that's not the reason." Just to be fair he added, "Not the only reason."

"You'd better have a good one, because I'm telling you now, Charlie Conyers is one of the best students in the group. He works hard, he listens, and he's determined to make something of his life."

Bob tried to speak, but Tom plowed on. "Sure he's rough sometimes, but only with the other boys—the ones who are big enough to take care of themselves." Tom turned and bounced the heel of his hand onto the fence rail a couple of times. "Why aren't you looking at Jake Perkins? He's the sort that would get a big kick out of watching people's houses burn."

"What have you got against Jake?"

Tom turned away. His turn to brace his forearms on the fence rail. "Saw him sneaking out of his house one night a couple of weeks ago."

Bob was on instant alert. "When the fires started?"

"No. It wasn't a fire night. I would have told you if that had been the case. Maybe a week before the fires started. He climbed out a second-floor side window—probably his bedroom—and shinnied down that big crape myrtle next to the house."

Bob knew that tree. The previous owners planted it not three feet from the wall. Stupid.

"He looked around like he was making sure he wasn't seen."

"You saw him."

"Yeah, but there wasn't much of a moon that night, and the only reason I saw him was because there were lights coming from the living room."

"You think that makes him a fire starter? Hell, Tommy, you and I used to sneak out like that all the time."

Tom opened his mouth like he was going to object, but all he did in the end was punch Bob on the arm and return the gift of the childhood nickname. "Right you are, Bobby. We sure did."

"I still want to question Charlie. Even if he didn't do it, he might know something."

Tom nodded and headed back to the front. "You do that," he called over his shoulder.

"Oh, I will," Bob said to the empty air, but his heart wasn't in it. Biscuit didn't know what she was doing, suspecting Charlie just because of where he came from. And because he acted like … like a boy.

Chapter 40

One Month Earlier:

YES. MOVING TO MARTINSVILLE HAD been the best decision they could have made, like a crocodile moving upstream to the perfect place, the place where his quarry had chosen to swim.

This meal was going to be delicious. Hunting was so much fun

Chapter 41

So, everybody at church was talking about
this great big fire
bigger than any of the others
sounded pretty spectakular to me

~~Ke~~ #3 and me think #1 must have set it
but he won't talk to #3 and me
and she's still not home
he's really worried I can tell
and he's not as good a cook

~~~~~

LUNCH WAS EXCEPTIONALLY QUIET. BOB seemed lost in thought. I had to ask him three times whether or not he wanted seconds. Cream of leek soup was one of his favorites, which is why I'd made it. During an investigation, he's under so much stress, he can use all the help he can get. I understand that. But he could have said thank you.

I felt a bit dumpy in the comfy gray slacks I'd changed into right after church. Peachie had refused to change clothes, so she was way too dressed up for a casual lunch. She'd worn a ridiculous-looking brown shawl—the color did nothing for her complexion. Rats! I stopped and pinched my arm. Again. Who was I to offer fashion advice? If my socks matched my turtleneck, I thought I was haute couture.

All through the meal she kept ignoring my comments and crossing her arms. I knew body language. That meant she was shutting me out. But why?

Maybe she'd picked up on some unconscious vibration and knew at a gut level that I thought her shawl looked dumb. Grrr! If I had to pinch myself one more time, I was going to scream.

Making conversation with two people who didn't want to talk was for the birds. I might as well shut up.

~~~~~

Peachie was perfectly aware that Biscuit kept looking at her funny. Biscuit chattered like a magpie all during lunch, but Peachie couldn't carry on a conversation. Not when the itching was getting worse by the minute. Thank goodness for this shawl. She didn't particularly like the color. It looked like dirt; why had she bought it anyway? But it was a godsend in a situation like this.

She probably ought to give in and make an appointment with the cat. With the doctor. Just to get some relief. She wasn't sure she'd be able to stand it if she waited until she got back home. She'd have to ask Biscuit for the number, and Biscuit would want to know why. She couldn't ask now, anyway. Not with Bob sitting there, although she was fairly sure he wouldn't even hear her if she spoke. He was off lost in another world. Peachie wondered if he did that a lot. Maybe he wasn't quite the catch she'd imagined he was.

So, if she didn't want to talk to Biscuit about it, maybe she could take a walk tomorrow and just happen to stop by the doctor's office. She remembered where it was. Down the street to the first intersection and turn right. Then walk about twenty-three miles. It had sure seemed like it, and her legs were still sore.

Okay, so maybe she'd ask Biscuit for the number. And a ride there.

~~~~~

Bob ate mechanically. He didn't usually worry about an interview beforehand. Maybe it was just because the Havershams were old enough to be his parents. It was kind of cute, he had to admit, the way Tim, like a white-muzzled old dog, still wanted to protect Emma.

He looked up from his soup bowl to see Biscuit looking at him. Protect her. She was such a strong capable woman, one of the things he loved about her. But he still felt a need to protect her.

"Bob?"

"Huh?"

"More soup?"

He looked at his bowl. Empty. "No. I have to leave." He stood and bent to kiss her cheek. "Stay safe."

He was out the door before he realized he hadn't even acknowledged Peachie. And he'd forgotten about Connie. Or rather, he'd forgotten Not-Connie. Again.

~~~~~

Tim couldn't walk as fast as he used to. It wasn't just age, either. He knew this dissension with Emma was getting to him.

Jimmy seemed unusually quiet, too. He trudged dutifully on Tim's right, not bouncing around the way Tim remembered him doing— when? Not lately, that was for sure. Maybe the boy was just too old to bounce the way he did when he was little, but there wasn't much animation to him in other ways. Jimmy had been such a happy little boy—before his parents died.

Maybe he just needed to give Jimmy time. Time healed all wounds, didn't it? Then why did his heart still ache so much for Timso?

The boy went straight into the kitchen as soon as they got home. "I'll fix us some lunch, Grandpa," he said. "I'll open a can." Tim took the opportunity to tiptoe upstairs. Even he could hear the pans clattering, so the boy wouldn't hear him.

"Emma?" He waited a moment. "Emma?" He knocked a little louder. "Please come out. I'm sorry for whatever I did to make you mad." He wasn't really. He didn't think he'd done anything, but it never hurt to cover all the bases.

He heard something in there. Doggone her. How could he coax her out? Maybe he should go out front and throw some pebbles at her window. It was right over the front porch. That would make her laugh. He'd done it when they first were dating, back in college. She was such a sweet little thing. She could be tough, though. He knew that for sure.

That was why it wasn't fair for that guy, whoever he was, to burn the car. Or the gang in Atlanta—the ones who trashed their house. Their former house. It hurt Emma, and he'd do anything in the world to keep her from being hurt. Only he didn't know *what* to do.

He raised his fist to pound on the door, but stopped it in midair. Sheffield and Garner would be here soon. They'd lure her out, and then she wouldn't be able to blame him for it.

Emma told the truth as she saw it, but she wasn't the kind to lay blame, a little piece of his mind told him.

"Then why isn't she talking to me?" He said it out loud. When he trudged in defeat back to the steps, he saw Jimmy at the bottom, looking up at him.

~~~~~~

Reebok walked up Magnolia Street thinking like crazy. As soon as he'd finished talking with Mr. Orrin, he'd gotten out his lists and his cards, and he'd made a note of every woman in town who was in her seventies. There were a lot of them. But then he'd gone down the list and cross-checked with his daily notes, and he'd seen every single one of them within the last day or so. Either that or somebody he knew had mentioned having talked with one or the other of them. This just proved the importance of good record keeping.

Maybe he could ask Mrs. Haversham today. She might know who the dead woman could be. If her husband hadn't been such a guard dog yesterday, they could have woken her up and asked her then. Only then, he admitted to himself, he hadn't seen the autopsy report. The decedent, it had said, wore blue jeans and a white knit shirt. The only reason the ME could tell that, was that the fabric directly underneath the center of the body hadn't burned. But everything else had. The only thing the jeans and white shirt told Reebok was that it wasn't Sadie Masters who'd died—she would have been wearing yellow jeans and a yellow blouse.

Ahead of him, he saw the Chief, coming down Fifth Street, ready to turn right onto the Havershams' front walk. Reebok speeded up his steps, came abreast of the Chief, and slowed to match his steps.

They both looked up when they heard a loud thump. A patch of bright red tumbled down the porch roof and hit the concrete just in front of them.

"It's a cardinal." Reebok bent to retrieve the fallen bird. He stretched out one of the wings and marveled at the intricacy of the barbed feathers. He took a step back and pointed at the steep pitch of the porch roof and the window above it. "Cardinals run into windows sometimes and knock themselves out. Sometimes," he lifted the limp body a fraction and the head lolled at a totally unnatural angle, "they hit hard enough to break their necks."

The chief raised an eyebrow and Reebok rushed to explain. "The males are very territorial, Sir. This one probably thought he saw another cardinal in the window and flew at it to scare it off. He didn't know it was just a reflection of himself." He laid the little body under a small shrub beside the path. "A raccoon will probably find it tonight and have a good meal."

The Chief's eyebrow went even higher.

"It's the natural way of life, Sir."

"Ring the doorbell, Garner. Let's see if Mrs. Haversham can shed any light on this investigation."

~~~~

Despite his words, Bob didn't think Mrs. Haversham would be of any help. There had been too much town gossip about the dead body. She couldn't have remained ignorant of what had happened. If she'd seen anything suspicious, she would have come forward before now.

Reebok didn't have to ring anything, though. The glass pane in the door showed Tim Haversham hurrying down the stairs and across his foyer.

"No," Bob said in answer to Tim's question. "We don't need any coffee. Or anything else. We'd like to see your wife."

Tim gnawed at his lower lip.

"She *is* home, isn't she?"

"Oh yes. She's here, but she's in her room. I heard her a minute or two ago."

"Did she say how soon she's coming downstairs?"

Tim pulled out one of his hearing aids and frowned at it. "She didn't actually say anything." He hemmed and hawed a bit and stuck the thing back in his ear. "You see, she's mad at me about something. She just slammed a book down on the table. I heard the big ker-thunk."

Reebok echoed Bob's thought. "The bird?" They both nodded.

"Mr. Haversham," Reebok said, "when was the last time you actually saw your wife?"

Good question, Bob thought. I should have asked that yesterday.

Tim considered the question for a few seconds. "Oh, uh, well… she hasn't been around much. Maybe a couple of days ago?"

Bob and Reebok headed for the stairs.

"This is good," Tim said. "She won't come out for me. Maybe you can coax her."

Bob took the steps three at a time. At the top, he found Jimmy, sitting there and crying, cradling a spiral bound notebook to his chest. Bob couldn't take the time to talk to him. He gave him a searching look, then ran past him to Emma's bedroom door, and pounded and shouted with no result.

~~~~

So, he must have called the cops
these two officers came back
one of them looked at me hard
I didn't give anything away
I couldn't say anything, could I?
if I did #1 would blame it all on me
am I wrong, Mr. Latham?
now they're busting down her door

~~~~~

Reebok had never broken down a door before. It was one of the most exciting moments of his life. He wished Miss Biscuit could have seen him. The only one watching, besides the Chief, was the boy, Jimmy. Except he didn't really watch. He just sat there scribbling in his notebook. Reebok had to ram his shoulder into the door as hard as he could. It only took three tries. Maybe he'd have a bruise!

But the room was empty. No Mrs. Haversham. Nobody at all. He'd expected to find her dying on the floor or in the bed. Maybe some blood scattered around.

"If she wasn't in here," he asked, "how did the door get locked?" He and the Chief both looked at Mr. Haversham, but it was Jimmy who stuck his head around his grandfather and answered.

"She has a key." He sniffed and wiped the back of his hand across his nose. "She always locks the door whenever she goes out."

Mr. Haversham looked down in surprise. "Why would she do that?"

The boy's voice came out high pitched, as if he were trying to hold back more tears. "She told me she didn't want anybody ruining anything ever again."

Mr. Haversham's face went as gray as the ashes that still coated the ruin of Connie's studio. He put an arm around the boy and tightened his hold. Through teeth clenched so hard it looked like he was trying to bite off his own tongue, he said, "She's the one who died in the fire, isn't she?"

The boy pulled away and ran to a room down the hall. He slammed the door behind him. Mr. Haversham sank to the floor and put his hands over his face.

Chapter 42

JUST AS SHE'D EXPECTED, IT was so easy. She didn't have to break into the house. That woman had walked out practically into her arms. She'd faded back behind a nearby tree and then followed that woman down the street. When she turned into a big old shed of a building and nobody else was there, well, it was just too simple.

> Follow her in.
> Tell her why.
> Hit her with the star.

Chapter 43

NO! NO! NO! NO! NO!
I ran to my room when he said it
I didn't want to hear it
What's gonna happen to me?
she's dead
and I know
#1 killed her
that was his spectakular fire
what do I do?
Telling won't bring her back
and grandpa might give me away
to an ~~orfanig~~ orphenage
to somebody else
if he knows what I did.

~~~~~

THIS WAS RIDICULOUS. I REFUSED to wait around any longer. "All right, Peachie. Out with it. What on earth is wrong?"

Why are you angry?

"Wrong?" She looked away from me, out the window, as if the bird feeder were the most fascinating sight in her universe.

"Yes. Wrong. You've spent three days here and have hardly said a word to me the last two. I'd like to know what's going on."

Peachie started crying, which was about the last thing I expected.

"I have … I think I have … there's a …"

This was getting us nowhere, fast. "Take a breath, Peach." I tried to moderate my voice so I wouldn't sound so abrupt.

Now you are puzzled. You are not angry anymore.

"Hush, Marmy. I'll feed you later."

Goat poop!

Marmalade sneezed, but at least she moved away so I could kneel next to Peachie's knee. "What's wrong? Tell me."

"For the … for the past few months, I've had this really itchy place…"

Her words ran down, and I patted her knee encouragingly. Lordy, it sounded like hemorrhoids.

"I can't seem to stop the itch, and … it looks … it looks all … scaly." Her sobs made her words almost unintelligible, but I put together the general idea. Still, if she had hemorrhoids that bad, how could she possibly look at them? A mirror, maybe?

"… thought the cat might be right."

"The cat? Oh! The cat. Right. You mean KorsaCat."

His name is GrayGuy.

"Didn't I just say that?"

"Sorry. You know me. But the good news is that they can do amazing things with hemorrhoids nowadays."

What is himroydz?

She reared back and stared at me with what looked like astonishment. She wiped the tears from her face. "Who said anything about hemorrhoids?"

"Isn't that what we're talking about?"

"Biscuit, Biscuit, Biscuit. Whatever am I going to do with you?"

At least she didn't storm off like Melissa.

Some day you will listen to me.

I patted Peachie's arm and stood up. "Give me half a minute to feed Marmalade. She sounds like she's starving."

~~~~~

The phone was insistent. Paula turned off the shower and grabbed a towel. All the fire and police chiefs in the county had her home phone number. When she'd first been appointed arson investigator, she'd been late to a few calls because her office had a hard time finding her. She made it by the fourth ring. Good thing all her curtains were closed. "Corrigan here." Her hair dripped shampoo-filled water onto her shoulders as she listened.

She glanced reflexively at her wrist, then up at one of the battery-powered clocks she'd put in every room in her house—even the bathroom—fifteen years ago to keep her from falling behind schedule. Almost half past one. "Probable ID? That's good. Thanks for letting me know so quickly. Are we still on for the meeting at four?" My hair will be wet, she thought, but I'll be there.

She'd long ago perfected the art of changing clothes, or in this case, drying herself off, while clutching a phone between her shoulder, in this case her *wet* shoulder, and her ear. She could do all that and take notes at the same time. Pretty impressive. "Be sure you find out the name of her dentist. The ME's going to need that for positive ID. ... Yeah, yeah, I know you know that. Never hurts to remind ourselves." She chuckled. Sheffield was one of the good ones.

"Better yet," she said, "how about if I come there? That way I can be in on the questioning. Do you think the old man will mind? Give me the address." She licked the tip of the pen. It wasn't writing very well. She put the pen down. "Yeah. I guess I can see that. You go ahead and talk to him then, and I'll go over the fire scene one more time. I've been wanting to do that anyway. You can join me there once you finish with Mister..." she looked at her notes, "Mr. Haversham."

She was about to sign off when she remembered one more thing. "Did you get the fax I sent you? ... Good. I want to talk about that last page."

~~~~~

Bob hung up the phone and pulled the autopsy report out of his pocket. He skipped to the back page and re-read it, wondering what he had missed. He was struck again by one of the final paragraphs, unusual because he'd never yet been involved in a case where the victim burned to death.

> Due to the extent of charring,
> the decedent is not a candidate
> for tissue donation.

And then there was the signature of the ME and all his titles and contact info and such. Why on earth would the Corgi want to talk about all this? Shaking his head, his refolded it carefully and put it back where it came from. Wouldn't do to leave the thing lying around where Tim or the boy might find it.

He walked slowly back into the kitchen, studying Tim as he went. The old man sat at the table, bolt upright in one of those ridiculously uncomfortable chairs. His posture may have been attentive, but his eyes were out of focus. "Mr. Haversham?"

Bob waited a few seconds and tried again. "Tim?"

When Tim looked up, Bob asked, as gently as he could, "Do you know when was the last time your wife had any work done on her teeth? Maybe fillings, or a crown?"

"Last winter. She broke a tooth. Bit into a pie, and there was still a pit in one of the cherries. Baked it herself. She's a great cook." He sounded distant, removed somehow from this whole process. And he still spoke of her, Bob noted, in the present tense.

"Who's her dentist?" He prayed it was somebody local. Some people moved around and kept going back to the dentist they had in the last town they lived in. He didn't want to do this long distance.

Tim thought a minute. "I can't remember his name. It's that guy here in town. We both have good teeth. Only go to him once a year for a checkup."

From behind Bob, Reebok spoke up. "Do you mean Dr. Foley, sir?"

"Yeah. Yeah. That's the name."

"Head down to Nick Foley's office, Garner. It's on the corner at Third and Juniper, right across from the Old Church. He lives right next door, so you should be able to find him."

"I know that, Sir."

Of course he did, Bob thought. He probably had one of those index cards on Doc Foley. And everybody else in town. He wondered vaguely whether Reebok had one on *him*. "See if you can get her records."

"I'm on my way, Sir."

Bob waited for the door to close. He wanted to ask how the man could possibly have not known his wife was gone for almost three days. Instead, he said, "Tim, we need to talk."

~~~~~

He knew his wife was dead. He didn't need Bob Sheffield or any medical examiner to tell him that. But there was just a part of him that couldn't believe it. Couldn't grasp how Emma, his sweet loving Emma, could be gone.

It wasn't fair. They weren't that old. Mid-seventies. They should have had another thirty years together. Well, maybe twenty.

She'd been so terrified when that maniac in Atlanta had trashed their house. She'd wanted them to leave, and he'd taken her away that very night, first to a hotel and then here. To Martinsville. He'd protected her as much as he could. He'd been as understanding as he could be when her fear paralyzed her. He'd held her at night when she woke up screaming. And he'd found out that she wasn't scared for herself. She was scared for him. Scared that the man who'd destroyed their house would come after him to finish the job. He'd loved her with all his heart. Why wasn't it him that was gone instead of her? It should have been him. And to think that she'd still had her fear, even after almost seven years. That was why she locked her bedroom door when she wasn't there. He hadn't had a clue.

He turned red-rimmed eyes to Bob. "Is the man who burned our car the one who killed my wife?"

"We don't know for certain that she was the one—" Bob's voice broke and he cleared his throat. "The one in Connie's studio. That's why we need the dentals records. So the, uh, the ME can be sure."

"I know what a medical examiner is, young man. You don't need to pussy-foot around with me."

"No, sir. I didn't mean to. It's just that …" Bob paused, as if he were unsure how to say this. "I knew—I know her, and I liked—I like her a lot. I don't want it to be her any more than you do."

Tim's eyes turned steely. "You *knew* her. You can say it. And you *liked* her. That's the truth. She's past tense now, you know." He'd known as soon as the young officer broke down the door.

"Did she have any enemies that you know of?"

"Enemies? Emma? You've got to be kidding. Everybody loved her." Even as he said it, though, he knew there was one person who hadn't. He just didn't know who. Or why.

~~~~~

Reebok had done this before, sat and waited while a dentist filled out a little chart with all the inked-in markings that indicated fillings and crowns and bridges and such. He didn't like it any more this time than he had the last time, but he knew how necessary it was.

He fingered the blank three-by-five cards in his uniform shirt pocket. He was so sorry he'd ever suspected her. What was he going to do with Mrs. Haversham's card now that she was dead? He knew he wasn't supposed to assume it was her, but really, she was the only person missing in town except for Connie Cartwright, but Connie wasn't old enough to be the dead body. She was nowhere near seventy. And Connie's car was gone, so she was probably off on a trip somewhere. She should have called him before she left, just so he could keep a watch on her house whenever he made his rounds. That was one of the services he offered.

Maybe if he'd known she was gone, he might have driven by

her house more often, just to check. He might have seen something. Or maybe just his presence, as a Police Officer—he straightened his spine a little more—might have served as a deterrent.

He shifted his weight on the padded leather chair and felt a distinctive crinkle in his jacket pocket. Reaching inside, he pulled out the copy he'd made of the autopsy report. There were marks he didn't understand showing fillings and what looked to him like a big fat crown. He'd broken a molar once, eating popcorn, and now he had a big gold tooth in the back to show for it. He wondered what his own dental chart would look like. He began to wonder if Miss Biscuit had ever had any cavities, but he brought his mind firmly back into line. He folded the report with more force than was strictly necessary and jammed it back where it had come from.

Daniel. Daniel Russell. That's who he'd think about. Why would anybody beat up a scrawny little kid like that? Not so little, Reebok amended. He'd shot up a good six inches in the last few months. Talk about a growth spurt. The Chief had visited the hospital the night Daniel was attacked, hoping to talk to the boy, but he'd been in surgery for so long, the Chief just gave up. Reebok sure hoped the boy recovered easily. And soon. The Chief had talked to the doctors the next day, and they said whoever beat up Daniel left him lying there in the gutter. It looked, they said, like he'd been there an hour or more before somebody found him, judging from the state of the blood on his clothes. All dried out the way it wouldn't have been if he hadn't lain there so long.

Reebok wanted to collar whoever had done that. Daniel had his moments, like any kid, and Reebok didn't like the way he hung around with Jake Perkins. That boy was heading for trouble for sure.

He pulled the report back out and skimmed over the section about the newspaper in the mouth. His mother liked to do crossword puzzles. Maybe she could help him figure out what all those partial words were.

He looked idly around the waiting room and saw a fabric-covered box, overflowing with toys. That was a good idea. He'd get a box of some sort, and put the cards of any deceased town residents in there. That was better than just throwing them away. Mrs. Haversham, if that's who the body really was—but he didn't doubt it for a bit—would be the first. Maybe he could light a candle for her or something.

~~~~~

"Nathan? It's Biscuit. I'm so sorry to bother you on a Sunday, but ... what? No, I'm okay.... So is Bob. ... Yes." I smiled. "So is Marmalade. ... Well, that's right. It *is* Ms. Rose. Korsi may be onto something." I met Peachie's glance and nodded my encouragement. "Is there a chance you could see her tomorrow morning? ...What? ... Wait a minute." I covered the mouthpiece. "He says he can see you in five minutes. All he has to do is walk downstairs and wash his hands, and he'll be ready."

Peachie looked panicked. "Will ... will ..."

"Yes, I said. "The cat will be there."

She nodded her assent and I turned back to the phone. "Give us ten minutes?"

GrayGuy is waiting.

"And be sure Korsi is there." I added.

He already is. I told you that.

~~~~~

What a shame, Nick thought as he walked the few steps from his dental office to his house. Why did such a nice woman have to meet such an untimely end? As a small-town dentist, he wasn't usually called on to provide dental records so a body could be identified. Most people around here died in their beds and there was never any question about who they were.

This was probably murder, though. Body all burnt to a crisp. Or so he'd heard.

He stepped through the back door into a kitchen redolent with the smell of apple pie. He could see the crust browning through the glass door of the oven. Apple pie was his favorite dessert, but he was afraid that smell would always from now on be linked to the thought of Emma Haversham's death.

He slammed his chair back away from the table.

"What's that for?"

He sank into the chair across from her at the square kitchen table and rested his clasped hands on the red checkered tablecloth. "Bad news. Emma Haversham was probably the woman killed in that fire. Reebok just came for the records, so it's not really official yet, but I'm afraid it might be her."

"Oh, Nick, that's awful. Such a lovely woman."

Nick wouldn't have described her as lovely. Sort of dumpy, if you asked him. But a pleasant woman for sure. And, except for that one broken right mandibular first bicuspid when she bit into a cherry pit, she had excellent teeth. He was sure she flossed regularly. He corrected himself—she used to floss regularly.

Chapter 44

SHE MADE IT ALL THE way home without being seen. Such a quiet town. She tucked into her most comfortable pajamas and fell right to sleep. That was when she started dreaming about fire.

Fire.

FIRE.

She woke with a jolt. Three fires already. What a grand idea. Incinerate the garbage. Then nobody would find that woman. Ha! That woman's corpse. She smiled. It was easy to sneak out of her house.

The big gas can for the riding lawnmower.

Easy to carry it back through the dark streets. She saw only one other person, that joke of a young cop, driving along, checking his town. Everybody in town knew his nightly routine. He'd be back at the station within minutes.

She pushed the heavy door open slowly, just in case, but of course there was nobody there. And then she heard a sound, and wondered if it might be a rat come to feast on the remains. The door had been tightly shut, though. So, not a rat. A faint light came in through the four big skylights. She advanced a step at a time until she saw a slight movement. Legs, twitching, scrabbling in slow motion on the concrete floor. That woman wasn't dead, damn her.

Thank God I came back, she thought. Too bad I left my hammer at home, but it was easy enough to soak the clothes, the hair, splash the walls, the workbenches, the wooden tables.

Before she splashed the outside walls, she thought of one final crowning touch. She pulled a scrap of newspaper from her jeans pocket, ripped it once, twice, three times, and shoved it in that woman's mouth. Let her eat her words.

A trail to the street.
A lighted match.
Poof!

Chapter 45

PEACHIE STILL HADN'T TOLD ME where the itch was. Not that it was any of my business, but I sure was curious. I bundled her into the car and drove the few blocks to Nathan's office. KorsaCat sat waiting on the front step.

Nathan, preceded by KorsaCat, took her first into his private office, a place where he'd counseled me some time ago. Marmalade followed the three of them.

I want to know what is happening.

So I sat and looked through old magazines. Nathan finally came out and invited me to join them.

"I explained to Peachie that Polly couldn't get here this afternoon, and that it was best to have another woman in the room if I was going to examine her. She said she'd like you to stay with her."

I looked at Peachie. "Of course I will." I thought a moment. "As long as it's not hemorrhoids."

We both laughed at Doc's puzzled expression. Once we explained, he laughed, too. He knew my habit of zoning out.

~~~~~

Reebok stopped by the station to fax the dental records to the medical examiner's office. That was the first priority. While he waited for the machine to do its thing, the phone rang.

"Martinsville Police. Deputy Garner."

When the voice on the other end told him what this was about, he sat down abruptly. He didn't want to believe it. Automatically, he pulled a particular index card from the alphabetically arranged file box on his desk. "What was the time of death?" He made a note and, even though he was pretty sure of the answer, he asked it anyway. "Did he ever regain consciousness?" Reebok had to take a deep breath. "Thank you. I'll inform the Chief."

The fax machine was finished long since, but Reebok sat in silence, his hands limp on the desk in front of him. Finally, he picked up Mrs. Haversham's index card, and re-ead all the information on it. He stared at the other card on the desk and worked his lower lip with his upper teeth. Eventually, he paper-clipped the two cards together. Just in case the deaths of Daniel Russell and Emma Haversham were connected.

Once this was over and everything was solved, he'd put the two cards together in the pretty box he planned to buy.

~~~~~

Peachie wasn't prone to fear. But something in the doctor's face made her gut ball up in a knot. It hadn't been as hard as she'd thought it would be, to have Biscuit there watching as he looked and touched, gently—at least he was gentle—and then he took a little sample, a scraping.

"I'd like for you to get dressed now," he said, and the compassion in his voice made her want to scream.

"What is it?"

"Let's talk in my office. I'll want to get the name of your family doctor, so I can have the test results sent to her—or him?"

Peachie shook her head. "Her. Is it an infection?"

"Not exactly. Why don't you get dressed? We'll join the cats in my office, and we'll talk."

~~~~~

Lorna Jean leaned her forehead on the base of her palms and groaned. These edits were a pain in the tail. She'd gone through the first group quickly, and all she had left was one chapter, but it kept slipping away from her, like an ice cube on a wet counter. Maybe a cup of coffee would help, she thought, and headed downstairs to the kitchen, just in time to hear the phone ring.

The last person Lorna Jean expected to hear from was Anita Foley. They hadn't talked in ages. "It's a good thing I'm taking a quick break from Chapter 23, or I wouldn't have answered the phone. How are you doing?"

Of course, Lorna Jean expected the standard Georgia answer: *I'm fine, how are you.* The first phrase wasn't usually true, and the second was never really a question. But Anita surprised her.

"Did you hear? They identified the body. It's Emma Haversham."

Lorna Jean sank into the nearest kitchen chair.

"Lorna Jean? Did you hear what I said?"

"I heard you. I just can't believe it, that's all."

"It was murder, you know. Who do you think did it?"

Lorna Jean held up her hand, palm forward, like a traffic cop, even though Anita couldn't see her. "I have to go now, Anita. I need to get back to my writing."

"Well, I just thought you'd want to know. You don't need to get snippy about it."

"I'm not being snippy. I appreciate your letting me know, but I need to hang up now."

It took three more exchanges back and forth before Lorna Jean managed to break away. She didn't go back to writing, and she forgot about her coffee. She just sat and stared at the tabletop for a very long time.

She wrote about murder all the time. But it had never before hit home like this.

~~~~~

Tim had never felt such anger, not even when that gang trashed his house in Atlanta. At least, then, he'd had Emma. The two of them had supported each other through that horrible time. And when they learned that their son had run his car off the road, and Timso and his wife died in the flaming wreckage, even that, horrible as it had been, was somehow mitigated by the fact that his Emma was safe. And the boy. The boy wasn't in the car. The boy lived.

But this? This wasn't fair. How was he going to raise this precious boy without Emma to bake cookies with him? How could he tiptoe into the boy's room at night without Emma there to tousle Jimmy's hair?

Even losing the car hadn't been that bad. Oh, it was awful to see it erupt in flames like that, but... Why? Why? Why?

Why had life dealt him four such blows? The house, their son, the car, and now, his beloved wife, his lovely Emma.

"Four times," he said.

Sheffield looked up from his notebook. "What did you say?"

So Tim told him about Atlanta. He didn't mention the star-shaped dents. After seven years, they seemed almost to be a product of his imagination. He did tell about the glass in their bed, though. And the photographs in the toilet. Those details seemed important.

~~~~~

It was better to get it over with quickly. Nathan Young could almost smell the fear emanating from both women as he ushered them into his office. He chose not to sit behind his desk. There was no need to distance himself from them, and all the reasons in the world to be available for physical contact if Ms. Rose wanted it. Of course, she had Biscuit with her, thank goodness. Biscuit was the one she would reach for, he was almost certain.

They walked directly to the gray couch, and he decided on the wingback chair closest to Ms. Rose. He watched as her hand strayed to her left breast.

She hurts.

"It's something bad, isn't it," she said without preamble. KorsaCat rubbed against her legs and settled himself firmly on top of her feet, curling his bushy tail around the back of her legs.

He is comforting her.

"It's something that's treatable, especially when it's caught early enough." He hated this. "Although there will have to be more tests to be absolutely certain, I'm fairly sure this is a case of Paget's disease." He spelled it for them.

"Paget's." Biscuit seemed to try out the word. "What is Paget's? I've never heard of it."

"That's because it's quite rare. It's a seldom-seen form of cancer." There. He'd said it. The word that always caused the heart to lurch.

Peachie clutched at Biscuit's hand, and Biscuit moved even closer to her and folded her other hand over Peachie's. That was good.

"I have to stress that, first, this is not a certain diagnosis, and second, that even if it does turn out to be Paget's, it can be treated with a very good chance of success."

What does that mean?

Marmalade meowed, and Biscuit disengaged one hand to put it on the cat's head. "If it's not certain, then why are you even mentioning it?" She sounded like a mama bear defending her cub. *Why are you scaring us* was what she was really asking.

Nathan thought of his best friend, who had come to him years ago while he was in his last year of medical school. "Nat," she'd said.

"There's something wrong and I'm afraid to go to a doctor. Would you... would you take a look?"

So, he'd taken a look, and once he consulted his textbooks, he'd told her and her partner what he thought it might be. I could be wrong, he'd told her, but you need to see a real doctor. She'd refused to get it checked out further. You said you might be wrong, she said when he tried to argue with her. I think you are. She'd just been afraid, that was why she sat back and let it consume her. Twenty-one months later, he and his best friend's partner had buried her.

"I have ... some personal experience with this disease, Biscuit. I've seen it once before." He turned his gaze directly on Ms. Rose. "I know that seeing your doctor when you get home may seem scary, but it is absolutely vital. The itching you've been experiencing is an early symptom. The scaly texture goes along with that. Like any disease, it can express in varying forms, but I strongly urge you to go to your doctor as soon as you possibly can."

Both women looked stunned. He wondered just how much of what he was saying even registered with them. If he repeated the most important point several times, they'd get it.

"If you'll give me your doctor's name, I'll have the initial test results forwarded directly to her."

Biscuit patted Peachie's hand and they both began to cry. KorsaCat leapt into Ms. Rose's lap and refused to budge for quite a while.

~~~~~

Once Tim got started, it had been like a faucet turned on all the way. Bob didn't want to interrupt the flow. He took quite a few notes just in case that attack had any bearing on the current case. Stanger things had been known to happen.

"...and the detective who investigated said there wasn't a match for any of the unknown fingerprints they found. He was thorough, very efficient, but he just never could solve it. Stephens, his name was, I think."

"Pete Stephens? Tall, stocky fellow, red hair?"

Tim nodded.

"I met him at a police training seminar a couple of years ago. Would you mind if I gave him a call?"

"Not sure it would do any good, but you're welcome to try. He interviewed the neighbors on both sides, across the street, nobody saw anything, heard anything."

Bob waited until Tim's voice ran down. Now he lifted his notebook from his lap and set it on the kitchen table. "Was there any known gang activity in your neighborhood?"

Tim rotated his head back and forth, like a marionette gone haywire. "No. Nothing like that."

"Then why were you so sure it was a gang that did it?"

Tim braced his elbows on the table and leaned his forehead into his palms. Bob couldn't help noticing how thick his hair was for such an elderly man. "I wasn't," Tim said, "even though there were indications that it could have been a gang. They'd put their gang symbol all over the place. So maybe it was a gang. But I said it mostly for Emma's sake, trying to convince her it wasn't anything personal, anything that might follow us wherever we went."

"And you think it's followed you here?"

"No." He raised his head, a bewildered look on his face. "No, I really don't. I can't see a connection. Emma thought it might have been …"

He paused for so long, Bob prompted him. "Might have been…?"

"I started a company when I was in my thirties, and it grew into something of a phenomenon. By the time I retired, the company was making a lot of money for a lot of people. I treated my employees well, and they were extremely loyal. My management staff was absolutely topnotch."

Bob wondered where this was headed, but didn't interrupt.

"When I decided to retire, I took a healthy package—a very healthy package," he added with some pride, "and sold the company. There were some people who thought I should have sold it to them. Emma thought they might be retaliating, but I never believed that."

Bob nodded. "I'd say what happened to your house sounds more…more personal somehow. Are you sure you didn't have any enemies who weren't business rivals?"

Tim ran a hand through his hair. "Emma and I didn't make a habit of annoying people."

Bob thought of the autopsy report in his pocket. "Sounds like one of you annoyed somebody big time." And it was probably Emma, he thought, since she was the one who was dead. He looked down at his notebook. "You said something about four times. What were you talking about?"

Tim ran his hands through his hair again as if he didn't know quite what to do with them. "Even though I know damn well it's nothing but coincidence, it just seems like we've had more than our share of bad luck." He raised a hand and ticked off the fingers one at a time. "First was the break-in I just told you about. And then our son died."

"Could that have been connected?"

"He drove the car off an embankment in a rainstorm. Probably hit a puddle and hydroplaned. There weren't any witnesses."

"Was your son a drinker?"

Tim scrunched his mouth to one side. "Occasionally, but he never overdid it."

"Did they test for blood alcohol?"

Tim apparently forgot that he'd been counting and rubbed his palms along the top of his thighs. Bob could hear the fabric going swoosh, swoosh. "The car went up in flames. Everything was incinerated, including my son and his wife."

Bob could have kicked himself. Reebok would have known a detail like that. Where was Reebok anyway? He should have been here by now. "I'm sorry," he said.

"It wasn't your fault. It really hit Emma hard. Me, too, I guess, but Emma had been doing so well. After Atlanta, she sort of curled up in a frightened little ball. Wouldn't go anywhere without me. Moving here was really good for her—for both of us. She'd been doing so much better the last couple of years, and then when Tim Junior died, she just fell apart. It's been like a roller coaster, up and down, up and down. Atlanta, she went down, she got better, Tim Junior's death, she went down, she got better, and then our car went up in flames just like Timso's."

"Timso?"

"That was Emma's and my pet name for him when he was a baby. As he got older, he hated it. Made us promise never to call him that in public. Which we honored." A ghost of a smile hovered around Tim's lips, but it disappeared. "We just called him that between ourselves. And now, we'll never be able to do that again."

Tim's voice rose in pitch on each syllable. Bob thought maybe this particular witness had been through enough for a while. He sure hoped there wasn't a number five waiting around the corner.

~~~~~

All I could do, for what seemed like forever, was to hold

Peachie's hand. And cry with her. Until practicality reasserted itself.

"It's treatable," I reminded her. "The whole thing sucks, but there *is* something that can be done." I glanced up at Doc who simply sat there, waiting for the grief and disbelief and anger to run its course for now. I was sure he knew there would still be plenty of those feelings to erupt later on. I turned back to Peachie. "I trust Doc implicitly. He's very careful, and he wouldn't lead you astray. I think you need to get home right away."

She squeezed my hand, took a deep breath, and finally raised her head to look at me. "Ancient philosopher say house guests like fish."

I like fish, too!

I ignored Doc's quizzical look and played along. "Okay, Peachie. How are guests like fish?"

"Stink after three days."

What does that mean?

After I told Peachie I didn't care what she smelled like...

She smells frightened.

...we explained Lah Tsa Phun to Doc. We all three laughed, but I could tell Peachie wasn't as light-hearted as she sounded.

She is pretending so you will not hurt for her.

... and through it all, Marmalade kept meowing.

242

Chapter 46

BOB COULDN'T SHAKE THE FEELINg that he needed to talk to Jimmy. The boy had known why his grandmother locked her door. Maybe he knew other things as well—like just what his grandma was really afraid of.

"Tim." He waited for Tim to look up. "I need to talk to the boy. I'd like to do it up in his room. He might feel more comfortable there."

Tim lifted his shoulders up almost to his ears and let them fall, as if he wanted to shrug off the weight of the world. "I ought to be with him anyway. I'm not the only one who lost somebody I loved." The old man put his hands down on each side of him and pushed against the chair to help lift himself to his feet.

Just one of the little signs of aging, Bob thought, and wondered how soon it would be before his own legs weakened to the point where he'd have to work at it anytime he wanted to stand up.

"You stay here for a while. Let me go up and talk with him for a little bit. I should have done that right away, but I was too caught up in my own fears to have a thought for him." He rubbed the back of his neck with his left hand and wiped at his eyes with the other. "Emma would have known just how to handle this."

"Go ahead. I'll be up in three or four minutes."

Tim had hardly made it halfway up the stairs when Bob heard a quick knock on the front door. Tim didn't react. Probably couldn't hear it. Wondering why anyone who knew Tim Haversham would bypass the clanging doorbell, Bob stepped into the hallway.

He motioned to Reebok to come in.

~~~~~

Sunday afternoon should be a time for families to get together and enjoy each other's company, I thought. Sunday afternoons should not be a time to find out an old friend has cancer. Might have cancer. No. Does have cancer. Doc was probably right.

I ushered Peachie into the front seat and went around to my side. Marmalade hopped onto the driver's seat and vaulted into the back. Here I went again with no carrier for my cat.

I am safe.

"Do you need help fastening your seatbelt?" Why did I feel like I had to treat Peachie as if she were so fragile?

"If I could think of something hammer-like that Lah Tsa Phun said, I'd be happy to hit you with it." She fastened it by herself, shoving the connection together with a good deal more force than was necessary.

So all I did was start the car.

No. That is not all you did. You fastened your belt thing first.

As I turned right up Magnolia, planning to circle around on Third Street to Beechnut Lane, Peachie spoke. "I want to tell Mary."

"Okay. You can call her as soon as I get you home."

"No. I want to tell her now. In person. Can we go there?"

My grandmother McKee used to tell me that when she was growing up, people felt free to drop in on neighbors any time of day. I certainly didn't mind if my friends stopped in—Glaze and Melissa were always welcome—although it might be a while before Melissa and I were back on that comfortable track with each other. And I'd be okay with half a dozen of the other women in the town stopping by without notice. But Mary wasn't such a close friend. I hadn't seen her in decades, and neither had Peachie.

"All you have to do is turn the car around." She sounded impatient.

"Actually, all I have to do is drive about another hundred feet. We're on Magnolia already."

"There. See? It's fate."

What are you talking about?

~~~~~

Running was just about the best thing in the world. Mary usually ran in the morning, but this Sunday she'd gone to the Old Church to hear that preacher. The sermon had not been particularly inspiring, but the running—now, that inspired her the way few other things did. It was like her own private church. And she didn't have to talk to anybody. She'd had friends before, rather a lot of them, but somehow or other, her own company satisfied her best of all. Maybe she never should have gotten married. But then she wouldn't have moved to Martinsville. Moving here had been a good idea. Of course, it had been her idea, but her husband had been the only one with the money to pay for it.

She rounded the corner from Fifth onto the top of Magnolia. Home to be with him? Or another circuit? She'd reached her second wind. Might as well keep going. She turned right on Fourth Street and headed the short block to Willow.

Yes. This would be a very good run.

~~~~~~

Before Peachie even got out of the blasted seatbelt, Biscuit had rounded the car and opened her door. "Good grief, Biscuit. You don't have to treat me like an invalid. I'm as capable this afternoon of opening a car door as I was this morning."

Biscuit looked thoroughly abashed. I shouldn't be so mean, Peachie thought. She's only trying to help. And Biscuit was probably just as confused as Peachie was about how to deal with this Paget's thing. "Let's just go talk with Mary, and then you can take me home and feed me some tea."

"Lapsang Souchong on the way."

"And you can have some of your rabbit tea."

Biscuit looked surprised. "That's what Bob calls it."

"Bob is smart."

They rang the bell, but it wasn't Mary who answered. That husband of hers opened the door about a third of the way. Peachie had a quick glimpse of a white table, maybe three feet long, with a long drawer. It sat against a stark white wall. Just beyond the table was a plain white upholstered wingback chair. Above the table there was a colorless abstract painting, but she couldn't focus on it in time before the man stepped into the open space, blocking their access. It's funny, she thought, how much a pair of eyes can see in just a couple of seconds.

"Wh-wh-who are y-y-you?"

It could have been an honest question, but—even with the stutter—it sounded more like a challenge. "I'm Peachie Rose and," she turned slightly to indicate Biscuit, who had stopped on the lower step. "And this is Biscuit McKee, and we stopped by to talk to Mary? About something really important?" She hated it when her voice went up like that. It sounded like she wasn't sure of herself. Of course, with him standing there like a bulldog, she wasn't sure of anything.

"She's n-not h-here."

Peachie opened her mouth to ask when she'd be back, but the man had already stepped back and closed the door. She distinctly heard a lock click into place.

Biscuit's eyebrows were creased; she shrugged and turned away.

Good idea. Tea sounded better than rudeness any day. Peachie raised her hand to scratch, thought better of it, looked around—anybody could be watching—and got in the car.

~~~~~

Reebok kept his voice down. No need to alarm the old man upstairs. Or the boy. "I knew you'd want to know right away, Sir."

"Right. Good thing you caught the phone."

More than ever, Reebok wanted to talk to the Chief about hiring another officer so there could always be someone in the office, but decided this might not be the right time to broach the subject. "They've been trying to reach somebody at the station for quite a while. He died several hours ago." All the more reason to hire another officer, he thought. "The family asked that we be notified, Sir. I got the impression from …" he glanced at his index card "…Ms. Sterling—she's the hospital person who called me—from what she said, that the family's pretty angry."

"Wouldn't you be too, if your son got beaten to a pulp?"

"Yes, Sir. I would be. But now it's our job to find out who did it."

"That's been our job from the moment the boy was attacked, Garner. It's just that this," he waved his hand toward the stair, "had to come first."

The Chief was right. Murder always took precedence. But now they had two murders on their hands. "Shall I go meet with Daniel's family, Sir?" It was the last thing on earth he wanted to do, but it was part of his duty. As a Police Officer. He raised his chin a bit, and couldn't help feeling a scant hope that his moustache showed to good advantage. It had seemed a bit fuller this morning when he looked in the mirror. Maybe he should trim it just a bit on the sides?

"You do that, Garner."

"Huh?" Had the Chief read his mind?

"Be gentle, though."

Reebok was always gentle when he trimmed his moustache.

Wouldn't want to take too much off.

"After all, they've lost a son."

Oh.

Reebok hung his head and left.

~~~~~~

Lorna Jean wondered again why she hadn't put her office in the basement. That way she wouldn't be able to swivel her chair to the left and look out the dormer window. It was too easy a distraction. At least she'd taken down those awful curtains. Now anybody could look in—except that the window was so high above the street, nobody *could* see in. Unless they were in Connie Cartwright's house. She could see Connie's own closed curtains on the top floor. Maybe Connie had killed Emma? Ridiculous. Maybe Connie was lying dead in her own house and nobody would find her for three months. Another ridiculous thought. Connie was away and due for a big shock when she came home.

Well, if Connie ever did come home, nothing could stop her from opening her curtains and looking into Lorna Jean's dormer across the street. Who cared? All she'd see would be someone hunched over a desk, sweating almost as much as when she ran.

She swiveled the chair and turned her back on the window. She didn't want to look farther down the street to the mess that still sat there like a 3-D inkblot. Nobody thinks of inkblots anymore, she thought. Not since parchment paper and quill pens went out of style.

Years ago she'd had a fountain pen that used to let out a plop of excess ink every once in a while, so maybe it wasn't just the quill pens to blame. She picked up her trusty ballpoint and made a slash through the last paragraph she'd taken so long to write. This chapter was the final change she had to make, and she could not get it right. Could not. Throwing the pen down in disgust, she hauled herself over to the dormer. And saw Mary's pink socks pumping down the street in manic rhythm. The socks slowed a bit as Mary came opposite the ruins. Such a sight would slow down anybody.

Something moved in the charred mess, and Lorna looked closer. That was why Mary had slowed down. There was someone in there, bent down. She could almost make out the name on the back of the firefighter jacket. The figure raised its head and turned to face the street. Lorna Jean could see the streak of white hair in front. The one that made her look like one of those short-legged dogs that Queen Elizabeth always had. A Corgi. That's what she looked like.

Satisfied that the arson investigator was still working the case, Lorna Jean relaxed a bit. Mary ran on down the street, and Lorna Jean's mind wandered to the last time she'd seen Emma. It was something so simple. They'd met outside the IGA. Emma was coming out with her arms wrapped around a brown paper grocery bag. Lorna Jean had been going in, her list in hand. Had it really been—what? Two weeks? Three? She couldn't even remember when exactly or what they'd talked about. Just a few seconds of pleasantries, each one of them secure in the knowledge that there would be ample time in the future to talk about anything they wanted to. She did recall it had been a bright sunny day. And for some reason she remembered seeing Biscuit and Marmalade walking toward them. That cat was something else.

Was that the last time Biscuit had seen her? Who else might have had that as a final look at Emma, without knowing it was the last time they'd see her? Tim was there, of course. They'd always gone almost everywhere together. He had two bags in his arms. But he'd seen Emma every day since then, so he didn't count for this list. Lorna Jean liked lists. They kept information organized. Connie, Sue (one of the many around here), Sharon, Mary, one of the Linda's, Easton, Maggie—had everybody in town converged on the IGA that day just as Emma and Tom Haversham walked out of it?

All those people around her that day, but then that poor sweet Emma Haversham had died alone without anybody knowing.

Anybody except the man who'd killed her. And incinerated her. Lorna Jean, struck with inspiration, dashed the three steps back to her desk and rewrote the whole of Chapter 23 so it led into the final chapter seamlessly. The last of her rewrites was finished.

Fatal fire as muse? What a ghastly thought.

~~~~~

The boy had lost both his parents and now his grandma—and all three deaths were fire-related. Bob hated like everything to walk up those stairs, but he had to talk to Jimmy, not only about his grandmother this time, but about Daniel Russell. Surely the boy would have said if he'd known anything for sure, but when Bob thought about those wide panicked eyes, looking out from behind his grandfather, he wasn't certain. Maybe the boy would just turn within. People all dealt with sorrow—or fear—in their own way. He wished he knew the kid better.

Bob decided he needed to interact more with the young people in town. He never knew when he'd need their cooperation. And he might learn a great deal. He was pretty sure Reebok had an index card on every single one of them. Maybe he'd see if he could review those. Once they solved two murders. Could the two homicides be connected? Were they looking for one person? But what could Daniel Russell possibly have in common with Emma Haversham?

Who knew them both?

Easy question to answer. Everybody in Martinsville.

But who had something against a young boy and an old grandmother?

Not so clear.

He knocked on the bedroom door.

"Come on in," Tim said. "We're here."

The boy sat on his bed with his back against the solid wood headboard, his arms encircling his knees. Bob could see the spiral edge of a notebook tucked between Jimmy's back and the head of the bed. His love poems to that girl at school, maybe?

Jimmy's eyes were red, of course, but the tears seemed to have dried up for the moment. His grandfather sat on the edge of the bed, hands between his knees, his back bent.

"Jim? I need to ask you a few questions."

The boy glanced almost reflexively at his grandpa, who nodded. The boy wrapped his arms tighter around his knees. "Okay."

His voice hadn't changed yet, Bob thought, irrelevantly. He's too young to have had all this happen to him. "I have some bad news." Bob cleared his throat. "Some *more* bad news. We just found out that Daniel Russell died a couple of hours ago."

Jimmy pressed his back farther against the unyielding wood. Bob had seen panic before. This was a prime example.

"Tell me what you know about it, Jimmy."

"Nothing, nothing. I didn't see it. I didn't. I don't know anything for sure."

"But you guess something?"

Jimmy's head went down onto his knees.

"Or you know somebody who knows more about it?"

"Grandpa!" The boy launched himself at his grandfather, almost bowling him over. But Tim caught the boy and wrapped his arms around him. The boy was all legs and elbows, but somehow Tim gathered them together and cradled him. Bob saw tenderness, and fear, and anger. And something approaching danger.

"You need to leave my grandson alone for a while." Bob had always scorned novels that referred to *steel in his voice.* But there *was* steel in Tim's.

The boy's notebook, disturbed from its precarious perch on the pillow, toppled to the floor, almost in slow motion, as its outstretched pages, like the cardinal's scarlet wings, cushioned the fall.

~~~~~~

Something bothered me, but I couldn't quite put my finger on it. I brewed the tea while Peachie fiddled with rearranging the contents of her purse. I watched as she took everything out and spread it around the little table. She carried enough stuff in there to start a store. And it probably weighed enough to sink a battleship. No wonder it had gone *thunk* when she dropped it on my hardwood floor the day she arrived. I watched as she removed keys, wallet, a notebook, her address book, a brush, a handful of what looked like cash register receipts. She moved the vase of flowers onto the wide windowsill to make more space, and went back into her purse, taking out another brush even larger than the first, a big can of hairspray, lipstick, another lipstick, a box of Band-Aids, a nail file. The pile continued to grow. Finally I told her, "There's not going to be room on the table for the teapot if you don't stop soon."

"I just feel like I have to get organized if I'm going to leave tomorrow. I don't have that much to pack, but this purse is in a mess."

"Why don't you put about half that stuff," I gestured to the pile, "into your suitcase?"

She looked doubtful. "I suppose I…" She poked around the mess and extracted the small brush and one lipstick. "I could pack these."

Not a lot of improvement as far as I could see. "Great idea, but why don't you pack the big brush and carry the small one?" I wished I could think of an Ancient Philosopher aphorism, but nothing came to mind. "Think how much lighter your purse will be."

She pursed her lips. "*Heavy of bag mean light of heart.*" She dropped the singsong tone. "Only I'm not." She started to rub her jaw. I could see the moment she realized subterfuge was no longer necessary, at least not with me. "If only it would stop itching."

"Put all that stuff back in there and quit worrying about it for now." I pushed aside two of her travel packets of tissues and set a mug in front of her.

"I wish Mary had been home."

"You can always call her."

She began packing things away in the voluminous bag. "No."

"Why not?"

"Why not what?"

"Why can't you tell her on the phone?"

"I don't like the idea of talking about ... about this ... on the phone. I need to be able to ... to look in her eyes when I tell her." She tucked the nail file into a side pocket. "But I may end up having to call her. I don't want to run into that husband of hers again."

I knew what she meant. He was truly creepy. I wondered if he...

"You don't suppose..." She paused.

"I was thinking the same thing."

"He killed that woman?"

"I hate to say so, but it really could be him. I can't think of anybody else who might have done it." Anybody except Larry the obnoxious barber, or that boy from Enders.

~~~~~

Reebok paused to let a jogger, that quiet woman who wore such bright pink socks all the time, cross in front of his car before he turned left from Second onto Willow, heading for Daniel Russell's house—Daniel's parents' house—near the bottom of the street. He wasn't looking forward to this, but if there were any chance at all that they knew anything, he had to ask. He doubted a family grieving the death of a son would think to call the station. He doubted they were thinking clearly at all, except maybe for thinking of revenge. But maybe they'd seen something. Or maybe Daniel had mentioned something that piqued their interest. They wouldn't be interested in anything now, except heartbreaking things like getting a funeral arranged and over with.

But he could hardly get in the Russell front door. Relatives and friends had descended on the family, bringing enough food for a weeklong ice storm. Women arranged covered dishes on a big dining room table spread with a white tablecloth and a covering of heavy clear plastic. It might have looked like they were preparing for a party, except for the somber faces and the tears.

Reebok was surprised when he spotted Sadie Masters standing beside the front window. He hadn't seen her yellow Chevy parked outside. She stood out in the crowd of black-garbed people in her dark yellow pants suit, more of a deep gold than her usual sunny shades. Some day he was going to ask her why she always wore yellow, and why that was the only color in her house, so he could add that information to her index card. But now didn't seem like the right time. He had a more pertinent question to ask her. He threaded his way through the crowd, thinking she might be the best one to direct him to Mr. and Mrs. Russell. They were probably somewhere here in the melee, but Reebok sure couldn't see them.

But Miss Sadie was little help at all. All she said was, "No parent should ever have to lose a child." He'd never seen her so distraught.

Eventually he found someone who could help, a Russell cousin from Braetonburg. "They've locked themselves in their bedroom and won't talk to any of us, no matter how hard we pound on the door," she said. "But we know if we hang around long enough, they'll come to their senses."

Reebok was glad Miss Sadie was standing too far away to hear such an inane comment. How could they come to their senses when their last sight of their son was when his head was bandaged so heavily you could hardly see his face? Or it might have been when he took his last breath. The ICU nurses only let one person in at a time, but maybe in this case they'd made an exception. He hoped so.

He knew he wouldn't be able to find the bedroom in that labyrinthine house. Like all the old homes in Martinsville, it had been built at a time when families were large. He was fairly sure, too, that he wouldn't be able to coax Daniel's parents either to come out, or to let him in to talk to them. He couldn't blame them for hiding. Who in his right mind would want to be inundated by all these information-hungry relatives?

The one exception, of course, being Miss Sadie. He wound his way back across the large front room. "Miss Sadie? Would you like me to give you a ride home?"

The relief in her eyes was immediate and heartfelt. "Thank you, Reebok. I'd appreciate that very much." She didn't even bother to say goodbye to the person who had driven her here.

He moved a bulky paper bag onto the back seat and helped Miss Sadie into the front, glad that he'd cleaned out the car the day before and had removed the stack of books he'd checked out at the library, even though he knew Miss Sadie wouldn't have minded waiting for him to move them. It sure would be nice if he had a real patrol car instead of just having to use his own vehicle. Not that he minded too much.

Well, yes, he thought as he rounded the back of the car, he did mind. Here he was in a uniform and all he had was his old brown Mazda. At least he had a blue light he could slap onto the roof if he needed it. He'd never needed it though.

As he fastened his seat belt, Miss Sadie heaved an enormous sigh. "Could you believe that circus? Delphina and I went over there to offer help," she said, naming one of the many Russell relatives in town, "and we found a zoo. A zoo! Not a person was there to offer any comfort. They just wanted to gossip and ... and eat."

Reebok didn't think a Police Officer should discuss such matters with a civilian, but he certainly agreed with her. It *was* worse than a zoo. It *was* worse than a circus. "Yes ma'am," was all he felt he could say, particularly since they were her relatives, not his.

~~~~~

Paula reached for some hand wipes in her kit. Didn't matter whether she wore gloves or not, her fingers seemed magnetized to attract ash and char. She leaned against her car and looked back at the fire scene. There wasn't anything there. Nothing. Nada.

Bob Sheffield pulled into the space behind her vehicle. "Anything?"

She threw the black-smeared wipes into the garbage container in the passenger's foot space and slammed the door harder than was absolutely necessary. "Nothing."

"What did you want to talk about?"

Was he being deliberately dense? He wasn't the kind to play games. At least she didn't think he was. "The hammer."

"What hammer?"

"The murder weapon. Didn't you read my fax?"

He pulled some folded sheets of paper out of his pocket. "Autopsy report, right?"

"Didn't you look at the last page?"

He riffled the pages and extracted one. Holding it out to her, he said, "Signatures? No organ donation? What's important about that?"

"I get it, Sheffield. Your fax machine is broken?" She pulled her own copy of the catalog page out and handed it to him. "Star hammer. Old mining tool. *That's* what's important."

~~~~~

Connie Cartwright felt good. Really good. She'd accomplished more than she'd thought possible. It wasn't just that she'd arranged a one-woman show at one of the most prestigious galleries in the Southeast; she'd been working on that deal for months. But the gallery owner told her he and the national association had somehow found the money to fund a tour of that show to seven cities. This felt like the chance of a lifetime, and she couldn't wait to get started. She had three months to turn out some more masterpieces—she didn't think that was too exorbitant a word. Top of her form, that's where she was right now. It had taken a lot of years to get to this point, but she was ready. None of this waiting around to die before the world discovered her. That was the trouble with art of any form. Everybody wanted fame, but she wanted it soon. And she hoped every one of the pieces would sell at an outrageous price.

As she downshifted going into the steep curve not too far out of Martinsville, she glanced at her hand on the steering wheel. Strong. Decisive. Powerful. Sure. When the other hand joined that one, she thought of a few more adjectives. These hands of hers had served her well.

I won't be able to afford the time to go to tap dance class, she thought as she passed the funny B&B sign with the rooster on it. She'd be working far into the night every night for the next few months. And she'd have to cancel some of her classes. Mark Hagstrom would be especially disappointed, but she'd let him continue to work on his own. He never interrupted her at inconvenient times. And he was making excellent progress. The others, Emma, Louise, Sue, would just have to wait. This show was a lot more important to her than trying to shepherd hobbyists. If she started now, today, tonight, she'd just make the deadlines the new show had imposed.

On a sudden impulse, she turned right onto Lower Sweetgum and left onto Second Street. She'd swing by the fire station to fill her brother in on the good news. Hoss would be happy for her.

She liked her little brother. Not so little anymore. Growing up, he never had a nickname. But when he hit his growth spurt around age thirteen, fourteen, growing taller and broader with each day, or so it seemed, he'd turned into a spitting image of that guy who played on *Bonanza*, and she was sure there were a lot of people who couldn't even remember her brother's real name. Some days she could hardly remember it herself.

She pulled her car into a free parking space next to the station. She knew better than to block the path of the engine. She hoped she had the day right. Sometimes he alternated day and night shifts, depending on who was out sick. She was pretty sure this week was day shift. Sometimes the firefighters parked in behind the station, so she couldn't tell whether or not his car was here. Anyway, most days he just walked to work.

She'd barely stepped out of her car when Hoss grabbed her from behind in an enormous bear hug. "You're alive, you're alive, you're alive." He kept repeating it. She thought he'd gone nuts.

Until he told her. And then Connie Cartwright was the one going nuts.

~~~~~

Bob retrieved the Corgi's fax from the bottom of his In-box. Sure enough, there was the catalog page. He studied the image again, wondering how a murderer would come up with an antique tool like that. Something that belonged in a museum. He walked over and set the page on Reebok's desk. He had something else to think about at the moment.

He didn't hold much hope that Pete Stephens, the Atlanta detective, would be on the job on a Sunday. If he was there, he'd probably be embroiled in a homicide or two of his own, but maybe he could take a couple of minutes. He might not even remember the Haversham break-in. Probably not after seven years.

He dialed the number, spoke briefly with the woman who answered. Before he hung up, he remembered to ask, "Would you tell him it's about the Haversham case?" He gave Tim's name and the date of the break-in.

Why did this have to be the one week Pete had taken a vacation? He'd be back in the precinct tomorrow, though. Bob scribbled a note to himself and leaned back in his chair.

Daniel and Emma. Emma and Daniel. Kids—or someone else— starting fires. Four fires. A trashed house. A fatal car wreck. An old woman dead, with a crazy X on her forehead from an antique mining tool. A boy beaten to death.

They had to fit together, at least some of them. But how?

He heard Reebok's distinctive step coming down the hall. Did that fellow never go home? If Bob didn't know better, he'd think Reebok

255

had moved in somehow. Maybe he slept curled up on his desk. Maybe he never slept. He looked up just in time to see Reebok frown. What was that about?

~~~~~

Reebok wasn't happy to see the Chief there. He carried the paper bag as casually as he could over to his desk and shoved it underneath. He'd have to wait until later.

Maybe once the Chief went home. To Miss Biscuit.

Reebok sighed.

The phone rang and he grabbed it, pushing aside what looked like a photograph of a hammer. What was that doing on his desk? "Martinsville Po—what? She's here?"

In his peripheral vision, he could see the Chief watching him. He pushed his shoulders back and lifted his chin. "Thank you for letting us know."

He set the phone down deliberately and turned to face the Chief. "Connie Cartwright is home safe. She hasn't seen it yet, but her brother told her what happened. She's madder than a wet hen, and she's headed here. Her brother thought we ought to be prepared."

~~~~~

My Gratitude List for Sunday
>   1. Peachie. I hope she rounds up all her friends at home to act as a support team for her while she's going through this whole process.
>   2. Bob, who isn't home yet, but he called a few minutes ago saying he was on his way. He sounded exhausted. I should go meet him at the front door.

I am grateful for
>   *Widelap, who will not write any more tonight*
>   *SoftFoot. He smells sad and angry*
>   *GoodHands*
>   *GrayGuy*
>   *this soft bed*

~~~~~

Reebok had thought for a while that Connie Cartwright would never leave. It had taken all the Chief's powers of persuasion to calm her down. The four of them—her brother had walked down from the fire station to join them—ended up going to inspect the scene. Reebok never knew a lady could use words like that. His mother certainly never spoke that way. Reebok didn't even know what some of those phrases meant. He was willing to bet Miss Biscuit wouldn't know what they meant either.

The gist of it, though, was that Connie Cartwright thought she was going to be financially ruined. There were only two pieces of good news, from what he could gather: the *show pieces*, whatever those were, were stored in her basement and hadn't been lost, and the building and contents were heavily insured. Motive for burning it down, maybe, but certainly not a motive for murder.

He looked out in the hall to be sure nobody from the Martinsville city offices would be coming in. Of course they wouldn't. Nobody worked on a Sunday. Except Police Officers. He flicked a slight piece of lint off his lapel. And firefighters, he added, just to be fair. He locked the door.

Then he locked the outside door as well. There was a buzzer if anyone needed him. He retrieved the bag from under his desk and, looking around one last time, although nobody could have snuck in without his having seen them, he carried the bag to one of the back rooms and shifted a small table away from a wall. They never used this room, and they certainly never used the big storage closet.

Reebok had been working on this project for some time, and it was almost complete. First he had to move the few supplies from the closet to other more convenient places. Staples went into his own desk drawer; rolls of toilet paper, of course, went in a cabinet inside the bathroom, next to the stall shower; the In-box, he'd installed on the Chief's desk, and a good thing he had. It was already in use.

He opened the bag and pulled out an alarm clock, a toothbrush and tube of toothpaste, a comb, and various other personal items. He'd get his sleeping bag and pillow out of the trunk after the town had settled down for the night. He straightened the clean extra uniform he'd already hung behind the door. It wouldn't do to look messy on the job when the Chief came in tomorrow, but he absolutely had to get a few hours of sleep. How soon would the Chief hire another officer? A junior officer.

Satisfied that all was in order, he went back to his desk to look at that hammer picture he'd seen there, wondering what it was all about.

Chapter 47

MONDAY MORNING I GOT UP early to make a big breakfast for Bob. No telling what time he'd get home this evening now that he had two murders on his plate. I ate with him, but there seemed to be very little to say. Before he left, he folded me into his arms and held me for a long time. I would have been content to stay there, too, but knew he had to get to work. "Good luck today," I said, stepping back a fraction. He touched my cheek and left.

I watched him walk down the front steps and tried to envision him catching whoever had murdered Emma. And maybe Daniel, too—it had to be the same person. But there was this little piece of my brain that kept reminding me of my garden shed. I wanted the guy caught because of what he'd done to my shed, much more than because of what he'd done to poor Emma. Of course, if Bob caught the guy who burned my shed down, he'd automatically have the murderer and I'd have justice, right? Funny how I could be more concerned with a shed than with homicide. But, to tell the truth, I hadn't known Emma that well. I'd hardly known Daniel at all. I felt bad about what had happened to them, but their deaths hadn't hit home the way my demolished shed had.

I closed the front door and wondered when to wake up Peachie. She'd said last night that she wanted to get an early start, but six in the morning was still too early for her to be driving. Anyway, I wanted her to break up the trip, driving fewer hours each day. A picture of the flaming car wreck that had killed Emma and Tim's son came into mind—Bob had told me about it last night. I shook my head to dispel the image. I wanted Peachie to drive safely and get home in one piece.

I decided to let her sleep for another hour, so I brewed myself a pot of licorice root tea and inhaled the sweet aroma. The morning chorus of bird song was in full swing by that time, so I opened the back door and leaned against the jamb, tea in hand, listening.

I am listening, too.

Poor Daniel Russell would never hear birdcalls again. At

fourteen, had he ever really listened to the birds, or had something like that been just a background noise to him as he went about his early teenage years? I could imagine him kidding around with his friends, maybe hoping to get a girlfriend, dreading homework or school exams, checking out adventure novels from the library.

I knew his mother, Ella, only because she had a library card. Biographies were her favorite, if I remembered right. I wondered how she and her husband were handling their son's death. Still, they had an extended family scattered throughout the town and the whole county, siblings and cousins up the ying-yang, so I knew they wouldn't be left to deal with this alone. I pictured Ella and—was his name Hank?—sitting quietly at their kitchen table, maybe with her sister or his brother, going through lists of what had to be done, dividing the tasks among them. And Marvin Axelrod would help with the funeral plans. How comforting to have a big family.

~~~~~

Bob had barely unlocked the door and walked into his office when the fax machine started clattering. Reebok wasn't there, probably was out on one of his morning reconnaissance tours around town. Bob couldn't imagine how many miles that deputy of his must put on his car every year. Heck, every month.

Bob smiled. Reebok was going to be ecstatic when the new patrol car was delivered, paid for with what Glaze and her crew called M-Money. M for Martinsville, M for Margaret Casperson, the town benefactress. Bob didn't care where the name came from, as long as the money was put to good use. And as long as he didn't have to be involved in tracking down the misuses he'd had to deal with in the past. Glaze was a good one to have in charge of that whole program.

The car should be here any day now. Bob could imagine Reebok's wide-eyed delight. Having the patrol car would most likely increase the number of times Reebok felt it necessary to drive around town. He'd be willing to bet Reebok would head up the valley toward Braetonburg the first day he had the car, just so he could turn on the lights and siren without disturbing anybody. He'd be like a kid with a new toy.

He dreaded the hiring process for a new officer. How would he select just the right person? What if *just the right person* didn't apply? Would he have to settle for the lesser of several evils? Maybe he should let Reebok do the interviewing.

With a chuckle, he hung his uniform jacket over the back of his desk chair and started the coffee pot, periodically eyeing the now-silent fax machine. Only about a page long, this latest fax. He'd be willing to bet his badge he knew what it was. It wouldn't take the ME's office long to compare Emma Haversham's dental records with what was left of the charred corpse. Everybody in law enforcement was lucky bones and teeth didn't burn up.

Coffee finally in hand, he took a look at the fax. Yep. It was Emma Haversham. No doubt whatsoever. Not that he'd had any doubt himself, not since Reebok had battered down that door and found the locked bedroom empty. This confirmation, though, meant he'd have to visit Tim Haversham again, just to let him know there wasn't any question anymore. And he'd need to help Tim through the process of claiming Emma's body—what was left of it—for burial. Maybe then he could talk to Jimmy again. He'd have to make that happen.

He and Reebok had talked to so many people throughout the town. You'd think somebody would have seen something. Well, Melissa had, but that hadn't turned out to be anything. He'd gone to the Perkins house and found Ken Potter hanging out with Jake Perkins. Two for the price of one. Bob told them they'd been seen—a bit of a bluff on his part—and they admitted they'd been the ones out that night headed for a walk around the block. Jake finally owned up that he'd gotten into his father's liquor cabinet and stolen some vodka. He'd even brought out the squarish book bag he'd hidden it in. Bob could see how late at night, the book bag might have looked like a gas can. And no, they hadn't seen anybody suspicious heading toward Beechnut Lane. Jake's dad called Ken's dad, and with Bob watching, both boys were grounded for a couple of weeks. But Jake's dad had punched his son on the arm in friendly camaraderie as Bob left. That grounding wouldn't last more than a day. Bob sure hoped Jake wasn't headed toward worse than drinking.

Reebok walked in, not from the front door as Bob had expected, but from the back hall. Bob handed him the fax. "Go home and get some sleep, Garner. Anybody would think you lived at the station."

"That's all right, Sir. I already—"

"I said go get some sleep, and I meant it. This investigation is going to ramp up pretty soon, and I want you on your toes."

Bob saw a funny expression cross Reebok's face, but he couldn't place what it meant. "Yes Sir. I'll just read this fax first, before I go."

Bob set his coffee down on the scarred desk his father had used when he was the only police officer in Martinsville. Hoping Atlanta detective Pete Stephens was an early-to-work kind of guy, Bob moved the In-box out of the way and dialed the Atlanta precinct.

~~~~~

Peachie woke with a start, disoriented and still sleep-sodden. Once she registered where she was, she stretched and scratched. And then she remembered what was going on. The gray cat. Doctor Nathan Young. This wasn't fair. Why her? What had she ever done to deserve cancer?

She was too angry to cry. He said it was treatable. Well, whatever the treatment was, it jolly well better be fast and easy. And effective. She threw back the covers and pulled herself to her feet. The room was too light for early, early morning. She'd overslept. One more reason to be in a bad mood.

Marmalade meowed outside her door, and for the life of her she couldn't figure out why it sounded like 'happy up.' But it did. Peachie thought of her Ancient Philosopher. What would he say at a time like this? Cat meow to happy be; you and me, we make three. Well, it wasn't very good, but if the cat and her old philosopher friend and she made three, then by golly they'd all have to be happy. Or else.

She rolled her eyes and got dressed.

~~~~~

Not only did Pete Stephens remember Bob from the training course they'd taken together, he told Bob he'd looked through his notes about the Havershams from seven years ago. "Not that I had to look too hard. That was one of those cases I remembered in my nightmares. I've seen a lot of anger in the cases I've worked, but this one had to be in the top ten. Why do you need to know about it?"

"There may not be any connection, but Emma Haversham was murdered last week, and her husband told me about what happened in Atlanta."

"Did he think it was the same guy?"

"No idea. He really doesn't think it's connected, but I keep thinking there has to be some reason why two such nice people were hit twice." He thought about the car. "Three times. Their car was torched a few days before she was killed."

"Sorry to hear that. If it is connected, then Mr. Haversham better watch his back, too. The whole house was nothing but rage. The only thing the guy didn't mess with was the bedroom. Don't know why, but I had a crazy hunch, and I pulled back the covers, thinking maybe he'd put a snake in there or something."

"Had he?"

"Not a snake. Shards of broken glass. Enough to have done some real damage when the Havershams climbed in for the night."

"Good thing they went to a hotel, then."

"I sure wouldn't have wanted to sleep there. The guy who did it didn't leave a single print. Must have worn gloves. Oh, there were lots of prints scattered around, but the Havershams said they'd entertained quite a bit. All the wife's records were trashed—she said she'd had all her invitation lists filed for future reference. Still, when I went to the hotel to interview them again the next day, they'd made up a list of pretty much everybody they'd ever invited in the past four or five months."

"Good memory," Bob said.

"Yeah. Most of them were business associates or church friends, so maybe it wasn't too hard to remember them all. I checked alibis for everybody on the list, and not a single hole."

"That's unusual." Bob knew most people couldn't remember where they'd been at a specific time.

"Everybody on the list had either a Day Timer or a social calendar," Pete said. "They were all filled out and airtight." Bob could almost see him shaking his head. "We had a tornado go through here in March of '75. Busted houses apart like they didn't have any nails in them. The only difference I could see was that the Havershams still had their walls left standing. And that one bedroom."

"I hoped … Scuse me a minute, Pete." Bob turned away from the phone. "Garner! Go home. Now." He watched his deputy head obediently for the door. "Sorry about that, Pete. With what you knew about the Haversham case, I hoped you'd be able to shed some light on what happened here."

Pete gave an audible sigh. "She was such a nice lady. My wife's a part-time painter, and she used to love Ms. Haversham's columns."

"Columns?"

"She was the art reviewer for the AJC. Didn't you know?"

"She never mentioned it whenever I talked with her. And Tim hasn't said anything about it."

"Well, she had a real good reputation. Very fair, but she didn't let anything get by her, either. She quit after the break-in and they moved away. To Martinsville. Tim sent me the address, but I never had any reason to talk with them again. I'm real sorry to hear she's gone."

Bob twirled a pencil between the first two fingers of his left hand. "I hear you talking about just one guy, and Tim said he didn't really believe there was a possible gang involvement, but he told me there were gang symbols all over the place."

"Nyah. It wasn't a gang. I've seen plenty of that. Their marker of choice is almost always spray paint, and the results are always at least two feet high."

"What was different about this?"

"Doggonedest thing I've ever seen. Little X's everywhere, 'bout two inches high."

Bob dropped the pencil. His fingers felt suddenly cold. "X's?"

"Yeah. You know? Like little plus signs? Stove, fridge, baking pans, kitchen counter, wood paneling, all the furniture. He even branded all the toilet seat covers."

Bob reached for the autopsy report. "Let me read you something, Pete."

He didn't read the whole thing, of course. Just the pertinent parts about the star-shaped fracture. And the newspaper stuffed in Emma Haversham's mouth.

~~~~~

Reebok thought he was perfectly justified in taking the time to drive up the valley to see his mother. It was part of the investigation. He was intrigued by what he'd heard of the Chief's conversation with that Atlanta detective. Part way through it, though, the Chief had motioned to him to get out, even interrupting his conversation long enough to say *go home now*. Well, Reebok was going home. Not to his own apartment, but to his mother's place. He'd copied part of the autopsy report—just the part with the photographs of the newspaper that had been found stuffed in Emma Haversham's mouth. He didn't want to expose his mother to the rest of the autopsy information, but with her being such a big crossword puzzle fan, he thought maybe she could help.

Of course, the minute he walked in the door, she wanted to feed him. "Not now, Mother. I'm on duty." He brought out the copy he'd made and explained what he needed.

"And you say these pieces were all that survived?" His mother sounded excited. She *loved* puzzles. He nodded.

"Well, the first one is pretty obvious."

Reebok smoothed his mustache, the way the Chief did, and stared at the paper. "It is?"

"Well, sure it is, honey." She pointed. The only newspaper I know that has n - a - l - hyphen - c - o in the title—it has to be a name because of the capital letters—is the Atlanta Journal-Constitution. That hyphen between the l and the capital C gives it away, too."

Reebok made a note on an index card. "What about the next part? It looks like just one word. Part of a word."

"That's right, sweetie pie. It could be *resents.* Or maybe it's *presents.*" She thought for a moment. "I can't think of any other words that would fit there. But look at this next part—*iece.* That could be *piece* or *niece,* definitely. I'm pretty sure those are the only two."

Reebok made more notes.

"Now, *Hated,* notice how it's capitalized. That's a funny word to start a sentence with. Right below it there's a space before e-x-a, which means the e probably starts a word. Now, I can think of a lot of possibilities right off the bat. There's *exam, example, hexagon...*"

Reebok knew what she was doing. She was running through an internal alphabet, trying out different letters to begin the words.

"...and there's *Rexall,* and *vexatious.* That's all I can think of."

Reebok leaned closer. "What about *Texas?*"

His mother looked inordinately pleased. "Aren't you smart? I missed that one."

Wishing he didn't blush so easily, Reebok pointed to the last groups of letters. "Do you have any idea what *eming* could be?" He was sorry that *flamingo* wouldn't fit. It was such a flamboyant word.

Eventually, his mother asked, "May I keep this?" She indicated the piece of paper. "Your grandmother loves puzzles, too. I'll see if she can come up with anything."

Reebok thought of how quickly Jimmy had lost his grandmother. "That would be great. Tell her I'll drive up there to visit her as soon as..." he straightened his back, "as soon as the Chief and I wrap up this investigation." He'd call her later on today, too. That was important.

~~~~~

Lorna Jean paced herself the short block on Third. When she rounded the corner into the middle of Magnolia Street, her stride was perfect. Just like those last two chapters. Life was good. And all was well.

Except, all wasn't well. Mary wasn't warming up on her front walk the way she always was. Lorna Jean wondered if she should stop and check, just to be sure Mary was okay, but she could see the lights were all blazing, which meant that her husband was home and Mary wasn't. So, Mary must have started out earlier than usual. Lorna Jean put on an extra burst of speed. Maybe she could catch up with her.

By the time she'd pondered all this, she'd run half a block past Second Street. Well, she hadn't run along Main Street in quite a while. She didn't like dodging cars, but maybe this early nobody would be out yet.

~~~~~

Mary made it a point never to get sick, but here she was coming down with something. She groped her way down the stairs. Her head was splitting and her stomach was queasy. Not a good start to the day. She hadn't slept much, what with all the tossing and turning, so it was later now, and she really ought to be outside warming up.

Every light downstairs was shining. The amount of electricity her husband used in a month would keep a small village supplied for a year. She opened her mouth to object, not that he'd hear her. She could tell from the clanking pans that he was at the back of the house, in the kitchen.

She turned left at the bottom of the stairs and happened to glance out the living room window. She saw Lorna Jean running past, halfway to Second Street already. The woman didn't even care enough to stop and see if Mary was all right.

This afternoon. She'd run then. She'd feel better by that time.

~~~~~

I'd halfway expected Peachie to be ticked off when she figured out how much later she was than she'd planned, but she was smiling when she walked into the kitchen. Marmalade trotted behind her.

I checked on her. She is less angry now.

"Guess you thought I needed some more sleep, huh?"

I raised my mug in acknowledgment. "A little extra snooze never hurt anybody."

She skirted me and sat at the little round table.

I joined her. "You look rested, at least."

"I guess I do." She looked faintly surprised. "I didn't think I'd be able to sleep last night, what with…" Her words petered out.

"Maybe now that you know what it is, you don't have to worry so much. You can just get it taken care of."

She didn't look a hundred percent convinced, but she sat back and said, "So, where's my tea?" The chuckle in her voice was heartening.

"Coming up. The water's already hot." While I turned the heat up to bring it back to a rolling boil and fiddled with the teapot, Peachie sat quietly and gazed out the window. The dawn chorus was long over, but there was still a healthy symphony of birdcalls from outside.

I heard her mutter something indistinguishable. "What did you say?"

"It's not fair, you know."

"You're right. It's not. But there's nothing any of us can do about it except deal with it."

Peachie leaned over to look at Marmalade. "Deal with it, she says. *She* doesn't have anything to deal with."

She has to deal with me.

The self-pity in her voice tweaked some sort of button. "Peachie, how can you say that? I slammed my nose into a cliff and broke it in two places. I almost died when somebody pushed me into the river. I spent agonizing hours looking for my sister when she went missing. I watched a friend die. Well, she was already dead by the time I got there, but I heard the shot and by the time I got there she hadn't been dead for long. My beautiful garden shed got burnt to a crisp. And on top of all that, I have a husband who carries a gun, who's looking for the madman who killed Emma, and what happens if he finds him, huh? Every day he walks out of here in the morning I have to wonder if he'll ever make it back."

You feel angry.

Marmalade let out a squawk, and I ground to a halt.

Peachie looked a bit stunned. "I'm sorry," she said. "I can't help feeling like I'm alone in this."

I ignored the whistle of the teakettle and crossed the room. I grabbed one of the hands splayed out on the table. "You're not alone. You're not. You have to believe that. And if I have to come visit you and take care of you while you recover from…from whatever you have to recover from, you just let me know."

I will come, too.

"This is not a good time to ask to be fed, Marmy."

Goat poop!

She sneezed, and I held Peachie's hand while the teakettle whistled a merry tune. All *would* be well if I had anything to say about it.

~~~~~

Bob found it hard to believe. "You think somebody stuffed Emma's own column into her mouth? Why on earth would anyone in his right mind do that?"

"You know as well as I do that people can kill over the stupidest things. And," Pete added, "the ones who do the killing aren't in their right minds to begin with."

"But an art column?" He hated to sound so incredulous, but he couldn't think of anything stupider to get murdered over. There was one way to solve this. He covered the mouthpiece and yelled, "Reebok! Get in here." But nothing happened.

"What are you hollering about?"

"Looking for my deputy. It'll take a full day, but I'm going to send him to Atlanta, to the AJC archives. He can look up Emma's old columns and find one that matches the bits and pieces we have."

"I just happen to have a little free time. I'll do it."

"You're just back from a week's vacation, and you expect me to believe you have some free time?"

"Well, it's free enough. I have to head that direction on another matter. No reason why I couldn't put in an hour or two. Save your guy from driving half the day here and back. And anyway, I'm pretty curious myself."

"Give me your fax number and I'll send you the report."

Bob felt a surge of hope. This was coming together. It wouldn't be long and he'd have this guy in cuffs. He pushed the In-box away. It seemed to have migrated back to the center of his desk. He needed to look at who were the artists in town. He needed Reebok's index cards.

Why had he sent Reebok home? Bob felt an irrational impatience as he looked toward Reebok's desk. The man worked every night shift and half the days as well. He never seemed to sleep. He could do without sleep for another day. Bob needed him now. Now.

Judging from past behavior, Reebok would be back at his desk in another two or three hours.

In the meantime he could call the Corgi and bring her up to date about the newspaper column and the X's all over the Haversham's former house.

~~~~~

Passing through Garner Creek, Reebok gazed longingly at the window of the Garner Creek Diner. He hadn't had any of their Brunswick stew in months. Maybe a year. He pulled into a parking space and looked at his watch. It was nowhere near lunchtime. But he hadn't had much of a breakfast. And the Chief didn't need him. Nothing much was happening. He could give the Chief the results of his mother's word sleuthing—there was a good term—in a couple of hours. It didn't have to be right now.

That settled it. He walked into the diner, anticipating a hot mouthful of their world famous stew. Well, famous in Georgia. To be truthful, maybe it was only famous in Keagan County. But that was good enough for Reebok.

~~~~~

Eventually Peachie settled down a bit. I knew these roller coaster mood swings could—most likely *would*—continue until she'd resolved the problem. All I could hope for was that I could support her emotionally and, if need be, with my presence. I'd miss Marmalade if I had to leave.

You are not taking me with you?

And, of course, I didn't even know whether I'd need to go.

Oh. Good.

I untangled my hand and stood up. First, the teakettle. Second, feed Marmalade. Lately she'd become very vocal whenever she wanted to be fed.

Mouse droppings!

I threw together pancakes and scrambled eggs for breakfast. Honey butter for me. Maple syrup for Peachie. She'd need good fuel for her journey. As we neared the end of the meal, I asked, "You're not going to try to drive straight through, are you?"

She shook her head. "I wouldn't do that. I know what happens when somebody falls asleep at the wheel."

What wheel?

She swallowed a final bite and leaned back in her chair, scratching as she did so. I guess she felt truly at home. "Maybe it's not too late for us to go visit Mary. Would you be willing to drive me there?"

I used a last bite of pancake to mop up the rest of the honey butter. "Knowing Mary—not that I do, but you know what I mean—she's probably out running."

"We'll just have to take a chance. If she's not there, I'll call her."

"You're sure?"

"Yep. Ancient Philosopher say *no home, need call.*"

"Oh, he said that, did he? I personally think the parsing squashly comment was more pertinent."

"It was certainly funnier," she admitted.

What are you talking about?

Marmalade's gurgle sounded so confused, we both laughed.

"Okay. You go brush your teeth and finish packing. I'll clean up here and be ready to go whenever you are."

Chapter 48

REEBOK HAD EATEN FASTER THAN he wanted to. He'd hoped for an hour or so away from his duties, but something in him must have felt the call to arms. That was a great thought, he thought. A call to arms. He liked that. He paid for his stew and walked at a leisurely pace to his car, wondering what it would feel like to have a real patrol car. Blue and white. Or maybe black and white. With real lights and a real siren.

Sighing, he opened the door of his brown Mazda—brown as dirt, he couldn't help but think that, or maybe brown as old tree bark—and saw the two boxes of index cards sitting on the passenger seat. Maybe he should take a few minutes to look through them, in case something inspired him. Not the ones listing all the Martinsville residents. They were in alphabetical order, and he practically had those memorized. The other box held what he liked to think of as the case cards. He shuffled them carefully, hoping to chance upon the right combination—two cards together that would spark a memory or a thought or a … or just anything. Reebok didn't like to feel discouraged, but he simply couldn't see any answers in this case. These cases. He'd combined the cards about Mrs. Haversham and the ones about Daniel Russell. He was sure, absolutely sure … well, almost sure … they were connected. He read them through, one at a time.

Then, no more inspired than before, he started the car and backed out of the parking place.

~~~~~

Bob knew it would be hours before he heard anything from the Atlanta detective, Pete Stephens, but he was reluctant to leave the office just in case. He needed to talk to Jimmy and his grandfather again. Jimmy knew something. He was sure of it. He just didn't know what. Did it have to do with Jimmy's grandmother? Did it have to do with the fires? That second option was more likely.

Garner had never managed to talk with Dick and Naomi Russell about Daniel's death. So he needed to go there as well. He grabbed up his car keys and set them down again. He couldn't make up his mind which was the most important task.

Jimmy. Jimmy had to be the priority. He wanted to ask Tim (preferably out of the boy's hearing) about the X shape and the newspaper, to see if Tim could make any connection between Atlanta and Connie's studio, but he hated to burden the old man with that knowledge. It would all come out during the trial. Bob knew there would be a trial—there would if he had anything to say about it. He *would* catch this guy.

He glanced at the quiet phone. He had time. He'd go talk to Jimmy and his grandfather. He scribbled a note on a yellow sticky pad. He locked the station door behind him.

~~~~~

Ron kind of liked mowing the grass. When he and Mary first moved to Martinsville, he'd had a hard time getting used to all that expanse of green. He was a city boy. Always had been. But then he got the rider mower, and it was just like a drive in the country. He'd go around and around. Sometimes he could get up enough speed for the breeze to blow his hair off his forehead. These lots were huge—a little more than an acre—and the house wasn't that big. Didn't take up very much room.

He opened the shed back by the fence and drove the big red Toro down the ramp. It would be good to get away from Mary's complaining, too. She wasn't sick very often, but when she was, he stayed out of her way as much as possible.

~~~~~

I couldn't imagine that Mary was going to be thrilled to have us stop by her house, but I suppose a sense of guilt propelled me out to the car. Peachie had cancer. I was perfectly healthy. Therefore, as twisted as the logic seemed, I needed to grant her request. I told Marmalade to stay and ushered Peachie to the car.

I will take a nap.

~~~~~

Bob's car was headed downhill on the wrong side of the street—he knew as a police officer he should park on the correct side of the street, but it was so convenient, no matter which direction he was coming from, to pull up against the curb right in front of the station and hop out. Nobody parked along here except Reebok and him; visitors to the town hall had their own parking lot.

Normally he would have driven up Juniper to Fifth and turned left to get to Tim's house, but he was already headed downhill, so he drove down to the corner and waited for two cars to pass. The second one was Biscuit's green Buick. He could see Peachie in the passenger seat. He'd thought Peachie was leaving early, but maybe he'd heard wrong. His mind had certainly been busy elsewhere ever since the fourth fire.

He flashed his lights and saw Biscuit's hand wave behind the windshield. The glare kept him from seeing much else. He pulled his car onto Second behind her and followed as she turned right onto Magnolia. About halfway up the block she slowed down and pulled over to the curb. She waved again as he drove past.

~~~~~

Mary Fleming walked around the house turning off lights. She glanced out the kitchen window and watched her husband careen around the corner from the side of the house into the back yard. The swath of mown grass was only out two or three strips from the house.

He was so predictable. He always started in a tight circle counterclockwise around the house, then gradually increased the diameter of his circles. He'd be busy for quite a while. She wandered into the living room and saw him circle from right to left across the picture window. Beyond him, a green car pulled against the curb. Mary recognized it. Maybe they were visiting somebody else. Maybe she could pretend not to be home.

Too late. Peachie looked up and waved.

~~~~~

Jimmy tried to run for the stairs when Bob came in the front door, but his grandfather grabbed him with an arm that looked to Bob to be surprisingly strong. He could see the muscles bulge out as the boy tugged to try to get away.

"All I need to do is talk to you," Bob said in what he hoped would sound like a reasonable voice. The effect was far from what he'd wanted, though.

The boy's face went ashen. "I can't. I can't. They won't let me. They'll ... they'll ..."

Bob thought he'd been on alert when the boy first started to run, but now he could feel everything tighten up even more as he readied himself to react with speed to any threat. What could be threatening about a scrawny boy, though?

His grandfather hauled him into the kitchen and sat him at the table. Tim sat next to him, between the boy and the door.

"It looks like you have something to tell us, son," he said.

Jimmy lowered his head, put his hands between his knees, and clammed up.

Bob fully expected Tim to grab the boy by the collar. Instead, he put his arm around Jimmy's shoulder. "We've both lost somebody we love, Jimmy. I know you're hurting, and I know you think there's some sort of problem that can't be solved. But you're all I have left now. I'll help you solve whatever it is."

Jimmy lifted his tear-stained face. "You won't give me away?"

Tim tightened his hold. "I'd never give you away, Jimmy, no matter what's happened."

"Promise?"

Bob had never felt so lost, not since Biscuit came close to death after being trapped in the river. He wondered how so much pain could be reflected in just one word.

"I promise. Cross my heart and hope to ..." Tim swallowed hard. "Cross my heart."

~~~~~~

"See? He's on the lawnmower," Peachie said as we got out of the car. "And it looks like he has a long way to go. We won't have to deal with him."

"She's probably out running."

"No. She's home." Peachie waved toward the house. "I see her in the window."

"All right, but we can't stay long. You need to get on the road."

Peachie took my arm as we crossed Magnolia, her heavy purse clanging against my leg. "If you'd wanted me on the road by now, you wouldn't have let me sleep so late."

She had a point. "At least you're well rested."

"I'm glad that husband of hers is outside." She let go of my arm, but leaned her head my way and said in a stage whisper, "I still think he might be the murderer. Did you talk to Bob about it?"

"No. There isn't any proof. There isn't even any reasonable suspicion, except that you don't like him."

"That doesn't matter. Bob can find all the proof he needs."

Ahead of us, Mary opened the door, so we closed our mouths and went in.

~~~~~

Jimmy clung to his grandfather. Bob felt like an ogre, pressing him so hard. The boy's grandmother had died by fire. And so had his parents. But something was going on here. Bob needed answers.

The boy's story was incoherent at first. Something about a club.

"Can you tell me more about it?"

Jimmy shook his head, and his grandfather leaned closer to the boy. "You can tell us, Jimmy. It's okay. I'll understand. I was a boy once, you know."

Bob almost laughed at the look of incredulity on Jimmy's face.

"And I know how boys act. Sometimes they do stupid things."

A lot of times they do stupid things, Bob thought, but didn't say it out loud.

"You won't like it, Grandpa."

"I like *you,* Jimmy. That's what counts."

"Well … so, there was this initiation. And, I wanted to have friends, and so I had to go along if I wanted to eat lunch with them. I didn't mean for anybody to get hurt."

Bob's stomach twisted. Had this boy killed his own grandmother just so he could eat lunch with some other boys?

"So, we each were gonna have numbers. I was the new one in town, so I had to be number four." He looked imploringly at his grandfather.

"Go on, Jimmy. You have to follow this through to the end."

"So, we each had to burn something down."

Bob saw Tim's free hand tighten into a fist, but his other hand stayed on his grandson's shoulder. Four boys, thought Bob, and four fires. "Go on."

"We had to do it all by ourselves, and Ken and Dan, I mean

number 3 and number 2, they cheated cause Ken—I mean 3—gave 2 the signal."

"You don't have to keep using numbers, Jimmy; I know Ken and Dan were involved." *At least, I know now*, he thought.

"You do? Do you know about Jake, too?"

The innocence of youth. "Yes, I know about Jake."

"So, Jake was number 1, and he said he saw num—Dan getting beat up by that lady…"

Lady? What did he mean? Bob's mind went reeling off, trying to make sense of a woman hitting the boy hard enough to kill him. Of course, if it was a big rock, the way the doctors thought … Bob came back in time to hear the last of the boy's sentence.

"… do anything, he didn't go get help and … so … Dan died and …"

"Dan set the car fire, the one that burned your grandparents' car?"

"I didn't know what he was planning. If I had, if he'd told me, I woulda talked him out of it. I got really mad at him when I found out, but I had to be home early that night and I didn't know until later. I didn't know!"

"You're the one who set the grocery store garbage bin on fire?"

"Yeah, but it didn't hurt anybody. And I hid kind of close so if anything happened," he looked up at his grandfather, "you know, if it spread or anything, I'd be able to get some help."

"That was a good plan, Jimmy," Tim said, "but you know you shouldn't have burned even a garbage bin. You're going to have to pay for it."

"I know, Grandpa, but … but I was so lonely."

Luckily, Bob thought, Jimmy had lowered his head by that point and couldn't see the stricken look on his grandfather's face. Fishing and cookies hadn't been enough.

"Was it Ken who set fire to my wife's garden shed?" Bob tried to disguise his disgust, but it must have shown through somehow.

"I didn't know he was going to, really. I never would have … she's a nice lady … she helps me find good books at the library … that's why I wanted to help clean up afterwards. I didn't know what else to do."

"If you felt so bad about it, why didn't you tell me? Or your grandfather."

The tears Jimmy had managed to get under control spurted forth again. "I couldn't. They said if I told, they'd tell everybody that the whole thing was my idea, and they said Grandpa would send me to an orphanage or somewhere like that."

"Jimmy! Do you really think I'd do a thing like that to you? I never would have believed them if they said that. I know you. You're so much like ... your dad, and he got into some awful scrapes when he was around your age."

Jimmy gulped. "He did?"

"Didn't he ever tell you any of those stories?" Tim paused while his grandson shook his head. "No, I don't suppose he would. Probably afraid you'd do something even worse."

Bob interrupted this stroll down memory lane. "Jimmy, do you know who set the fourth fire?"

The tenuous connection that had begun to build evaporated. Jimmy drew away from the two adults, his head bobbing up and down as if a demented puppeteer pulled invisible strings. The puppeteer, thought Bob, was guilt.

"So, you have to believe me, I didn't know anything about it. But number—Jake—told us before that his fire was gonna be spectacular, and it was and then when I found out it killed Grandma, I couldn't ... nothing I ... it wouldn't ..." He shuddered convulsively. "I couldn't do anything to bring her back." He slid off his chair and dropped his head on his grandfather's knees. Tim leaned over to envelope the boy, patting him on the back, but saying nothing. The old man raised his head to look at Bob over the prostrate form of his grandson.

There wasn't much else Bob could do there. He excused himself, not believing for a moment that Jake had killed Emma. Jake was rough around the edges, and would probably turn into as useless a man as his father, but somehow Bob couldn't place him as a murderer. Maybe he'd set the fire, but Bob was pretty sure he hadn't known Emma was already knocked out cold inside.

If Jimmy was right and it was a woman who had killed Dan Russell, then maybe it was a woman who killed Emma Haversham. He still needed to find out about the fire, though. Jake might have seen something. If he'd left his friend bleeding in a gutter, who knew what he might have seen and might not have reported before the fire ate the building up.

Bob headed for Jake's house, wondering how Jake's father would excuse the fact that his son had left a friend to die without calling for help.

~~~~~

Reebok felt thoroughly refreshed after a good night's sleep and a good meal. He ought to do that more often, take a little time to stop during the day and eat something he enjoyed. It had been almost as good as his mother's cooking. Not quite, but almost.

He heard the phone ring inside as he stuck his key in the front door lock. Dashing in, he dumped the two index card file boxes on his desk and grabbed the phone on the fifth ring. "Martinsville Police. Deputy Garner."

"Is Sheffield there? This is Pete Stephens from ..."

"I know who you are, sir. I was here when the Chief called you. He's not here right now. Can I help you?" He tried to get the hopeful note out of his voice. He thought it made him sound inexperienced. But he *did* want to help solve this case. He fingered the index card he'd just pulled from his pocket and laid it on his desk. Maybe these notes about those partial words would help.

"... found the art review in the AJC, the one that was stuffed in Emma Haversham's mouth."

"You did?"

"I just said that, didn't I? All the phrases match words in the article. I already made a copy. I'm going to fax it up to you."

"That's great, sir. Thank you."

"Need to tell you this, too. I called Fleming, the gallery owner mentioned in the review. He said his son moved to Martinsville last year, maybe two years ago. Does that name mean anything to you?"

"Fleming?" He fumbled for his index card file. There was a Fleming who lived on ... was it Juniper? There it was. Magnolia. "Yes sir. We have one Fleming couple here in town."

"That must be him. He may be able to shed some light on this. Good luck with it."

"Thank you for your help, sir. I'll let the Chief know right away."

He studied the notes he'd made at his mother's house. It wasn't *seeming*. It wasn't *teeming*. It wasn't *deeming*. It was Fleming. He'd made such careful notes of everything his mother had come up with. He'd even written down his own contribution. *Texas*.

Sighing, he tore the index card in half, and half again.

Reebok didn't know anything about the Flemings except that they lived on Magnolia and Mr. Fleming stuttered. That didn't bother Reebok. He used to have a friend in grade school who stuttered. Reebok would always just wait for his friend to get through a sentence, no matter how long it took. Mrs. Fleming ran a lot. He saw her around town all the time, running like some demon was after her. Reebok thought about that. It made a good picture. He'd have to tell his grandmother about it when he called her. He looked back at his index card on the Flemings. Mrs. Fleming always wore pink socks. He smiled. That was kind of cute. He didn't really know them, though. Reebok thought maybe he should wait for the Chief so they could question Mr. Fleming together.

Usually the Chief left a note saying where he was. He looked for a sticky note on the Chief's desk. The Haversham house. That made sense.

The fax machine gave its characteristic clatter, and Reebok headed that way. He read it once and felt very glad that he wasn't the poor artist who'd painted that black and white painting. He thought about *I Hated Him,* and wondered if whoever the painting was about would recognize himself if he saw the painting. Dyslexic puppy. Probably not. He'd be willing to bet the painting was ugly. He wondered who'd written the review. Was it a man or a woman? It sounded like whoever wrote it was very sure of himself. He examined the top part of the fax, but it was smudged. Technology was great, but when it messed up, it really messed up. Still, he knew from his mother what the top said. Atlanta Journal-Constitution. What else did he need to know?

It didn't really matter who'd written it, but he'd hoped there'd be a readable date. That could be a clue. Somebody would have had to buy the paper. Maybe he could track down the places that sold the AJC in Keagan County. He scratched his ear. No, that might not help. The guy could've had a subscription, had it mailed to him every day. He thought about calling Detective Stephens back and asking him when the review was dated, but decided against it. Detective Stephens had probably told him the date while Reebok was thinking about the words he and his mother had discovered.

He picked up his two boxes of index cards and headed for the door, pulling his keys from his pocket. It would be more fun to drive to the Haversham house in a real squad car.

~~~~~

Paula Corrigan couldn't help but remember Sherrie's screams. She sat at her desk, looking over Emma Haversham's autopsy report and mulling through her notes about the fire—fires—in Martinsville, but her mind was back in her eight-year-old body as her big sister, backlit by a raging fire at the top of the staircase, calmly picked her up, kissed her, and tossed her out the window. Paula remembered landing in a jumble of her own arms and legs and the branches of the soft wax myrtle shrubs that surrounded the house. Within seconds her little brother was on the bush next to her. "Move out of my way, move, move," twelve-year-old Sherrie shouted, "I don't want to land on you!," but they had trouble getting untangled.

And then, by the time they scrambled away from the bush, away from the house, Sherrie's hair was on fire. Her clothes were in flames. Sherrie was screaming. She threw herself over the windowsill, but when she hit the wax myrtle bushes, the fire that was eating her ignited the waxy leaves. Twenty-eight years since Sherrie had saved their lives, and Paula could still hear her sister's screams as clearly as if they were coming from her own mouth.

Why didn't everybody with kids buy escape ladders? And why would anyone in their right mind plant such highly flammable shrubbery around their houses?

Her parents, who had been at a party next door, heard the sirens and came out to look, in time to see their first-born a living torch. They'd divorced soon after the funeral. Paula had heard that a lot of marriages couldn't manage to survive the loss of a child, but at the time, she hadn't known the reasons. She'd simply been bewildered by what had happened, and her solace lay in caring for her brother, who was only two years younger than herself, but who had reverted to sucking his thumb and wetting the bed in the aftermath of the fire. He'd been practically a full-time job for little Paula for the next three years. It was a wonder she hadn't gone into nursing, or day care, or something like that.

But the flames, and the unfairness, the sheer wastefulness of her big sister's death, had propelled her into the fire service.

She looked again at her sketches of the fire. Either this guy was very knowledgeable about how fires spread, or he was just plain lucky. She thought of a more graphic description. Asshole or not, she was going to catch him.

~~~~~

I sat down beside Peachie on the white couch at the end of the room, her enormous purse between us. Mary chose the white wingback chair, probably because it was the only other seat in the living room.

Living room. Something bothered me, and I couldn't put my finger on it. I heard the lawnmower outside pass in front of the big window, but I couldn't see it because I was sitting down. Living room. That was what was wrong. Why call it a living room when everything in there looked dead, from the lifeless white of the walls to the sickly white of the furniture.

"I'm leaving today," Peachie said. There was no response from Mary, not even a *sorry to see you go*. "I wanted to tell you something before I left, though."

At least she cocked an eyebrow. There against the white wall, with that black and white abstract painting behind her head, she looked like an extra on a movie set. I tried to see what the signature was on the painting. Two names. The second one almost looked like Degas, but all those ballerinas he painted had form and shape and life. This monstrosity just looked like something an amateur had slopped on in a drunken haze.

Oh phooey. I pinched myself. I'd tried painting once, and the result had turned into a joke between Bob and me. It was good for a laugh any day. We called it *Jaundice Behind Bars* because of the black stripes and yellow swirls. It was supposed to have been bright yellow flowers, heavy on their shadowed stalks. Ah well. I felt a smile coming on, but I stopped it when I heard Peachie say, "...so he says I have Paget's disease."

When Mary didn't answer, Peachie plowed on. "He says it's a rare form of cancer, but it's treatable, and he told me I have to get back home right away and see my doctor."

The lawnmower made another noisy pass, and Mary waited until the sound diminished. "Oh, you poor thing."

Somehow, Mary's voice, soft as it was, didn't seem to back up the words. She sounded ... glad. No, it couldn't be. She was just too quiet, that was all.

But Peachie must have heard the same tone. "Didn't you hear me? It's cancer! Aren't you sorry?"

Mary shifted to the edge of her chair. "Why should I be sorry? You're the one who deserves this. The only thing I'm sorry about is that you didn't get it sooner."

"I don't believe this," I said. "This is Peachie, your friend for decades. How can you be so ... so cruel?"

Outside I heard the lawnmower sputter and die.

~~~~~

Bob pushed the doorbell, but didn't hear anything from inside, so he knocked loudly, three sharp raps. Jake's mother answered. "Bob? What can I do for you?"

"I'm here on business. I need to speak to Jake. I'd like you and your husband, if he's here, to sit in on the conversation."

She looked confused rather than concerned. "Is this more about that walk in the park the boys took the other night?"

"Not exactly. I'll explain when everybody's together."

She opened the door farther and pointed through an archway toward the living room. "I'll go get them. Have a seat."

"That's okay. I'll wait here for them."

The last thing he wanted was to be sunk down in some overstuffed couch and hear the back door open. He didn't think Jake would try to run, and he halfway wanted to go look for the boy himself. That wasn't necessary, though. Everybody showed up within seconds, Jake's father looking truculent. "What's it about this time?"

"I have something to discuss with the three of you. Can we sit down somewhere?"

"No. I want to hear what this is about right now. You come in here disrupting our family, I want to know why."

Jake's mother stepped forward. "Let's be civilized. We can go in the living room. Or the kitchen. Which would you prefer, dear?"

Bob remembered Biscuit telling him about how she used to ask her children at bedtime, *Do you want to read a book before you go to bed, or do you want to have a drink of water before you go to bed?* It had worked with Sandra, but she'd told him that Sally looked her square in the face once and said, "I want to read a book and have a drink of water and play a game, and I don't want to go to bed."

Jake's father was not as smart as Sally, apparently. "I guess we can go in the kitchen. I need some coffee anyway."

Bob made a point of selecting a chair that was between Jake and the back door.

"Jake, I need to tell you that you've been identified as the one who started the fire that burned down Connie Cartwright's studio."

Jake jumped to his feet. "I did not!"

"Sit down. You've also—"

"Wait a minute," Jake's father said. "Who said such a lie about my son?"

"We've also learned that you watched your friend Daniel being beaten almost to death and you left him there and didn't call for help."

"My boy wouldn't do something as terrible as that," his mother said.

"Nonsense. These are all lies," his father roared.

Bob ignored him. "You told a friend of yours that you'd seen Daniel getting beaten up."

Jake sat down. "But I never set the fire. I never did. You have to believe me. I never did!"

Bob waited, while Jake's parents turned in unison to look at him. His mother leaned forward and put her hand on his shoulder. Her fingers gripped so hard her knuckles were white. "You saw what happened to Dan? And you didn't try to help him?"

The tough guy demeanor didn't last for long in the face of his mother's utter incredulity, but he tried his best to squirm out of it.

"It was the other guys that set the fires. I didn't. I never did."

"Because you didn't get a chance? Or were you too chicken to try it?"

"I was not! I could have. I just couldn't find a ..." His voice petered out and the silence went on a very long time.

~~~~~

The lawnmower ran out of gas as Ron rounded the right front corner of the house for the sixth time. God, this yard was enormous. He trudged around to the shed at the back of the property. He'd filled up the big red five-gallon container last week. He'd hate to stop now right in the middle of the mowing job.

He looked behind him at the expanse of yard. He loved it even though he was going to have to lug that heavy gas can all the way to the front of the house. Growing up in apartments, fancy apartments, but not a yard anywhere, he'd never thought he could enjoy living out away from the city like this. Atlanta was a great place, but this ... this was *his*.

His and Mary's, he amended. It wasn't that he kept forgetting her. It was just that all they ever seemed to do together now was turn lights on and off. It had started as something of a joke, but when he found out how much the lights irritated her, he just couldn't quite help himself—he kept hoping she'd see how funny it was. He hadn't meant for it to turn into a quiet war. Quiet because Mary hardly ever said anything above a whisper. He wondered yet again if something was wrong with her vocal cords. Not that it mattered. Between her inaudible voice and his stutter, they didn't either one of them talk to many people. They just turned lights on and off, on and off. It wasn't much, but it was something they had in common.

Maybe he should start telling her a joke every day. She used to like his jokes. At least she used to laughed at them.

He grabbed the handle of the gas can and heaved, knowing it was full. But his arm retracted so fast he thought he'd drop the can. He sloshed it experimentally, but there wasn't even a gurgle. It was empty. Empty? He knew he'd filled it.

Then he remembered the fires those kids had been setting around town. They'd done it with his gas. They'd stolen his gas. Well, the first thing he was going to do was get a lock for the shed door. No, the first thing he was going to do was take this can inside and show Mary. It wasn't anything to laugh about, but maybe she'd at least say something.

~~~~~~

Reebok wondered as he walked up Mr. Haversham's front steps whether he should maybe wait for the Chief to finish inside and come out on his own. He knew an investigative interview could be touchy sometimes, and he didn't want to interrupt, but he really thought the Chief should know about the Fleming connection. He paused a minute on the top step to be sure he had the fax from Pete Stephens. Of course he had it. He'd folded it into his jacket pocket just before he left the office.

This was too important to wait. It might be a clue, although he couldn't see what something in the Atlanta newspaper had to do with Mrs. Haversham's death. Except for the fact that it had been shoved down her throat.

He rang the bell. After a few long moments, Mr. Haversham answered. "Bob left a little while ago."

"Do you have any idea where he went?"

"No. Not for sure. But he might have gone to see Jake Perkins and his parents."

"Thank you. I'll head there right away."

Reebok hurried down the stairs, wondering how long it would take Mr. Haversham to get over his wife's death. He looked awful.

~~~~~~

Mary looked positively livid. "You think I'm cruel? You want to talk about cruel? You're a fine one to talk. You're the one who called me Mousie all the time behind my back. You thought I couldn't hear you. You thought you could get away with it. Just because I can't talk as loud as you can, you think you're better than I am."

She was right. Not about my thinking I was better than she was. But about the thoughtless way I'd branded her like that? She was right. "I'm sorry," I said, but Peachie jumped in on top of my words.

"Biscuit's your friend. I'm sure she didn't mean—"

"Such good friends. Ha! You've never been my friends."

"I have too been your friend. I read all about all those awards and wrote you to congratulate you on every single one of them." Something dark flickered in Mary's eyes, but I couldn't tell what was wrong.

Peachie must not have noticed anything. "I sent you a birthday card every single year, even if you didn't write me back every time. I was—"

"And what about Gus?"

Peachie closed her mouth, as much at a loss for words as I felt. "Gus? You mean the Gus I dated our senior year? That Gus?"

"You know perfectly well who I'm talking about. The Gus you dated. The Gus you stole from me."

"You stole Gus from Mary? I thought you said you met him in a donut shop."

"I did."

Mary made a rude sound. "He was with *me* that day."

"He was?"

Poor Mary. Always invisible.

Peachie must have had the same thought. "I'm sorry, Mary. I had no idea."

"Sorry, sorry, sorry." Her voice actually had some volume to it. A part of my brain registered how much louder she was. Did anger do something to vocal cords?

Peachie spread her hands. "Mary, can't we let all this just wash away? You know? Water under the bridge?" Apparently encouraged by the fact that Mary didn't say anything, Peachie went on in a rush, "We came here today for two reasons. One was to tell you about the Paget's, but the other one was really more important. Even if you're not being very nice to us, I think you should know that Biscuit and I think you need to be very careful."

"Careful? Why should I be careful?"

"We've been putting together a lot of evidence, and…"

"What are you talking about, Peachie?"

"You hush, Biscuit. Mary, we think you may be in danger. You know all those fires around town?"

Mary's eyes narrowed, but she didn't say anything.

"We think it was … was your husband that started them all."

Mary's mouth opened, but before she could say anything, that very husband walked into the living room, an enormous gas can in his hand.

Peachie jumped to her feet, knocking her purse off the couch. The contents splattered across the room. I was on my feet, too, this time, but I stepped on one of Peachie's lipsticks. As I went down, straight onto my tailbone, Peachie screamed, "Don't let him set us on fire. Stop him! Stop him!" I landed in a pile of her purse debris. I could feel the prickly bristles of her brush digging into the back of my right knee through my light pants. The lipstick rolled one way, the can of hair spray spun away to my right, the address book skittered a foot or so to my left. Why was I even noticing stupid details like that?

"M-M-Mary? Wh-wh-what's …"

"You idiot! Why'd you bring that in here?" Mary turned in a blur of movement and ripped open the drawer of a small white table. She spun around and knocked her husband to the ground. I saw a spray of bright red blood. It splattered the ugly white painting. Just what it needs, I thought. A touch of color.

But then Mary was headed toward me, a hammer raised high overhead. "You've ruined everything. Everything!"

"We haven't ruined anything." Peachie's voice seemed to come from far away. "We wanted to save you from that maniac husband of yours." I tried frantically to get to my feet, defend myself somehow. The hammer swept down in a deadly arc. I'd heard that when you're about to die, everything goes into slow motion. I could see a distinct X on the head of the hammer. I wonder what that's for, I thought. I threw my arm out in front of me and felt the crack as the hammer shattered my forearm. Screaming didn't seem to be of much help, but I tried anyway. Mary paused only long enough to be sure I was down for the count. "I'll be right back to finish you off." Her voice was the loudest I'd ever heard it. I hoped she was lying. "But right now, I have to take care of one more piece of business." For good measure, she kicked me in the face as she turned. Above her shoe, I saw the neon pink sock. I tried to avoid it, but even in slow motion, everything went too fast.

"Mary," Peachie cried, "Mary! Don't!"

I curled into the tightest ball I could manage, trying to protect my face. Just before I passed out, I heard another scream. Peachie?

~~~~~

Bob studied Jake long enough that the boy began to squirm in his seat. As much as he'd love to arrest the kid, Jake hadn't really done anything against the law. He hadn't set any of the fires. Sure, he hadn't reported the attack on Daniel, but Bob couldn't throw him in jail for it.

"I'm not going to arrest you, Jake, but you'd better understand that Deputy Garner and I will be keeping very close tabs on you."

Jake nodded. Rather sullenly, Bob thought. "What are you going to do about the lady in the pink socks?"

"What do you mean? What lady in pink socks?"

"The one who beat up Daniel. Shouldn't you be getting after her instead of coming after me?"

Bob stood up so fast his chair fell over. "You little … Why didn't you tell me this the day it happened?"

"Don't talk to my boy like that."

"If you and your wife had instilled even a modicum of decency and self-discipline in that son of yours, he wouldn't have left a friend dying in the gutter."

Bob ran into Reebok on his way out the door.

~~~~~

When I came to, I was swathed in white, enough so I wondered for a moment if I'd died and gone to heaven. Bob was there, so obviously it was heaven, although I seemed to be able to see him out of only one eye.

"She's awake." Somebody sounded delirious, but I couldn't identify the voice. Tenor. Reebok? I tried to look around for him, but Hoss stepped into my line of vision.

"Excuse me, Bob. Back up, please. We've got to get her in the ambulance."

I saw a stethoscope around his neck. "Did you change into a doctor?"

Everybody laughed. I didn't think it was that funny.

"No ma'am. All us firefighters are trained as paramedics. I've just been taking your blood pressure again."

I tried to move, but my body wouldn't cooperate. The pain in my arm felt like a volcano had exploded in there. "Don't wiggle, Bisque. You're tucked into the stretcher. They've got to transport you up to the Montrose Clinic. Your arm is ..."

He paused. He looked more distraught than I'd seen him in a long time. Not since I'd almost drowned. Hoss and the other firefighters had taken me to the Montrose that time, too. "This is getting to be a habit," I said, even though it hurt to talk. "And I don't like it."

"Try not to say anything, ma'am," one of the other firefighters said from behind me. I couldn't tell which one it was.

"What happened to ..."

"I'm fine." Peachie appeared in my peripheral vision, then moved to the foot of the stretcher so I could see her better. "Don't talk. Your poor face—it must hurt like the dickens."

"What's ..." I remembered Mary's kick aimed at my nose. I turned my head just as her foot connected. "My eye," I said. "I can't see out of my left eye."

"It's okay, sweetheart. It's just swollen shut. You'll be fine."

He called me sweetheart. He never called me sweetheart unless something was wrong. "Don't call me that," I said, but I was in too much pain to tell him why, to tell him how scared I was.

It must have been an hour later—or two or three—that I woke enough to make some sense of what was going on. Twice before, this room—the very same room—I recognized the painting on the wall— had hosted the entire McKee and Sheffield contingent.

I looked at each face gathered around the hospital bed. One person was missing. Melissa. I felt a pain in my heart that had nothing to do with what had happened in the last few hours. Before I had a chance to melt down, Melissa elbowed her way into the room and grabbed my hand. "You do anything like this again, and I'm going to divorce you."

"Am I forgiven?"

"What's to forgive? We all do it."

Dr. Prescott walked in on the last of her comment. "Do what?"

"Tune out when people are talking to us." Melissa moved to one side, but didn't let go of my hand until Dr. Prescott took it away from her to feel my pulse. A few moments of silence while she did that, and then everyone started talking again.

Dr. Prescott held up her hand. "You and your sister seem to want to hog this room."

It was true that Glaze and I had both been patients here, but it wasn't like we planned it. "It's not my choice," I said, "although if I need you, I'm sure happy you're around." I felt my face gingerly. The enormous, puffy bandage over my right eye was something of a shock.

"Don't worry." Dr. Prescott sounded like she meant it. "Heavy laceration to the eyebrow, and a lot of swelling. I had to take some stitches, but you'll be fine in no time."

"Then why am I here? Why can't I go home?" Behind her I saw Glaze walk in. Instead of coming up to my bed, though, she moved quietly behind my mother and aunt, and Dee and Maddy. It felt like the whole town was here. No. Just the most important part of the town.

"… tomorrow. We're keeping you overnight to be sure you don't have any brain trauma. The tests look good, but it won't hurt to be cautious. I'll check on you first thing in the morning." She patted my knee and left. Her place was filled immediately by a swarm of family and friends. Glaze pushed her way through the crowd and placed Marmalade on my tummy.

You smell funny.

"See? She's saying she's glad to see you."

"I'm glad to see her too. Did you have to smuggle her in?"

She snuggled me in.

"I tucked her tail up out of sight and held her real close under my sweater. I figured it was better to ask for forgiveness…"

"…than to ask for permission," everyone else chimed in.

I tired out quickly, though, and Bob shooed them all away. All except my sister and Peachie. He let them stay.

And me, too.

Melissa gave me a big hug before she left. That was good. All was well.

Bob dragged a chair up close for Peachie to sit in. He perched on one side of the bed, and Glaze sat on the other side, down next to my feet.

"You're supposed to be on the road home, Peachie." I stroked Marmalade's silky head.

That feels good.

"I'm staying till you get home, so hurry, will you?"

"What … what happened?"

Glaze squeezed my hand. "You must be better. I wondered when you'd get around to asking."

"The last thing I remember is being kicked and Peachie screaming."

"That wasn't me." She sounded indignant.

Bob reached out and smoothed the hair off my forehead. "You're lucky to have a good friend defending you while your dumb husband is off chasing dead ends."

"What?"

I chase my tail sometimes, when I feel silly.

He laid his hand along my cheek. "Your friend…"

"…the magnificent Peach herself," Glaze inserted.

"…employed a weapon I've never heard of before."

Glaze nodded. "Super secret weapon."

"I'm thinking of outfitting Reebok and myself with it on our duty belts."

"Peachie," I said, "help me out here. These two aren't making any sense at all."

I will help you.

"Glaze, did you think to feed Marmalade before you brought her here?"

Oh, mouse droppings AND goat poop, I am not hungry!

"No, but I think she might be afraid of all the smells in here. I'll feed her when I take her home just in case."

Peachie raised an admonitory hand. "Do you want to hear the rest of the story or not?"

"I'm waiting with bated breath."

"Do you remember when I stood up so fast and my purse fell on the floor?"

"You hit her with your purse?"

"No. That little thing never would have stopped Mary. I didn't realize she was so strong."

"That purse of yours is most assuredly not little."

"Too little to do the job we needed. Shy Mary turned into a maniac."

"So, what happened?"

"I sprayed her with hairspray."

I looked at her, trying to tell if she was spoofing.

"Right in the eyes."

"That's what the screaming was?"

She nodded her head slowly and even rolled her eyes. "And to think you wanted me to pack it in my suitcase."

I looked from Peachie to Glaze to Bob. "I wish I could tell you how glad I am."

"Yes." Peachie's voice took on a singsong tone. "Ancient Philosopher Lah Tsa Phun say, the family that sprays together, stays together."

The End
not quite

Fran's Gratitude List

I so enjoy being able to thank people who help me get my books out there. For **GRAY as ASHES**, I'm particularly grateful to:

- Gwinnett County **Arson Investigators Wade Crider** and **Charlie Bryson**, who showed me photos of closed cases and answered numerous questions;
- my sister, **Diana Alishouse**, author of *Depression Visible: the ragged edge*. She is an invaluable pre-reader. If I ever get to the point where I can't write a book she'll enjoy, I'm going to give up writing;
- **the Gwinnett County Citizen Fire Academy**, where I had a chance to learn how to don turn-out gear in a couple of minutes, crawl through a "burning" building, open a fire hydrant, cart hose up three stories, use a fog nozzle, and a dozen other skills that are second nature to seasoned firefighters;
- **Gwinnett County Firefighters** from Stations 24, 10, 16, and 15, who answered numerous questions about fires and firefighting each time I went on a ride-along with them;
- **Jill Sensiba**, my go-to plant expert, without whose knowledge of wax myrtle, Paula Corrigan and her brother might never have survived being thrown out of a third-floor bedroom window;
- **Lorna Jean Hagstrom**, who bid on a high-ticket silent auction at the 2014 biennial celebration of the National League of American Pen Women, and won the chance to be in this book. I gave her the choice: *murderer or local denizen?* You can see which one she chose. "My grandchildren are going to read these books someday," she told me when I interviewed her;
- My friend and fellow writer, **Lynda Fitzgerald**, author of the wonderful *LIVE* mystery series, who offered valuable suggestions about story flow and convinced me to delete a lot of deadwood;
- **Mike Palenik**, owner of Whistle Post Antiques in Canon City, Colorado, who assured me that I hadn't invented a star-shaped hammer out of whole cloth. There actually was such a thing. He even drew a picture for me.
- **Dr. Seuss**, whose *Horton Hatches the Egg* I quote briefly;

➤ **Mikki Root Dillon**, artist friend and NLAPW compatriot, whose nearly constant "when-is-the-next-Biscuit-McKee-coming-out" kept me writing through weeks when I felt pulled by the ScotShop series;

➤ my archivist, the late **Patricia Gerard**, who was unfailingly supportive through all the ins and outs as I wrote two books (from two different series) at a time. She was also a darn good brainstormer. She came up with the name *Peachie*, as well as the "parsing squashly" quip. (Surely you didn't think *I* was the one who thought that up!)

➤ **You**, for having picked up this book and read it all the way through. Writers would be nothing without readers, and we absolutely adore people who take the time to write reviews online and who brag about us to their friends;

➤ and, as always, **Darlene Carter** for the layout and design of all my books.

--Fran
with deepest gratitude
from my home by a creek on
the back side of Hog Mountain,
northeast of Atlanta
August 2014 / 2020

Resource List
for the Biscuit McKee Mysteries

Depression

Depression and Bipolar Support Alliance
http://dbsalliance,org
1-800-826-3632

National Institutes of Mental Health
(for a depression self-check list)
http://nimh.nih.gov
1-866-615-6464

Depression Visible: The Ragged Edge by Diana Alishouse
http://DepressionVisible.com

Green Cemeteries

I highly recommend the book *Grave Matters: A Journey through the modern funeral industry to a natural way of burial* by Mark Harris ©2007
http://gravematters.us
http://memorialecosystems.com

Suicide Prevention

1-800-SUICIDE (1-800-784-2433) or
1-800-273-TALK (1-800-273-8255)
http://suicide.org
This website provides links to other suicide prevention sites.

Suicide is never the answer.
Getting help is the answer.

Childhood Sexual Abuse Prevention
Rape Abuse & Incest National Network (RAINN) is both a hotline and a referral service to direct you to an approved local resource.

> 1-800-656-HOPE (1-800-656-4673)
> http://RAINN.org
>
> Prevent Child Abuse America
> 1-800-CHILDREN (1-800-244-5373)
> http://preventchildabuse.org

Animal Communication and Ethical Treatment of Animals
There are many fine organizations out there These are two that I regularly support through contributions.

> Noah's Ark Animal Sanctuary
> http://Noahs-ark.org
>
> The Humane Society of the United States
> http://hsus.org

Ecological Responsibility:
> Mother Earth News
> http://motherearthnews.com
>
> The Nature Conservancyhttp://nature.org

Fire Escape Ladders
> Kidde 13-ft. 2-story – This is one Fran has (but hopes she never has to use)

Fire Resistant Plants
There is no such thing as a *fireproof* plant. Any plant can burn if it's dry enough, but some plants take longer to dry out and therefore may be less susceptible to catching fire easily.

Note: Since plants resistant to fire vary so much from one area of the country to another, I encourage you to search the Internet for "fire resistant plants in X." Plug in your state's name where the X is. Believe me, you'll end up with a lot of information.

If you're in southern California, for instance, you'll be able to plant Nevin's Barberry, but that plant won't grow well in northern Michigan, where Serviceberry or Flowering Quince will do you more good.

American Red Cross Blood Donation
800-REDCROSS (800-733-2767)
Please donate blood as often as possible.

Please note: *Websites listed here were correct when this book went to press, but may have changed in the time between then and now.*